ALTERED

BOOK ONE

JACQUELINE BROWN

Also by Jacqueline Brown

The Light, Book One of The Light Series
Through the Ashes, Book Two of The Light Series
From the Shadows, Book Three of The Light Series
Into the Embers, Book Four of The Light Series
Out of the Darkness, Book Five of The Light Series
"Before the Silence," a Light Series Short Story
Awakening, Book One
Gifted, Book Two of the Awakening Series

To receive your FREE copy of "Before the Silence,"
please visit www.Jacqueline-Brown.com.

For Ray ~ who passed from this life into the next as I was
preparing this manuscript for publication. I'm so grateful
for your life and honored to have been there as you
neared your eternal home. Thank you for helping to make
Daniel into the man that he is.
You are dearly missed and forever loved.

I exist to serve.

Some level of peace comes with knowing the truth of one's life—an acceptance ... a resignation. I don't need to strive for better, as so many borns and vintage borns do. I must accept my life as it is. Never changing, never altering.

I could be envious of those whose sole reason for existence cannot be summed up so easily. Those who were not created to be a slave. I could spend my time, as my skin bakes in the withering sun, imagining how different my life would be if I had been born, if I was a person, but such thoughts are not allowed. Gestates were not created to think or feel—we exist only to serve.

"Are you daydreaming again?" young Hastings teased as he came toward me while holding the smoothie I'd made for him.

"No."

I'm not allowed to lie, but I do it anyway. I do many things I am not allowed to do. Though, I would never lie to Hastings if the band on my wrist was not always listening.

"Then what're you doing?" he asked.

Beads of condensation had formed on the metal straw he held to his pink lips, which were surrounded by freckles. His mother detested those freckles.

"I was contemplating the watering needs of these dandelions. They are supposed to do well in all soil types, but they are struggling here."

It amazed me how easily lying came to me, how easily it had always come, and yet I never took pleasure in it. Certainly not when I lied to Hastings, and not even when I lied to his parents. Lies were necessary. I realized that almost as soon as I arrived here as a young gestate, but still I did not like it.

Hastings crouched beside me, his uncombed red hair sticking up in various directions. His hair color was so dull it barely looked red at all—nothing like the vibrant red hair of the altered borns. Though that, along with everything else about him, would change soon enough. Hastings was a young vintage born, only nine, and so, too young for alterations. In another seven years he would be eligible for alterations. Then he would no longer look like a gestate and his mother would not be so embarrassed by his appearance. Maybe then his parents would be more engaged with him.

It always struck me as odd that before the age of sixteen, the gestates, the lowest of humans, were virtually indistinguishable from vintage borns, the purest of persons. Though it wasn't actually true. Gestates always wore their gestation firm's band around their wrist, our clothes were tattered rags, and our eyes trained to the ground as we were taught to keep them. Vintage borns—even without alterations—were nothing like us … they were free … they were people.

"It's probably too much water. See how wet the ground is here?" Hastings said, his knees bent tight, his butt hovering a few inches above the ground. He slurped his smoothie while studying the yellowing leaves of the dandelions.

"We've had a lot of rain this summer," I said.

He was right, of course. This property had very poor drainage. It was the reason Hastings's family unit lived here. They were not eligible for anything better. It's the same reason they had me for their gestate.

They obtained me when I was seven, a few days after Hastings was born to Ms. Parker. This is what made him so unlike the rest of his family. He was conceived by his parents and his biological mother carried him and birthed him. A vintage born child from born parents. It was an odd occurrence, but one which was highly encouraged. Ms. Parker was praised for such an immense sacrifice; birthing a child was something few born women did. It was fairly common among the vintage borns, and of course those gestates who were created to birth the borns did it all the time. But a born woman birthing a child was far from typical. Hastings's family unit, in general, was far from typical. His parents had now been together for over twelve years.

"It could be too much salt as well," Hastings added thoughtfully.

"Yes, this land has far higher salt content than other areas."

He stood, still pondering the dying dandelions. "We live so close to the reclamation zone," he said, raising his eyes beyond his house, where the ruins of the reclamation zone haunted the eastern skyline.

He was so unlike the rest of his family unit. He was always asking questions, never satisfied with watching his screen. He wanted to run and play—a true sign he was unaltered. That was probably what bothered his parents the most about him: not his appearance, but his behavior. They caught him, once, climbing a tree … and I was severely punished.

I got to my feet. At our ages I was more than a foot taller than him. If I ever saw him once he was full-grown, he would tower above me. But it would never happen; I would never see him again once my year turned sixteen, a month from now. Then, I would be removed from his family unit, which paid only the government subsidy for me, and placed with those who could pay more.

"I bet the land of the reclamation zone is really salty," Hastings said, nodding his head vigorously to himself and making a goofy face.

He did such things to make me laugh. I was not supposed to laugh, but it was not a punishable offense, only a strongly discouraged behavior. But with Hastings, I couldn't help it.

"Yes, young sir, I am sure the land by the ocean is quite salty."

"Stuff still grows over there, though," he said, going up onto his tiptoes.

How that helped him see more, I wasn't sure.

"Not particularly valuable plants," I said. "From what I can tell, it is mostly vines that do not appear to be edible. The saw palmettos and grasses are not edible, either. Only the scrub oaks hold any real value."

"Silly, the sea oats are edible, not the scrub oaks," he said, and took another sip from his smoothie.

"Yes, but no one is allowed to eat sea oats. People are allowed to eat acorns," I said, making a silly face at him. It made him laugh so hard he accidentally spit some smoothie onto the ground.

"We don't eat acorns," he argued.

"Everyone is asked to leave them for the wildlife, and your family unit complies with the request, but you are allowed to eat them."

Hastings giggled. "We comply because my father detests things made from acorn flour."

"Perhaps that is true," I said, winking at him. I was secretly grateful that Mr. James detested acorn flour; it was so difficult for me to make. I much preferred the various flours that were delivered to the house—those I did not have to soak or shell or grind.

"Can I help you hoe the garden plot?" he asked as I picked up the hoe and moved from the dandelions to the raised section of amended soil where I grew the designated vegetables.

"You know better than to ask such a question," I said to him, though I wasn't angry. It was a kind gesture, but one that could never be allowed—not with the cameras watching and my band listening.

"You let me when I was younger," he said, following me into the bright sun.

The temperature seemed to instantly rise fifteen degrees. "Yes, when you were much younger, on cooler days your mother asked me to keep you outside. I had no choice but to allow you to help me. But today is far too hot for a vintage born to be outside and you are too old for such menial labor."

"You aren't altered against the heat and you stay outside all day," he said.

"Master Hastings," I said in a scolding tone expected to be used when a young born or vintage born spoke in such a dangerous way, "never compare your valued life to mine."

Hastings's face grew dark. "I hate it when you say things like that."

"There is no reason to hate the truth. We must accept it and make the most of it," I said, moving him to the shade cast by the patch of scrub oaks. His pale skin should not be outside in the intense sun. My skin, though unaltered, was not pale and freckled, as his was. My skin darkened in the summer sun; his turned red and then peeled away. Such a sight enraged his mother like nothing else.

"That's not the truth," he said, his bottom lip quivering.

"Oh, please do not cry, sir," I said, pulling him into me, the only action that could stop his tears.

The band on my wrist changed from blue to green. No doubt the cameras were trained on us as well.

"It is okay," I said, petting his sweat-soaked hair.

"It isn't, though. You'll be transferred soon and I'll never see you again." He began to sob. "I wish you were my sister, instead of that red-eyed monster."

It didn't matter that he was upset and a vintage born. To say such a thing was far too dangerous. I held him tight, thinking as quickly as I could.

"Oh, young sir, your skin is burning hot. This heat has made your mind unsteady. Come now, you must go inside to the cooled air. It was wrong of me to let you stay out as long as I have. Come quickly, before you have heatstroke," I said, leading him toward the house.

He shuffled his feet; he never wanted to go into the house if I wasn't there.

"Will you come with me?" he asked.

His miserable tone made my heart ache. How I wished I could say yes. How I wished I could control how I spent my time.

"No, sir, not quite yet. I'm scheduled to go in at five, in order to have dinner prepared by six thirty." It was the same every day; he knew this.

"I don't see why you have to do what they say," he said, his face in an angry pout.

"You have been taught how important order is," I said, guiding him closer to the house.

His shoulders slumped in defeat. I hated being right.

"Go inside. Go enjoy your free screen time," I said, making my voice sound as cheerful as possible.

He didn't answer. He didn't need to. He hated his screen. He was such a strange person, or perhaps it was something about being a vintage born. He and Mr. Northup were the only vintage borns I knew, and they both preferred being outside. They were very strange in that way.

Hastings plodded up the step to the side door—the same one I used to enter the house from my pod.

"I'll be in soon, sir," I said with a smile.

He turned to face me, his eyes speaking what his lips could not. My heart was breaking from his unspoken words.

TWO

The door closed behind Hastings. I left the slim shade provided by the narrow cover above the door. The walkway from my pod to the house was not covered, but at least there was a slim overhang of shade. Thunder boomed; my band vibrated. A weather alert lit up the tiny screen, indicating the storm should arrive within the hour.

Perhaps I would be inside a little earlier than expected. Hastings would be pleased. And I would be glad to contribute to his happiness.

The wind was picking up when I made my way toward the front of the property. The wind was the true issue with storms in this area—though lightning was always something to be cautious of. I'd never been struck by lightning; I had been struck by falling debris.

Condominiums: that's what the buildings were called long ago. Places people lived, with no yards—a bizarre, old-fashioned idea. Mr. Northup said so many people wanted to live by the ocean that there was never enough land for everyone, and so people built structures tall and lived within the same building, as if they were bees or ants or some other insect.

Once people realized how irresponsible their actions were—not growing their share of sustenance and encroaching onto the precious sands near the ocean—such buildings were outlawed. It was decided to allow the buildings to remain because taking them down would have caused more environmental damage. Leaving them as they stood allowed nature to take back what it wanted.

All over the country there were areas like this. I'd seen pictures once, when Hastings was learning in school about the reclamation zones. Whole cities were once foolishly built on land that could not sustain the population. There were cities in the desert where people drained rivers to water non-sustenance vegetation, simply because they liked the appearance of such vegetation. When the rivers were gone, people drained lakes and more rivers; eventually, the age of systematic reason took over and those ill-conceived cities were abandoned.

The same happened with coastal cities built below sea level. After flood upon flood, the people who lived in such places were told they either would move or receive no government assistance. Most moved. However, I overheard Ms. Parker saying there was still a population of sorts in those cities. It was a hushed conversation between her and a co-worker. Her words had confused me because, based on what Hastings told me, those cities were now deserted. Those who once lived there wisely chose not to isolate themselves from the rest of the nation. How anyone could live without government assistance was beyond my understanding. Why anyone would want to was also beyond me.

The wind increased. Strands of my dirt-brown hair pulled free from the tight braided bun gestate females must wear. I turned to face the wind, the hair blowing from my face. When the wind came from the reclamation zone it was heavy and thick. My skin became covered in a thin layer of salted air. Winds like this had made fairly quick work of the condominiums that dotted the ocean's edge near us. Every storm brought more rusted metal flying across the crumpled asphalt, onto the property occupied by the Parker-James family unit.

Above the wind I heard: "Azalea Rose …."

It was the name Mr. Northup had created for me. I stopped watching the clouds and went toward the banana trees that the Parker-James family unit shared with Mr. Northup. Since Mr. Northup and the Parker-James family unit were assigned to grow them, they spanned both properties. This was a reasonable decision by their assigned naturalist, given that the trees spread underground and did not know where one property began and another ended. Since Mr. Northup did not have a gestate, I was the one who maintained all the trees. Technically, he was supposed to maintain his portion. When I was among the large, broad leaves, the cameras could not see me and it was easy enough to strip the yellow leaves and aggressive vines from the ones on his property, along with the ones on the Parker-James property. I was not allowed to assist Mr. Northup, but I did so as often as I could.

"Azalea Rose, what're you doing working outside? Don't you know a storm is coming?" Mr. Northup called, coming out from his covered porch—where he spent most of his time.

I knew very little about his life before the age of uselessness; we were not allowed to talk about such things. I do remember when he entered that age, it was a few years after I arrived, though even before then he was often on his back porch or tending his beloved roses or his garden. Since then it seemed that was all he did.

The light on my band changed to green. The borns were listening again; they always listened when he spoke. It had always been that way, perhaps because I was not his assigned gestate and so the AIs alerted the borns every time we were near each other.

"Mr. Northup, sir, you know that isn't my name," I answered, though we both knew I only said that out of necessity. In truth, I appreciated the name he had gifted me. Gestates were assigned numbers by the gestation firms. To have been given a name, even by someone as remote as a neighbor, was an unusual occurrence.

"How are you today, Azalea Rose?" he asked, his long, thin fingers lightly touching a banana leaf.

"I am well, sir," I answered, "and you?" It was the scripted answer and follow-up question.

He hesitated, glancing at my band. I put my hand in my pocket. It would not cover his words completely, but perhaps with the wind ....

"I've been feeling a bit off lately," he said, his voice low but concerned. "I'm not sure what's going on." He was rubbing his forearm as if it was sore.

"Have you been to the doctor, sir? Perhaps you need an alteration." I kept my voice equally low. If they heard me make such a suggestion I could be reprimanded, though only if the born I made the suggestion to was offended by it and asked for me to be punished. Mr. Northup would never do such a thing.

He said, "I've made it eighty-six years without an alteration. I'm not going to start now."

"No, I suppose not, sir. But perhaps you could receive a checkup. Perhaps you don't need an alteration, just some medication," I said with concern.

Mr. Northup was too stubborn for his own good. His stubbornness kept him from having a gestate, which is why he had to work so hard tending his garden and roses. The sun was too hot in this part of the country. If he was younger it wouldn't have mattered, but he was far from young.

"Maybe I will make an appointment," he said.

His words sounded funny. His hands went out, catching me on the shoulder as he tried to keep himself from falling to the ground between the broad leaves of the banana plants.

"Mr. Northup, sir," I called as I went to the ground beside him. I lifted his head and shoulders onto my thighs.

He groaned. "I'm all right," he said, pushing himself up.

I helped him stand with me. "Here, lean on me," I said. My heart pounded with concern as I kept my grip tight around his chest and led him across his yard, toward his house.

I'd never been so close to his house—not even when I broke my arm when I was ten, and he had cared for me until the medical unit arrived to set the bone.

My band glowed green. They were still listening and undoubtedly tracking my steps away from the property I was assigned to. I was allowed, in extreme circumstances, to venture onto another family unit or, in this case, a single's property. Mr. Northup's falling down practically on top of me met that extreme criteria.

"Here, sir," I said. I helped him tentatively go up the first and then the second step to his expansive covered porch.

His house was obviously built long ago. It was nothing like the other houses around here, which were constructed of poured concrete walls and painted gray. His house was built by his parents, who bought this property. That was why he was allowed to keep such an odd house and why he was allowed to grow ornate, wasteful roses. He owned this property; it was not the government's. Though, why anyone would buy property on such salt-infested land, I didn't understand.

"I'm not sure why I fell," Mr. Northup said, his voice sounding groggy.

"Sir, the ground by the banana plants is uneven. Those plants are always trying to shoot up to make new plants. Your foot probably caught the edge of a new shoot," I said, hoping I was right. I twisted the doorknob and helped him step into his house.

My breath caught.

This place was wholly different from the house the Parker-James family unit occupied. Wholly different from anywhere I'd ever been before. Pictures hung on the walls, fabric couches and chairs were gathered in a common area of the house, and they looked like they'd been used often. Mr. Northup had a family unit once. They must have sat on this furniture together. How strange to sit together … not to mention all the wood. There was a wood table, chairs, coffee table, shelves, and even bright white painted wood around each door and window, and even around the base of the wall and at the top—as if framing the light blue walls, heavy wood doors, and clear windows.

"Help me sit," he said as he reached for a navy-blue wooden chair. A dark wood table sat in front of it, atop a lovely navy-blue and cream patterned rug.

I helped him sit as I released him, and reached my hand for the wooden table. I shouldn't have done such a thing, but I couldn't help it. I'd never seen a wood table before. The grain of the wood was so alive, so unlike the cold metal of every other table I'd ever seen.

I wanted to speak, but I dared not. I was sure it was a crime for a gestate to be in a place like this.

I tried to be still and not see such things I was not allowed to see, but I couldn't help it; the beauty called to me. Near the row of windows was a narrow table, not very long, filled with photographs in frames of all different shapes and materials. I'd never seen so many photographs displayed like this. My eyes went from picture to picture.

"Is this you?" I asked. It was a horrible thing to ask a person anything that did not pertain directly to work, and this did not. I glanced nervously at my band; they were still listening. I wished they would stop. I wished for a moment I could be a person instead of a gestate.

His eyes lit up. "Hard to tell, isn't it? Yes, that's me, with my wife and our son, when he was no older than your Hastings."

Wife. It was an old-fashioned term, one I hadn't heard since my early days of training. "I did not realize you were married," I said, using an equally old-fashioned term, but the one I was instructed to use when a born or vintage born used the words "wife" or "husband."

"I was, for fifty-nine years. She passed away a few months before you arrived here." His voice caught for a moment at the mention of his wife's death. "That's our son as an adult, there in the next picture, with his wife and their kids."

The picture showed a man probably in his thirties, with brown hair and brown eyes. He looked a lot like a younger Mr. Northup. Though when I compared the man in that picture to the picture of Mr. Northup when his son was young, the two were only slightly similar. The expression on Mr. Northup's face was so different. In that picture with his wife and young son, Mr. Northup's eyes were hard and uncaring; his expression was nothing like the man sitting before me. It reminded me of Mr. James. The skin colors were different, but the look of coldness was the same.

I went back to the picture of Mr. Northup's son and his family. The woman had lighter hair and lighter eyes. The boy in the picture matched her blonde hair and pale blue eyes—natural colors, not the altered kind. He was no older than Hastings. Mr. Northup's son held an infant girl in a dress with roses embroidered along the hem. She had dark hair and eyes that matched her father's.

"They appear kind," I said, accidentally allowing the words to slip from my lips.

"They are"—he glanced at my glowing band—"or were," he said sadly.

"They're no longer living?" I blurted out.

"They died soon after that picture was taken, a bizarre accident," he said, his voice cracking.

I lowered my eyes. Because of my impertinent questioning I had caused a vintage born to experience emotional pain. "I'm sorry, sir," I said, my eyes focused on the light wood of the floor.

"You didn't know," he said kindly.

I shouldn't have spoken; I should not be here. "May I get you anything before I leave, sir?"

"A glass of water, please. My glass is there, by the sink." His voice was steadier.

"Yes, sir," I said, filling the glass from the faucet.

This house was designed so differently. It seemed as if the food preparation area was here, in the middle of the house. I wished I could spend hours exploring, or really, I wished I could be assigned here. It would be a privilege to work in a house such as this. It would be a gift to work for Mr. Northup, but then I would not be with Hastings. At least now I could see Mr. Northup outside on a frequent basis; if I did not work for the Parker-James family unit, I would never see Hastings. The thought brought pain, followed by a prickle of tears in my eyes. I would be leaving them both so soon.

"Goodbye, sir," I said after I placed the clear glass of water on the table near his hand.

"Thank you," he said, moving his torso in order to make me look into his eyes.

It was forbidden to do such a thing.

"I was created to serve," I answered obediently, keeping my eyes focused on the wood floor.

I stepped out onto the porch, but before the door closed, Mr. Northup spoke. "You were created for much more," he said solemnly.

I closed the door. Something was rising up inside of me. Feeling unsteady, my hand went to the wooden column that held up the roof of the porch. I felt something … a sadness, a longing. I glanced back into Mr. Northup's house. The white wooden shutters on the inside of the windows were closed on most of them, not allowing others to see in, but from where I stood, I could see through one of the windows. Mr. Northup was sipping his water, rubbing his fingertips slowly back and forth across the surface of the table.

I stepped from the porch. The air was cooler now. The wind blew harder, pulling the Spanish moss tight against the limbs of the low scrub oaks. Rain tried to wash away the emotion rising within me … it failed.

Three

I should've run to make my time in the rain as short as possible, but I did not. My band was no longer green. There was no longer anything for the borns to listen to other than the thunder. The holes in my shoes filled with water, soaking my threadbare socks. The clothes I wore—little more than rags— clung to my body. The air felt cool against my wet skin.

The lights of the Parker-James house lit up the storm-darkened afternoon. I stopped, turning to face Mr. Northup's house. The light glowed from his windows as it did from all the other windows of the other houses around, yet the light from his house was different. A lump formed in my stomach. I did not want to move forward. I did not want to go to the Parker-James house. Never had I felt like this.

I was trained not to feel. I was told emotions did not belong to gestates, that we had no right to them. It was wrong, these things swirling inside of me, raging like the storm. I forced a step forward. It was wrong to have such thoughts. I was assigned to the Parker-James family unit; I must serve them. My eyes stung. Tears came.

I did not want to go back. I did not want that life.

I wanted a different one. One that Mr. Northup had. Though he was old and becoming feeble, his life was different.

My band vibrated. It was five. I should be inside the drab concrete structure. I raised my chin, allowing the rain to wash away my tears.

The door in front of me swung open.

"There you are," Hastings said, grateful to see me.

I smiled at him—I could always smile at him. He was the bright spot in my life of darkness.

"My mother is going to be mad. You're all wet," he said with concern.

"I got caught in the rain," I said, though it was obvious.

He studied me for a second and then disappeared. I stepped onto the relatively dry space beneath the slender covering above the side door. My pod was right beside me. I could go inside and dry off, even change into dry rags, but then I would get wet again on my way back to the house.

The door opened and Hastings reappeared. He held his finger to his lips as he handed me a towel. It was not a towel I should use; it was his towel, one made for a born, not a gestate. It was illegal for me to use such a thing, but at this angle, in the rain, I doubted the cameras could see me. If they did, the AIs monitoring the system would probably not realize this was a towel I was not allowed to use. I quickly took the towel from Hastings and stepped into the house, drying off as much as I could to at least keep from dripping throughout the house.

Ms. Parker would still be angry. She hated it when I was caught in a rainstorm. She said it showed how lazy I was.

Hastings whispered, "Your shoes."

He was right; there was no way to dry them. They would leave puddles everywhere I went and, more than that, they would make a squishing sound. Another thing his mother could not tolerate. I slipped off my shoes and socks. I would be reprimanded for being barefoot. Perhaps she wouldn't notice.

I opened the door and put my shoes on the narrow concrete step. The socks I put in the rain. Nothing cleaned as well as rainwater. They would not be noticed—Hastings and I were the only ones who ever used this door.

I rubbed the towel roughly over my body one more time, squeezing it against my hair to dry it as much as possible. The tight braided bun would look the same as it always did, only darker.

Hastings whispered, "Maybe the conditioned air will dry you out before anyone notices."

"Thank you, sir," I said, giving him the towel. "I'll prepare dinner now."

He gave me a hug, which was not allowed, but now that I was fully inside, the cameras missed this corner. Hastings had been the one to figure out the various camera dead zones inside and outside of the house. He was young, but smart. He tapped into the camera feed one day and studied it. He was the one who told me the camera in the food preparation room was broken. This was the most important dead zone of all.

He released me and ran off to hang up the towel before anyone noticed. A filthy gestate using the towel of a young vintage born … if I was at the gestation firm, I could be whipped for such a crime. Here I could not be whipped, but there were other ways they could punish me.

Hastings was right about the conditioned air. The air in the house was always cold, a stark contrast to the near one-hundred-degree heat outside. The hard vinyl floor sent chills through my bare feet. Small bumps rose on my arms and legs. That was part of the difference between Mr. Northup's house and this one; his felt warmer—not just the air, but some other way. It felt warm and … as if it wanted me to be there.

I'd never felt that this house wanted me to be in it.

The house was quiet, as usual this time of day, and in general. Only after dinner, when they went into their personal rooms and used the larger viewing screens, was there noise—or if twelve-year-old Salt was in a mood, which she often was. But that wasn't random noise, it was screaming.

At this time of day the house was exceptionally quiet; each member of the Parker-James family unit had their assigned viewing, which they typically did on their handheld screens with wireless ear speakers in. They very rarely interacted with one another; only Hastings ever seemed to have any interest in the others. During training, we were instructed that most individuals within family units were too busy with their own tasks to spend much time focusing on one another. That was one of the many reasons family units required gestates. The exception, they said, was unaltered vintage borns, due to their lack of focus on assigned tasks. This would be another aspect of Hastings that would eventually be altered away.

Gratefully, I made it to the food preparation room without being noticed. I felt relief; perhaps only Hastings would realize how wet I was. He would join me soon, as he always did, but maybe his mother and sister would not. I tapped the screen on the front of the refrigeration unit. The internal scan told me what ingredients to remove. The screen next to the stove then lit up with the instructions for the meal. This was not a meal most in the Parker-James family unit cared for. I would hear the complaints—but ultimately it was not my decision what they ate. The state nutritionists made that decision. If all adults in the house agreed that they preferred not to have a particular meal, they could petition to have it removed from their menu options, but Mr. James enjoyed this meal and so he had not agreed to remove it from the menu.

The wind grew louder and the rain pelted the windows. I thought of Mr. Northup, of his welcoming house that somehow kept out the sounds of the storm. A longing bubbled inside me. I filled a pot of water and set it on the stove. I rinsed the quinoa, scooped it into the pot, and placed the lid on top.

"Ugh, what's that smell?"

I didn't move my head; I remained focused on chopping the cauliflower.

"I'm talking to you, girl," Salt said in a repulsive tone.

I could feel her red eyes boring into the side of my face. I should care, I should try to appease her. When she was in moods such as this, it meant trouble for me. But something about the afternoon made it impossible for me to care about her disgust of me.

"How can I assist you?" I said, though I sounded anything but accommodating.

She stepped back, startled, not used to hearing me respond in such a manner.

"You smell disgusting," she said after a few seconds of my staring into her blood-red eyes and her glaring into my mud-brown ones. I was not allowed to look in the eyes of borns unless commanded to do so, but I didn't care—not today.

She was searching for a fight … maybe I was too.

The members of my assigned family unit were not allowed to physically reprimand me; that was reserved for those employed by my gestation firm. But Salt was different. Born and vintage born adolescents were sometimes difficult to control, and she, in particular, was a challenge to her parents. If she hit me, there was nothing anyone could do about it, or so that is what my company had determined. If she caused a broken bone or deep laceration needing medical attention, though, her family unit must pay for that. As a result, Salt no longer used weapons against me. The scar on my thigh had cost her a new screen; she was furious at me for weeks about that. Now I relished the thought of her attacking me and my returning the aggression. Power coursed within me as I felt my muscles tensing, preparing for what I was sure would come.

"You're wet," Ms. Parker's shrill voice said reproachfully when she entered the food preparation room, screen in hand.

I lowered my eyes, the tension in my arms fading. "Yes, ma'am. I was caught in the storm."

"She smells so gross! Can we please get her altered?" Salt said, gagging.

"We've had this discussion," Ms. Parker said, still observing me. "That alteration is not allowed in gestates. If they do not sweat, they could die in the Southern heat."

"So?" Salt said blankly to her mother. "What difference does a dead gesty make?"

I clenched my hand. I wanted to hit her more than I ever had before.

The sound of boiling water came from the pot of quinoa, snapping me out of myself. I relaxed my hand and reached to turn down the burner to keep it from frothing over. Salt shoved me, but I did not fall backward as she'd expected. She was bigger than me, but in every other fight I did not fight back; I was merely her punching bag. That would not happen today.

"I wasn't done speaking to you," she said, but in a tone that told me her anger was mixed with fear; she could sense I wasn't backing down, even with her mother present.

I raised my gaze to hers—I was not allowed to be so disrespectful. "No, ma'am. I'm sorry, ma'am," I said, my voice far more threatening than hers.

"That's enough," Ms. Parker said. "I don't know what's gotten into you, but if you aren't careful, we will send you for reeducation."

My band glowed bright green. I swallowed hard. "Yes, ma'am," I said timidly.

Ms. Parker and her family unit may not be allowed to physically hurt me, but those employed by my gestation firm certainly could. They took pride in how loud they could cause us to scream.

"Come with me, Salt. I'd like to eat dinner sooner rather than later," Ms. Parker said, her purple eyes matching her daughter's purple hair. They turned to leave the narrow room. "Be sure you shower as soon as dinner is prepared. And never come into my house smelling like a wet pig again."

"Yes, ma'am, I'm sorry, ma'am."

Her body became rigid. "Are you barefoot?" Her tone of disgust surpassed that of her daughter's.

"My shoes were filled with water, ma'am," I said, wondering how I ever could've been so brash as to come into the house barefooted.

She moved closer to me. She towered above me, as all adult borns did. "Never … allow … your filthy gestate feet … to touch my floors again," Ms. Parker said, her voice shaking in fury.

"Yes, ma'am," I whispered without lifting my head.

She remained where she was, breathing heavily, as if she, too, wanted to attack me. I doubted I could fight them both off … I doubted I would try.

Finally, she stepped away, taking her screen from the counter. "Salt," she said, "finish your assigned viewing."

Salt emitted a low grunt as she stomped her way out of the food preparation area, her long purple hair flowing in soft waves.

I swallowed. Tears of fear were stinging my eyes. How could I have been so reckless?

I trembled, thinking of what she could've done, what she may still cause to be done to me. I would be here only a month longer. Each of these things was being noted in my file. I would be punished when I returned to the gestation firm.

The oven beeped. I opened the oven door, my hands and arms shaking as I slid in the roasting pan of cauliflower. The heat offered me momentary warmth.

Four

I did my best to think of the greens in front of me, not the memory of Salt's glaring red eyes. I used the most tender dandelion greens from around the garden beds, where the soil was richest. Still, few in the family unit would eat the tender greens, which they were mandated to grow … or, I was, on their behalf.

Salt's eyes popped into my memory. She hated me so much, it was unsettling. Though she always had. She was only four when I arrived. I tried to engage with her as I was instructed to, but I had replaced the previous gestate. If their relationship was anything like the relationship Hastings and I had, then I understood why she would be angry when I arrived, taking her familiar gestate's place.

Though I doubted Salt could ever show the kindness toward anyone that Hastings showed toward me. With her red eyes, flat nose, and high cheekbones, it was difficult to imagine her ever looking kind. Only her hair had any softness to it; the purple was subdued—not as bright as some purples— and it flowed gently around her shoulders. She was, I suppose, less intimidating than her mother, who was at least half a foot taller than me, with the same high cheekbones as her daughter, but with a sharper nose. Her hair was the red of her daughter's eyes, and spiked. Ms. Parker reminded me of an angry porcupine. In truth, they each looked a lot like every other female of their respective generation.

In training we were told that borns have as much natural variation as the gestates and vintage borns, but because of the alterations they all end up looking like their generational prototypes. Salt had the same hair as every other girl her age. It was thick and smooth, with the perfect amount of waves. Many borns her age even had the same purple hue. Purple and teal were new additions to the alteration options when she was selected, so those were the two most common colors for boys and girls her age. It was the same for her parents; they matched the coloring, size, and shape of almost every other born their age. There were different color combinations, but for the most part, body sizes and shapes were exactly alike.

The borns are designer people, designed by those who selected and raised them. Hastings, being a vintage born, was different. I exhaled, sadly realizing that someday soon he would look like them. He would be eligible for those alterations in less than seven years. I doubted I would even recognize him then. The thought of his kind brown eyes and freckled pale skin being gone, turned into who knew what, was disturbing.

When he got older and moved away from his mother, he could choose not to maintain his alterations and after a few years would revert back to his natural state—if he wanted to. He probably wouldn't want to, but as a vintage born he had that option; his alterations would have to be maintained. Even the borns, if they wanted, could choose to override the alterations their parents had selected for them and be altered in different ways. Though none of them ever seemed to opt for it.

Gestates are the opposite. We remain unaltered for life, except for the two alterations we were given during our gestation. The alterations that, along with being gestated by a machine, make us less than people. First, we are unable to truly emotionally attach at the level which borns and vintage borns are able to attach or care for one another; and, second, we lack free will. We are altered to be overly compliant, a sort of robot in a human body. Perhaps that is why Hastings gets so frustrated with my following orders. He is free. His mind doesn't make him comply.

The oven beeped. I removed the roasted cauliflower, ladled up four bowls of tomato soup, and placed a heap of quinoa and cauliflower in each bowl. I swiftly took the food to the designated eating spaces and pressed the tiny button which would send a message to each of their devices that the evening meal was prepared. Mr. James was not home yet. He preferred to spend as little time with his family unit as possible. As a result, he typically did not take the first transport unit and so ended up on the second one, which did not arrive here until after the family unit's set mealtime of 6:30 p.m.

This was a source of great conflict for Ms. Parker and Mr. James. Ms. Parker felt it unfair that she spent more time with the children than he did. Other family units were allowed to leave their children with their gestate, but because Salt had been reprimanded so often for physically attacking me, my gestation firm would not allow me to be the one left in charge of her. This was an extreme hardship for Ms. Parker, in particular.

I returned to the food preparation area before any of the family unit arrived in the dining area. I would've liked to see Hastings, but given that I was still barefoot, it was best I avoid his mother.

Thunder reverberated through the house, and I wondered for a split second how thunder sounded in Mr. Northup's house made of wood and soft fabric furniture. He even had fabric hanging from the sides of the windows. In this house, everything was hard … even the people.

I heard the members of the family unit enter the dining area. They were quiet; each likely had a screen in front of them, with ear speakers turned on. I took a deep breath and stepped quietly into the dining area, as I was obligated to do. I stood far back, against the wall, trying not to be noticed.

Young Hastings saw me and gave me a friendly blink because he had not yet figured out how to wink. I returned the gesture, and we both grinned a little.

Each of them had a screen in the screen holder at their seating area. They watched assigned viewing material as they ate in silence, as always.

Ms. Parker finished with her salad. I went to the cold metal table where they sat, silently removing her salad bowl.

"Take mine too," Salt commanded without glancing up from her screen.

I swiftly removed it.

"You can take mine too," Hastings said.

Neither of the children had touched their salad. They rarely did. I was careful to note which had been Hastings's and which had been Salt's.

I entered the food preparation area. I placed Ms. Parker's bowl into the sanitizer, the remains of Salt's salad were placed into the composter, and her bowl into the sanitizer. I quickly began eating the contents of Hastings's bowl, sprinkling an extra hint of salt onto the olive oil and lemon juice dressing.

I was not supposed to eat their leftovers; those items were supposed to go into the composter. I was supposed to drink my daily sustenance powder and nothing more. But when I drank only the powder, I was hungry all day. It may have all the things necessary for me to live and even grow, but my stomach apparently did not know that. I felt bad for any gestate who did not have borns who disliked many of the meals prepared for them, and a camera dead zone in the food preparation room.

I placed Hastings's empty bowl into the sanitizer and returned to where the family unit sat upon the metal stools at the metal dining table. From where I stood, I could view Ms. Parker's screen. She was watching a series specifically designed for mothers. This one seemed to be about raising children who did not rely on their parents. No one wanted children who continued to need them past their nineteenth birthday. By then, parents were considered free of any obligation they had to their child, and the young adult moved into housing that was associated with whatever career they were best suited for. But if the person struggled there and was not living according to guidelines, and if the behavior was egregious enough, the parents could be fined.

Based on Salt's current behavior, Ms. Parker and Mr. James had reasons to be concerned. No wonder Ms. Parker was assigned such viewing material.

I heard the front door open in the distance. Mr. James was now home. I stepped into the shadows, doing what I could to blend into the wall. His shoes squeaked. Hastings looked up with some degree of excitement as his father entered the room, but he was the only one who did.

"Welcome home," Hastings said.

"Thank you," Mr. James said as he went to the hand sanitizing station. He placed his hands into the cuffs, triggering the ultraviolet light. He pulled out his hands and sat down near Hastings.

"How was your day?" Hastings asked, still the only one who had acknowledged his father's entrance.

"Ah, nothing too interesting happened, until the very end," Mr. James answered.

"Oh, what was it?" Hastings asked, trying to engage his father, who was already flicking on his screen.

"Nothing that concerns you. I'll tell your mother about it later, but nothing you or Salt need to think about," Mr. James said, eyeing his family unit partner who never lifted her purple eyes from her screen.

"What about you?" Mr. James asked. "How was your day?"

"My day was good, a bit boring," Hastings said, still trying hard to keep his father focused on him, not the screen he was slipping into the holder.

"That's great. What's on your screen tonight?" Mr. James asked, leaning over to see Hastings's screen. "Ah, math video songs. I used to enjoy those when I was a kid."

"You can watch with me," Hastings said, his voice hopeful.

Mr. James turned away. "I'd better not. I have my own programming to watch." He took a bite of the salad.

This was the end of their conversation and Hastings knew it. His shoulders slumped. After a few minutes of silence, with the rest of his family unit staring at their screens, Hastings stood and left the dining area.

I wished I could follow him and tell him I would interact with him, but such actions were not allowed. Instead, I removed Hastings's mostly full bowl of soup and Mr. James's empty salad bowl.

As soon as the food preparation room door closed behind me, I lifted Hastings's bowl to my lips. The gloriously rich tomato soup warmed my mouth and filled my stomach. I quickly scooped chunks of roasted cauliflower into my mouth, followed by what remained of the quinoa covered in tomato soup. When I finished his bowl, I retrieved a drinking glass and filled it with water from the sink. Not limited to how much water I could drink, I quickly guzzled one glass and then a second. I wiped out Hastings's bowl and placed it in the sanitizing machine.

I went back into the dining area. Only Mr. James and Ms. Parker remained.

They were arguing, so I stepped back into the food preparation area, busying myself by wiping down the shelves of the refrigeration unit. Mr. James and Ms. Parker often argued, but no one faulted them for this. They'd been together far too long, far longer than was natural.

It was expected that family unit creation partnerships dissolve after their child reaches three years of age, when the pair can legally separate. The Parker-James family unit was an anomaly, both in having so many children and in the number of years together.

They had no one to blame except themselves. They had conceived a vintage born child. The parents of borns were only mandated to stay together until the child was three. And then parenting responsibilities were split evenly between them or their gestates. In contrast, the parents of vintage borns were required to be together for ten years. It was said this was because vintage borns didn't have the proper modifications and so needed additional parenting support. To be together for ten years … few could imagine such a thing.

The arguing had stopped. This was my cue to reenter the dining area.

"That's what I heard, six more weeks at the most," Mr. James said, his dark green hair and brown skin always causing me to think of a tree.

Ms. Parker was calmer than she typically was after an argument. Whatever he was telling her must be of particular interest.

I was not allowed to interrupt and ask if they needed anything; my job was to stand as still as possible until I noticed something they needed or they signaled for something.

"That will be good," she said, tapping her burgundy nails on the metal table. "It didn't make sense—them letting him live for as long as they have. It would be quite understandable with alterations, but without them … what can he do? How can he contribute?"

"He can't," Mr. James said, stuffing a piece of cauliflower covered in tomato soup into his mouth. "That's the reason. It's strange, though, he's not that old, only in his mid-eighties."

"That's comparable to a hundred and ten with alterations," Ms. Parker responded.

"That's exactly what they were saying at the office."

"Well, that is certainly interesting," Ms. Parker said thoughtfully.

"See, it's good I worked late. I wouldn't have heard any of that if I'd caught the first transport," Mr. James said.

"Yes, today it paid off. Most days it does not, but today it did."

"Do you want me to apply for his property?" he asked, slurping his soup.

"You?" she said. The skin between her eyes pulled together.

Most of the skin on her face didn't move, but occasionally, when she was unclear about something, that part of her face did.

"Hastings is already nine," he said, wiping his tomato-stained lips on the cloth napkin. "You know how long property paperwork takes to go through. And by the time they build a new house on the site, he will be ten and our family unit will be dissolved before it's all done." He conveyed this information with so little emotion it caught me off guard, though why it did, I wasn't sure.

Ms. Parker's back straightened, her face growing even harder than it typically was. "Is it that easy for you, the end of our family?"

"The end of our family *unit*," Mr. James said. "We will still have our children, which is why I thought you might prefer I live nearby."

"*Our children?* Since when do you do anything with *our* children?" she said coldly.

"What're you implying? I paid my equal share. I signed off on each of them, just as you did. I live here, as is mandated. What more do you want me to do?" There was no anger in his voice. There rarely was. He was complacent in his interactions with his partner … complacent in life.

"Yes, you signed off on them, but you did not give birth to them, and you interact with them and me as infrequently as possible."

"You chose to birth Hastings. That was your choice. As for Salt, we made her selections together, and I helped care for her as much as you did when she was a baby."

"I chose to birth Hastings because removing an already implanted embryo from one woman and placing it in another is rarely successful. He would've died if I hadn't decided to birth him, and you know that level of waste is not acceptable," she said defensively.

"It was a noble decision, but one *you* made," he said, finishing his soup.

"And *you* signed off on," she said, her purple eyes flashing hot.

"Yes," he said, slamming his hands on the table. His orange eyes flared with rare emotion.

My body began to tremble as he stood, his tattooed arms bulging. From the corner of my eye, I saw movement and the hint of purple hair hiding in the hallway.

"I did sign off on the birth of *my* son, and I've been here every day since, as it's mandated for me to be, but I will be here no longer than is mandated. We have now been together twelve years. It is an unnatural length of time. I will be gone the day after Hastings's tenth birthday." He stood taller, his shoulders falling back, his breaths slowing. "If you would prefer for me to live close to this location—assuming you will be remaining in this house—please let me know and I will apply for the Northup property."

I jerked at the words "Northup property"; they were speaking of Mr. Northup. This whole time, when they were speaking of an old man who was better disposed of, they were speaking of Mr. Northup. I quickly lowered my head, my heartbeat thumping in my ears.

"Will you create a new family unit?" Ms. Parker said with a scratchiness in her voice.

Mr. James let his head fall forward and he sat down. "I'm only fifty-four. It's difficult to predict what I will do, with such a vast future ahead of me. At this point in time I do not wish to sign for more children. Perhaps I'll change my mind. They're quite adorable when they're young, though exceedingly difficult when they're older," he said with a simple smile.

"But you would not sign for any more with me?" Her arms were folded.

His fingers touched the table as if he might reach out to her, but he did not. "No, not with you," he said solemnly.

Ms. Parker stood, flipping backward the metal stool she'd been sitting on. She stormed from the room. Mr. James was still for a moment. Then he scraped the bottom of his bowl, swallowed what remained in his mouth, and placed the spoon in the empty bowl. He stood, taking his screen as he went toward his personal room.

In the hallway, I heard something that sounded like someone was crying.

I remained still for longer than I should have; gestates were never allowed to be idle, but that's what I was doing. It was difficult to steady my thoughts. Mr. James said Mr. Northup was going to be dissolved or perhaps already was being dissolved. Six *more* weeks, he'd said. Mr. James worked in the dissolution department. I'd known this for several years, but he rarely discussed his work with Ms. Parker. Though in this case, it made sense for him to share this information. I tried to process the information. Mr. James would be moving out of this house in a little less than a year. If she wanted him to, he would try and take possession of Mr. Northup's house.

My chest pulled tight; my mind swirled. I must move, I must not be idle. I lifted the chair lying on its side. In a daze I took the dishes to the food preparation room, mindlessly wiping them clean before placing them in the sanitizing machine.

Mr. Northup would be dissolved, his beautiful house torn down, and one like this and all the others, would be built in its place. And his roses … his wasteful, ornate roses that he loved so much would be killed … just like him. My chest tightened so severely I gasped for air. I bent over the sink, placing my mouth beneath the faucet, allowing the water to flow over my face. The warm liquid helped ground me. I dried my face with one of the cloth napkins before I loaded them and the dish wiping rags into the rag cleansing machine and started the cycle.

I wandered through the house with a broom and dustpan in my hands, sweeping from time to time. Near the front door, Mr. James's umbrella had left a pool of water. I took a rag from my back pocket and wiped up the water. On the other side of the wall, Hastings sat alone in his room, watching his screen. I wanted to go to him to tell him of Mr. Northup's impending death, but that was a ridiculous thought, one that would cause my back to be torn open with lashes. Never, under any circumstance, could a gestate reveal what was said by her born masters.

I could hear the muffled sounds of each of the large viewing screens in the personal rooms. Hastings's was telling him to brush his teeth. It would turn off soon, telling him a short bedtime story as the light in his room dimmed and then darkened. At that point, all others in the house would be required to use their ear speakers.

Typically, at this time of the evening when I was still cleaning, the loudest sounds from the screens came from Salt's room. Tonight, her room was silent. I wanted to open the door to see if the screen was on, to make sure everything was okay. That was something I was mandated to do: to ensure the health and safety of my assigned family unit, as best as I could. But Salt did not want me in her room any more than I wanted to be there. I moved on to the next room. It was Ms. Parker's. Typically, her room was the quietest. Tonight, it was the loudest.

Five

The heavy rain pelting the corrugated aluminum roof of my pod helped drown out the noise of my mind. There were so many thoughts it was difficult to know what I was thinking. I was grateful for the empty darkness of the metal storage container, as Mr. Northup called the gestate pods. It didn't matter what they were originally designed for. A light bulb, metal sink, toilet, and showerhead had been added and now the storage container was what gestates lived in. So different from Mr. Northup's house. No wonder it always seemed to bother him that I lived in a pod. Though even the born houses were nothing compared to his house.

The house that would be destroyed in a few months when he was gone. I pushed my hands against my scalp, trying to drive out the thoughts.

Lightning flashed in the window, partially covered by the Spanish moss I'd hung in a feeble attempt at privacy. My body contracted into a ball. Mr. Northup dead. Hastings no longer mine. I couldn't stop the tears.

I didn't try.

Thunder reverberated against the metal around me, breaking my useless thoughts. Something hit the side of the pod. Debris. It was always debris. The pieces were not large enough to do any real damage to the concrete houses borns lived in, but the pods of gestates were often no match for flying spears of rusted metal.

I wanted to stand, to pace back and forth, to move my body. My band was dark. Even the AIs weren't listening. It was the middle of the night and I was supposed to be asleep. As long as I didn't move much, they would think I was asleep and I would have privacy. Not that they ever read my mind, but something about the darkened band made my racing heart slow.

Thunder shook my pod. I turned over on my side, my face pressed against the old shirt filled with moss. A gift from Mr. Northup that he was not allowed to give me ….

If I told Mr. Northup they were killing him, could he leave this place before the effects were too far gone? If he went somewhere the government didn't control, would he be okay? Did such a place exist? I had no idea … maybe he did.

I stared up at the rusty ceiling. It was pointless. There was nothing I could do. No law was as strictly enforced as the law that demanded the silence of the gestates. If I told Mr. Northup, or even hinted about it … my mind pulled away from the thought.

I'd been punished before; my back bore the scars. But those punishments were nothing compared to what would be inflicted for a crime such as this. A crime that would be discovered as soon as it was committed. My band was always monitoring everything I said. If that was overheard—I'd be better off dead. Even if I stole a piece of paper from Hastings's room and tried to slip him a note, the cameras inside and outside of the house were sure to notice. And what if the paper was found.

I stared at my banded wrist resting on the makeshift pillow. Bands could be removed. They weren't adhered to our skin or anything, and we were allowed to remove them for up to five minutes to clean the skin. Any longer than that without a heartbeat detected, an alert would be sent to the gestation firm enforcers about a possible runaway. Each of the gestates whose backs were shredded in front of me, had been trying to escape. The firms always punished runaways in front of the young gestates … searing their screams into our memories.

The only gestates punished more severely than the runaways were the ones who told the secrets of those they served. They did not make us watch that punishment. A tear slipped from my eye, falling onto the ragged shirt stuffed with moss.

I pulled my legs up, my back arching as I wrapped my arms around my legs. To warn Mr. Northup was impossible.

My mind jumped—then you will watch him die.

I whimpered.

My band began to glow as it turned on to listen to the storm that raged within me.

Six

The band around my wrist vibrated.

My eyes blinked open. My body ached, the consequence of not enough sleep—I'd thought too long last night. It was right that gestates were instructed not to think. There was no use in doing so. Our thoughts didn't matter, and by allowing our minds to wander late at night, our bodies didn't get the needed rest.

The band vibrated again; I hadn't moved enough to make it stop. I sat up. The sun wasn't up. It was never up when I was awakened. Even in the peak of summer, when the sun rose early and set late, I was up long before and long after it was.

The air was cooler this morning than it had been yesterday—an appreciated change from the near hundred-degree weather. The summer temperatures in this area were severe, but it was the ninety-plus percent humidity that made the air so heavy it was difficult to breathe. This was the time when the most gestates died—in the South, at least. In the North, it was the winter that took them.

I shuffled the few feet to the one narrow shelf in the pod. I opened the tin of sustenance powder, careful to pour only two scoops into the metal water bottle I drank from. If I used more than two scoops, I wouldn't have enough to last me for the entire month. I learned that the hard way when I was seven. I filled the bottle with water from the sink and swirled the liquid inside until it was dissolved. The smooth metal felt good against my lips. The food powder was without taste or substance. It was designed to keep us alive … but never satisfied.

I brushed my hair with a hard plastic brush. My hair was jagged and thin, nothing like Salt's thick, flowing hair. Some pieces were long, stretching to the middle of my spine. Many others were broken at my shoulder blades or higher. That didn't matter; I wasn't created to be beautiful, I was created to serve. I braided the hair into one long braid and tied the thin end with a bit of old cloth. Then I twisted the entire braid into a bun at the base of my neck, using the assigned metal clip to hold the braid in place. The clip was old and rusted, often snapping strands as it held the straggly hair in place.

I went to the metal sink to wash my face. The sink stood so close to the metal toilet that my left leg touched its rim as I splashed the chilly water onto my face. The showerhead dripped one giant drop of water onto my head. It always did this when I turned on the sink beneath it. I guzzled the rest of my nourishment drink, brushed my teeth, and was out the door fifteen minutes after waking, as trained.

The walkway from my pod to the house was dark, normal at this time of day. No one inside was awake. I heard scurrying and could make out the back end of an opossum waddling away from the compost pile. It was hunting for the bugs that helped decompose the garden waste. I passed the animal most mornings on my way into the house. When I first came across it, I made the mistake of approaching it, and it fell onto its side as if it was dead. I was so afraid I'd killed it and would be punished. I'd slipped back out after the family unit left for the day, to bury it quickly in the compost heap. There were few cameras on this part of the house, so I hoped I might be able to get away with my crime. But when I returned, the animal was gone and I saw no sign of it having been eaten by a predator.

The next morning, to my great relief I saw it again. A few days later I brought it up to Mr. Northup as casually as possible, not saying I had been the one to scare an animal almost to death, since it was illegal to kill an animal of any size.

Mr. Northup chuckled. "Azalea Rose, haven't you heard the expression 'playing possum'?"

Then his face fell, as if he'd remembered something he wished he could forget. "No, I suppose you wouldn't have heard that. Who would you have heard it from? Oh well, in the case of an opossum, its body pretends to be dead. It's an involuntary reaction to trick predators into leaving it alone."

I listened now as the opossum was eating grubs. The giant owl was hunting nearby. The opossum never worried about the owl, but the mice did. They scurried as the owl swooped low overhead. During the day, it was the hawks that got the mice

… or the snakes. When the day was clear, I could see the osprey that nested in the rusting buildings. They didn't care about the mice; they preferred the fish of the ocean.

Across the distance of the properties, there were lights in the gestate pods but not in the houses, except for one. Mr. Northup was awake. He was always awake early in the morning. It was due to his age, he'd told me. He couldn't sleep very soundly or very long.

My throat felt tight.

A few more months and there would be no light in that house. There would be no beautiful house at all. It would not be fair for one person, or even a family unit, to have something so nice if everyone could not have the same.

I held my band at the scanner. The door lock clicked open, and I entered the house. I slipped in as quietly as possible to the food preparation room. My shoes remained damp from the day before, but that could not be helped. They at least did not squeak as I closed the door and turned on the light. There was a mess to be cleaned; someone had eaten a bag of crisp salted sweet potatoes during the night. These were not part of the assigned government food, but such items could be bought and consumed in moderation, if desired. If consumption reached an unhealthy level, nutritionists monitoring waste samples from the house would deny such spending options.

I removed the clean dry rags from the rag sanitizer and used one to clean up the mess. After that, I emptied the dish sanitizer as silently as possible. I checked the time: six twenty-five. Mr. James would be emerging from his personal room in a few minutes. I inserted the coffee pod into the machine. The rich, bitter smell permeated the tiny room. I put two scoops of coconut sugar in and stirred it around. I took the mug to Mr. James's preferred dining spot.

When I returned to the preparation room, the screen on the stove lit up with instructions for mango millet. I began by boiling the water on the stove. I placed eight pieces of dried mango into the water and two brimming-over cups of millet. This was one of their favorite breakfasts, and mine, so each of my measurements was a bit more than called for. I was hopeful Hastings wouldn't be hungry this morning. Though given how little he had eaten for dinner, he would probably eat all of his breakfast. Hopefully, Ms. Parker would not.

I glanced at the time and placed the second coffee pod into the machine, allowing it to fill the mug for Ms. Parker. She didn't want sugar, only a drop of nut creamer. Her definition of "a drop" changed often. Regardless of how large a drop was, I always did it wrong. I now served her coffee with the creamer on the side to allow her to do it herself. This had been her idea, one I would've gladly suggested years prior if I was allowed to suggest such a thing … or anything.

Mr. James was sitting, sipping his coffee, staring at his screen. As I placed her coffee on the table, Ms. Parker entered the room.

I returned to the preparation room to finish cooking the millet. A shriek came from Salt's room. I didn't respond; neither did her parents. As much as I strove not to be noticed, Salt sought attention. I hurried on, mashing the mango into tiny portions, along with the creamed millet. I placed a few scoops of coconut sugar in the pot and continued mashing everything until the mango had turned the millet a faint orange color. I put one large spoonful into my mouth—I was allowed to taste meals to ensure quality. Though that was meant to be a minuscule amount on the tip of the spoon, not the largest of spoons brimming over.

I filled four bowls full. A little still remained in the pot. I quickly shoveled it into my mouth so that no one would realize I had cooked too much. How grateful I was the camera in this room didn't work and no one cared enough to get it repaired.

I placed the empty pot in the sink, and then carried two bowls and spoons out to Mr. James and Ms. Parker, who were sitting at opposite ends of the table, ignoring one another as they stared at their screens. I put a bowl in front of each one. Mr. James noticed, Ms. Parker did not; I was pleased by her indifference. It meant there was a chance I would get more than a few bites of breakfast this morning.

"Did you check on Salt?" Mr. James asked me as I was starting back to the preparation room.

"No, sir," I answered.

"Don't you think you should?" he asked in a condescending tone.

"Yes, sir. I'll do it right now," I answered, because there was no other way I was allowed to answer.

"That gestate is useless," I heard Ms. Parker grumble as I went toward her daughter's room.

It was odd that her words upset me. I expected nothing more, yet every time she spoke that way I felt the slightest of pains … a physical prickle of pain in my chest.

On my way down the hallway, I picked up the various garments that Salt had thrown from her room.

When she saw me, she screamed, "How dare you touch my clothes, you filthy gest."

She ripped the discarded clothes from my hands.

"You're way filthier than she is," Hastings yelled from his room, though he knew better than to challenge his sister.

She was as cruel to him as she was to me. However, for any cruelness shown to her brother, she would be punished.

Salt screamed, "You sorry excuse for a—"

I stepped in front of her, blocking her from entering her brother's room. She went silent, her mouth still open. She'd grown taller than me in the last few months, but her height didn't matter. I was much stronger. I was stronger than most borns, though their alterations caused them to appear stronger.

"May I assist you?" I asked in the manner I was instructed to.

None of this was unusual; it happened at least once a week—more, lately.

Salt yelled, "How dare you look at me!"

I lowered my eyes. Near my shoes which had holes in them, lay several stray shoes, all barely worn. None of them were good enough for Salt. This was the reason for the screaming; she didn't like her clothing choices. Her parents were not fazed by her screams or her demands for a new wardrobe. They were not fazed by most of what she did. Perhaps that was why she screamed so often.

Salt slammed the door in my face. I exhaled, grateful to be able to leave her alone.

"Thank you," I mouthed to Hastings.

He slipped his hand into mine. How I wished I could spend my life holding his hand. How I wished I could be his sister and he could be my brother. Then I could take care of him for life and not have to leave him alone in this wretched place.

We walked silently together toward the dining area. As soon as we were within view of his parents, I squeezed his hand and released it. A glum expression came over him, but he knew such behavior was not allowed. Not once a born child was older than six could they hold the hand of a gestate.

"Has she dressed?" Ms. Parker asked when she saw me.

"No, ma'am," I answered.

"Why not?" Ms. Parker glared at me.

I wanted to say, for the same reason she isn't dressed most mornings by this time, but instead, I lowered my eyes to the table. "I'm not sure, ma'am. She did not want my assistance."

Ms. Parker slammed her screen on the table. "I cannot handle that girl in this house for one more second. I want her dressed and on her way to the transport."

Mr. James lifted his eyes from his screen, his voice calm. "If she's not ready in time, the school will deal with her. You don't need to worry. She'll suffer the consequences, not you or me. The law is very clear in this respect. It's not our job to get her to the transport unit on time. She's now twelve, and it is *her* responsibility."

Ms. Parker studied him. "Perhaps you're right," she said.

Mr. James smiled. "Of course I am. You've always been an overly involved mother, which is wonderful, but it does make it difficult for you to understand where to draw the line."

I slipped out of the room and returned carrying a bowl for Hastings and one for Salt, if she came to the table.

"Why are you dressed like that?" The disgust in Ms. Parker's tone meant she could only be speaking to me.

I placed the bowls on the table. Hastings took his and began eating. He knew better than to defend me to his parents.

I lowered my gaze to the floor. "I-I have caused my clothing to wear out, ma'am. This is the best that I have."

"Her shoes are awful, as well," Mr. James said. He could see my feet from his side of the table.

"Ugh," Ms. Parker moaned, "I wish you took better care of your things. My day was already so busy, and now, to have to place an order at the gestate store. I hate that site."

I kept my head lowered.

"She'll be leaving us soon. Maybe it could wait," Mr. James suggested.

"That means they'll be inspecting her. We can't send her back wearing rags," Ms. Parker said, rubbing her head in exhaustion.

"You should give her some of Salt's old clothes," Hastings said before he took a bite of millet.

"Salt's old clothes?" Mr. James said.

"Why not?" Hastings said while chewing. "Salt is bigger than her, so the clothes would fit, and then Mother wouldn't need to spend time ordering clothing for her."

Already losing interest, Mr. James lifted his screen. "Seems like an obvious solution to me. Gestates are to wear whatever they're provided."

Ms. Parker leaned back. "It would save me from placing an order. Besides, why spend good money on clothes for someone who's so irresponsible with them."

"I think that's wise," Mr. James said.

Ms. Parker turned her attention to me. "When Salt is at school today, take two of each clothing item you need from her discard pile, but only those that are most worn or with a stain or rip or something. Don't you dare take clothing we could trade in for new."

"Thank you, ma'am. That is very generous," I said.

"What about shoes? She needs shoes," Hastings said between bites of breakfast.

His mother stood to examine my shoes. She groaned and sat back down.

"Give her a pair of Salt's old shoes," Mr. James said, not looking up from his screen. "Those cost the most and, like you said, if her company did an inspection right now, we wouldn't be happy with the outcome."

"And whose fault is that?" Ms. Parker retorted.

"Hers, of course," Mr. James said. "I'm saying we may as well let her take a pair of shoes. It will save us the effort of ordering a pair and then we won't have to think about this again. She'll be gone before they wear out and maybe our next gestate will be better at caring for their things."

"Is she leaving that soon?" Hastings said, trying to hide that he cared.

"I got the notice yesterday," Mr. James said. "Her year turns sixteen on August first. They will send a transport for her a few days after that, depending on availability. And will drop off our new gestate a few days after that."

"A few days after?" Ms. Parker said, raising her eyebrows. "There won't be an overlap? This one won't be able to train the next one?"

"Of course not. You know there's an additional fee for that," Mr. James said.

Ms. Parker sighed in exasperation. "I wish we could have a better gestate. The new one will be seven, just as useless as *she* was. They do such a poor job at that age. Well, at any age, but especially when they're that young."

"I wish we could keep this one," Hastings said timidly.

His father made a slight laughing sound. "To keep a sixteen-year gestate would require us to have a much higher income or one less child," he said, with a meaningful glance at his youngest child.

Hastings slumped back in his chair. I hated that his father had said that. Ms. Parker and Mr. James were rightly burdened by having such a large family, but it was not Hastings's fault.

"August first?" Ms. Parker studied her screen. "That's less than a month away."

After a moment of silence, she spoke again. "Take the items from Salt's discard pile, but I'm warning you—take the worst, I'll be checking." Her glare confirmed how little she trusted me.

"Yes, ma'am, thank you for your generosity. It is far more than I deserve," I said, keeping my head bent low.

Ms. Parker snorted and replied, "You can say that again."

Hastings languidly lifted his spoon to his mouth. He looked as if he would cry. I left the room before the thought of leaving him overcame me.

Seven

Salt was the last to leave the house. In a rage she kicked metal debris from the reclamation ruins that was strewn across the property by the previous night's storm. Between cleaning up her room— which she left in a worse state than ever before—and the yard, I wasn't sure how I would also clean all the bathrooms as was mandated to be done on Sundays.

I should start on the debris first, to avoid the hotter temperatures later in the day, but I was not assigned to outside work until later. It was as if whoever scheduled my work shifts wanted me to work outside when it was hottest. Of course, that wasn't true. My gestation firm cared very much about my health; they efficiently staggered the gestate times in this area. They told us in training they avoided all gestates in an area being inside or outside at the same time. They said it kept the area better watched; in case outsiders tried to come in, the gestates would notice. I'd never heard of outsiders in this area, but perhaps there had been.

That didn't matter. The debris would go unnoticed by the family unit—the state of Salt's room would not.

I went quickly to work picking up the articles of clothing thrown down the hallway and throughout her room. I gathered the hangers from the empty closet and began hanging the clothing and folding the others. After an hour or so the clothing was back in order, along with the shoes. She had not, thankfully, taken the clothes out of the discard bag. This I removed from the back of her closet and knelt on the soft rug that rested at the foot of her queen-size bed. The personal rooms were so spacious and comfortable compared to the rest of the house, where everything was made of metal. In the personal rooms everything was soft and plush except for the floor, which was made of cold vinyl, softened by the rugs. Technically I was not allowed to sit on any personal items, even the rug, but there were no cameras in any of the personal rooms.

I emptied the clothing discard bag onto the rug and began the search for damaged clothing. Ms. Parker was correct. Her family unit was gentle on clothing; there were few damaged items. Could be because they did very few activities that would cause damage to the items and a new wardrobe was allocated every nine months. Typically, their new items were previously worn by other people. This system is what allowed them to have so many new items so often and kept anyone from falsely believing that they had better items than anyone else.

I removed a pair of shorts that were longer than most of the shorts Salt wore. They were not stained, but due to their length they would not be desired by other borns. I examined a short-sleeved shirt that was looser fitting, even on Salt, who was larger than me. It had a small stain. I found two pairs of undergarments, including socks, that were clean. These items were never reused by borns. They were always given, instead, to the gestate store. Those I found in Salt's discard pile were by far the least stained I'd ever had. I then found a pair of loose cotton pants the color of lavender blossoms and a long-sleeved button-up shirt of a light fabric, in the same color, that wouldn't be too hot but would help protect my skin from the sun and insects. These items were in good condition, as were all the other items. I hesitated. Ms. Parker did not typically notice what I wore and, likely, by the time she noticed this outfit it would be stained or torn from my work outside.

Next, I found the lone pair of shoes Salt was discarding, that had a flat sole and close to no elevation. I slipped them on. She must've gotten these before her most recent growth change. They fit me well. They were made of a thick fabric material that was comfortable and durable. They laced up high over my ankles. The perfect work boot. I smiled as I admired them on my feet. I quickly slipped them off and finished tidying her room before moving on to her bathroom.

Every personal room had its own bathroom, and hers was always the messiest. As I entered I stooped to pick up the burgundy towel and dirty clothes on the gray tile floor. When I lifted my head, I gasped. Falling backward against the open door, I stared at the mirror. Written in bright red were the words *I wish you were dead!*

My hands trembled as I spun around to ensure I was alone and she was not waiting to kill me in the silence of what I thought was an empty house. I stepped into the hallway, listening. I heard nothing except the song of birds outside. I returned to the bathroom, hung the towel I was still holding, and used the rag I always kept in my back pocket to wipe away the frightening words. Why did she hate me so much?

After the mirror was clean, I wiped the rest of her countertop and quickly left her room. I didn't care if I was supposed to clean the bathrooms today. I couldn't stay in that house another minute.

I practically ran out the side door and into my pod. I placed my new clothes onto my mat and went to the outdoor storage room for the debris collection containers.

Outside, placing large chunks of rusted metal into specified debris containers, I was calmer. I always felt better when I was out of the Parker-James house.

The air was extra humid after the rains. My ragged clothing began sticking to me almost as soon as I stepped outside. I should've changed clothes to avoid anyone seeing me in the rags I wore—which would cause Mr. James and Ms. Parker to be fined—but I was afraid of what would happen if Salt saw me in her clothing.

Mr. Northup became visible as I neared his property. My heart sank; the day continued to get worse. I lowered my head, as mandated whenever a born came into my vicinity.

"How are you this morning?" Mr. Northup called out to me.

My band glowed to life. Were they curious about his health? Is that why the borns always listened when he was around? Did they wonder how fast he would be dissolved? I felt as if I would be sick.

"I am better than I deserve," I answered with the scripted response. "What about you, sir, are you feeling better this morning?"

"Somewhat," he said with uncertainty.

My stomach spasmed. He was feeling the effects already. His dissolution was already beginning.

"Are you sure you're all right, Azalea Rose? You don't look well," he said, stepping closer.

He stared into my face, that I was sure had lost all color. I fought the urge to fall to the ground … the world was spinning as I thought of him, of how soon he would be gone.

"I-I must deposit this bin of debris for the waste removal."

"Yes, yes, don't let an old man keep you," he said lightheartedly.

He was watching me, glancing down at my glowing band.

There was more he wanted to say and much more I should say to him, and yet neither of us spoke. That was how it was with us. So much went unsaid, by mandate. Yet he was always watching, always doing what he could to protect me. Several times over the years, Ms. Parker had been irate over something I'd done, and Mr. Northup had casually wandered over to where we stood. His presence instantly distracted her. It was odd for anyone to go onto another's designated property. His presence was enough to make her stop yelling at me and go inside. After each of these times he said what a beautiful day it was and gave me a wink.

I could never thank him. Somehow, he understood I was thankful. He always seemed to understand what I could not say. Even now he knew something was wrong, that there was something I wanted to tell him, but neither of us said a word.

Eight

I willed myself to go back into the house. I cleaned the bathrooms one after the other, finding no more surprises. Hastings's was always the cleanest. He did his best to keep his area as clean as possible so I wouldn't have as much to do. I took extra time arranging his stuffed animals on his bed, the way he preferred. His room was the one place in the house I didn't mind being.

After I left his room I went back to my pod, stared down at my new clothing, and forced myself to change into it. I put on the shorts and short-sleeved shirt. The clean socks and undergarments made me feel almost like a vintage born—never had I had such luxuries. The shoes, too, were amazing. To have a pair of shoes worn by only one born? It was unheard of for a gestate to have such nice items.

When Hastings arrived home he commented on the clothes, telling me how I looked so much better in them than his sister. That was all the comments I received. Even at dinner, where I stood off to the side, clearly visible to Salt, nothing was said. She didn't notice the clothes I was wearing, nor did she notice the next day or the next or the next. She seemed to not notice me at all. Except, every morning after she had left for school I found more and more frightening notes on her mirror. *You should die. Kill yourself already. You're worthless, nobody cares about you. Nobody wants you here. I hate you. Die!*

Every day I wiped them away and did my best to pretend I never saw them. It's possible … likely even, that I was the only one beside Salt to see them. There were no cameras in any of the personal rooms or bathrooms; even in gestate pods they were not allowed. Family members never went into one another's private spaces. Very occasionally, Ms. Parker or Mr. James went into the other's space, but that had not happened in a long time. Even with young ones such as Hastings, his parents didn't go into his space; it was considered an invasion of privacy. I was the only one who went into every room of the house.

So I was the only one she could be leaving those messages for.

Days went on and the violent messages continued, but I got used to them. After a week I stopped jumping at every sound and found myself interested in what new ways she would think of to tell me she hated me. In truth, the messages never changed much. She hated me, I should kill myself, I was ugly. This was what each note said in some way or another.

Despite her wishes, it was not my life I was in fear of, it was Mr. Northup's. Every day was bringing him closer to death. Anytime I had thoughts of trying to help him, I forced myself instead to accept reason. He was incredibly old and not particularly useful—as Ms. Parker and Mr. James had pointed out to one another on multiple occasions. Plus, his house was far too large and it was outdated to live in such a place, even if it was beautiful. That was where every thought ended … in me focusing on the beauty. The beauty of who he was and what he had created, and I could not—no matter how much I tried—convince myself that Mr. Northup should be dissolved.

"Zelie, hey, Zelie," Hastings's voice called from far up the property.

He had not used his name for me in years. When he was very young, he heard Mr. Northup call me Azalea Rose. That had been too much for him to say and so he called me Zelie. Then his mother heard him and he and I were punished. I shivered at the memory of his tears.

Why would he be using that now, out in the open? Behind him, his sister walked slowly from the transport. She could hear him, but she didn't seem to care.

"Zelie, guess what?" Breathless, he beamed up at me.

"What?" I said, trying as best I could to suppress a giggle at his exuberance.

"A hurricane's coming!" Hastings shouted, despite my standing right next to him.

"A hurricane?" I asked, looking instinctively toward the east.

"Yes," he shouted with sheer joy. "I have to go to school tomorrow, but after that it's closed for at least a day! But me and some other kids think, longer. Plus, they think the power will go out, so we won't even have to do school on our screens!" He whooped and threw his backpack into the air.

I laughed and said, "My goodness, I had no idea a little hurricane could bring you so much happiness."

We had them often. Rarely did it result in any more than a few hours of free time for him.

He shook his head. "It isn't little at all. It's huge"—he spread his arms wide—"massive."

"Massive?" I said with concern.

"Yep, it's already destroyed half of the Caribbean," he said as though this was the best news he'd ever heard.

"I'm not sure you should be pleased about such destruction," I said.

"If it means I get out of school, then I should be pleased," he said, and swung his bag alongside him, whooping as he went into the house.

When Salt walked past she shoved me, anger brimming from her. I watched her slam the door.

***

Later that evening I caught glimpses of Ms. Parker's screen during mealtime. She hadn't mentioned the hurricane to her children; she hadn't mentioned much of anything to them.

I wondered how bad school must be for Hastings to prefer being here in this silent house.

The newscaster on Ms. Parker's screen zoomed in on the path of the storm. I opened my mouth and quickly closed it. It was indeed a very powerful storm, with the eye predicted to make landfall only a few miles north of here.

Mr. James entered the house. "Hello," he called cheerily, sounding as excited for the storm as his son.

"Hi, Dad," Hastings responded.

His mother and sister were silent, as usual.

I retreated into the food preparation room and returned with Mr. James's plate of black beans, mango salsa, and coconut rice. This was a meal they all, unfortunately for me, enjoyed.

Hastings asked excitedly, "Did you hear there's going to be a hurricane?"

"Yes, I did. What do you think of it?" Mr. James said, taking his fork in hand.

Ms. Parker focused on the exchange between her child and her partner. Salt remained intently staring at her screen.

"I'm happy to have a break from school," Hastings said, stuffing a large bite of mango-drenched black beans into his mouth.

My stomach growled. I wished they didn't enjoy this meal so much. Salt's plate was practically untouched, but I didn't dare eat her leftovers, no matter how hungry I was.

"I bet you are!" Mr. James said. "It's a shame you have to go to school seven days a week. It wasn't that way when I was a boy."

"It was a waste for us … not studying harder. Besides, now that offices are open every day, it would be too difficult to arrange childcare for all those children," Ms. Parker said, less sympathetically.

"I understand the reasons," Mr. James said coolly. "I only meant that I remember how nice it was to sleep in on Sundays. I'm sorry our kids don't get to experience that."

"We could opt them out, but I'm not going to be the one to stay at the house with them," she said with an edge of anger.

"Nor I," he said quickly, matching her tone. "But I'm excited for the boy to get a few days' break."

"You understand you will need to be with them since I'll be staying at the office," she said.

"Yes, I received your message this afternoon. I'll work tomorrow, and then I'm cleared to be here for as long as I'm needed."

"Your supervisor didn't have a problem with that?" Ms. Parker said with some degree of skepticism.

"No, no, she's very supportive. She would like a child of her own someday. I've shared with her some of the joys and hardships, to help her make a more informed decision."

"I see," Ms. Parker said with an expression that made him turn away.

Salt glanced at her mother and then at her father. She stood up, her stool making a scraping noise against the vinyl flooring.

No one but me watched as she left the room.

"After dinner," Hastings asked his father, "do you want to play on my screen with me?"

He'd had some success in the past getting his father to play with him, when they played games on his screen.

"Not tonight. We'll have plenty of time for that when you're home from school," Mr. James said excitedly.

"Yay!" Hastings said, leaping from his stool in excitement. "One more day and I'm free!"

"Honestly," Ms. Parker responded, "aren't you getting carried away?"

"Never," Hastings called as he ran from the room, his father laughing deeply.

I removed his plate and Salt's. Hastings left a few morsels. I scraped them carefully into my mouth and Salt's into the composter.

When I returned to the dining area the conversation had shifted.

"It's working faster than expected. His waste samples show the toxin is well ingrained in his system," Mr. James said.

My stomach lurched. It was impossible to pretend I didn't know who they were speaking about.

"Is it in his ventilation system?"

"No, no, that wouldn't work in his house. His system is different from the new houses. It's in the water," Mr. James answered.

"But not our water," Ms. Parker asked, raising an eyebrow.

"Of course not. The system is much more precise than what you're thinking."

"It must be," she said, with implied skepticism.

"He's as good as dissolved," he said as he chewed a large bite of food.

"Is there nothing that could be done for him at this stage?"

"Do you care about him?" he said, raising a green eyebrow.

"No, but I can't help thinking … what if it got into our water by mistake. Could anything be done to correct the damage?"

"We are altered, so the type of toxin we're using on Northup wouldn't affect us."

"Hastings is unaltered," she said with concern.

"I told you we're fine, and yes, there's a lot that could be done. If he stopped drinking the water with the toxins in it, he'd probably recover. Hastings certainly would, since he's a child. Northup is so old he might not, but that's sort of the point. He's old, he needs to go."

My heartbeat filled my ears; my knees became weak. I leaned against the wall to keep from falling to the floor as the world spun around and around. I took a deep breath … and then another. Finally, the spinning stopped.

"Are you concerned about this storm?" I heard Mr. James ask his partner.

Ms. Parker leaned back a little. "We're always somewhat concerned. It's predicted the electrical system will go down, at least in this area, where it's expected to be the worst."

"That is troubling."

"It will only be for a few hours, a day at the most."

"A few hours without cameras … that could be dangerous," he said, sounding nervous.

She took a sip of her water. "The bands will still work. The gestates will remain closely monitored. Peacekeepers will be deployed and the gestation firms are getting people in place to be deployed if there are issues, which there won't be," she said calmly.

"There have been in other areas," he said quietly, as if he didn't want me or anyone else to hear.

I did hear him and so did the AIs listening to my band. And the cameras in the room would pick up the movement of his lips.

"Other places are different," she said. "We've never had the slightest of issues. The firms around here do a better job of altering and training than in some other areas."

"I suppose you're right," he said.

"Of course I am. Will you be here when the kids get home from school tomorrow?"

He nodded. "I'll get the early afternoon transport. What about you?"

"We're all prepared to stay a few days. It will depend on how bad things get. I'll keep you updated."

"I know you will, you're very good at communication," he said, smiling at her.

"As good as your new supervisor?" she asked with something that reminded me of anger, but different.

He didn't answer. Instead, he placed the remaining scoop of food in his mouth and rose from the table. "I'm going to bed," he said, staring at his screen as he walked away.

She tapped the table with her finger, her mouth contorting tightly.

After a few minutes, she seemed to remember where she was. She sat straighter. "Don't just stand there," she said harshly.

"Yes, ma'am," I said, jumping to action. I took the empty plates from the table to the food preparation room.

In the quiet of the food preparation room I heard her seat violently scrape across the vinyl floor. I shivered, wondering if Ms. Parker's action contained the same anger that Salt's held earlier in the evening.

Nine

That night I lay on my mat, listening to the stillness. There was no wind, no croaking of frogs, only the rustling of the opossum outside my pod, a pod that would never survive anything more than a Category 1 hurricane. There had been stronger storms to hit this area before I was gestated. I'd been told about them briefly, in training. Many gestates were lost because of the damage done to their pods and they were forced to seek shelter.

After that, new laws were enacted mandating that borns allow their gestates into their house when such storms arrived. We were told about this law in training, but we were also told to do our best to avoid using it. If we did feel our lives were in danger, we could seek shelter in the house, but typically, standing against the house provided more than enough protection. If the storm hit during the day, when we were expected to be working, we could be in the house.

I wasn't worried about my personal safety; I would be fine. I had experienced several hurricanes and tropical storms. Most of the damage was due to the rusting condos in the reclamation zone. If the hurricane actually made landfall as close as expected, that would be the first time in many decades. Most ended up hitting north or south of us. Occasionally I heard of problems caused by the tornados they created, but even those were contained. It was odd to hear Ms. Parker speak about the likelihood of the power going out; that had never happened before, as far as I was aware.

I rolled over. The band on my wrist was dark, but that didn't matter; they were still there. The band would continue to work even if the power was out for days. It would continue to charge itself from the movement of my arm. It was virtually unstoppable.

Moonlight streaked in through the strands of moss hanging across the window. The moss probably served the same function as the fabric that hung beside the windows at Mr. Northup's house.

I rolled over, my mind bouncing between thoughts of Mr. Northup—whom I had been avoiding these last two weeks—and the comments Mr. James and Ms. Parker had made. What sort of problems were happening in other areas? Did they mean problems with gestates? That seemed impossible, and yet, based on how Ms. Parker responded with how that doesn't happen here because the firms around here train us better … what else could Mr. James have meant?

The wind picked up; the roof of my pod rattled. My pod … all of the pods would be destroyed. That destruction and loss of power would take out many of the cameras that encompassed the properties. Ms. Parker had said as much, but because of the bands, they weren't worried.

What was there to be worried about?

Something, if peacekeepers and people from the gestation firms were being deployed. They must be expecting some gestates to run. It was foolish to even consider such a thing. They could track us with our bands. If we took off the band and there was no heartbeat, they would immediately begin a search. The gestate might have a few minutes' head start, maybe even an hour, but that's it, even in a hurricane.

If a gestate slipped the band on someone else, they could get more of a head start, but no born would go along with that and no other gestate would allow it. The punishment for helping a gestate run away would be almost as bad as the punishment for running. I cringed at the memory of the girl who was getting her back flayed open in front of my training class. She'd run away … and been caught.

My heart beat faster.

The wind was calm. I heard rustling outside. I sat up, listening more carefully. They told us the bands monitored our heart rates and could tell if something was off. But would that matter during a hurricane? Would anyone go out in the storm if a gestate's heart rate was acting weird as a hurricane tore her pod apart?

Without fully meaning to, I crept to my feet as silently as possible. I opened the door beside my sleep mat and slipped out into the darkness. The opossum was there; I knew it would be. I inched toward it. The animal quickly rolled to its side, emitting a horrible smell. I lifted it by its tail, trying to hide the disgust I felt for this hideous little creature. It wasn't right to feel disgust for any part of nature, but I did. I went noiselessly back into my pod and closed the door. I lay the opossum, on its side, at the farthest corner of the pod away from my mat. It was only a few feet away from me, but the slight distance made me feel better.

I lay down on my mat. I stared up at the corrugated metal of the ceiling. My actions made no sense and yet I'd done them. So much of what I did and thought made no sense. I was broken; I'd always known this. If I were not, I would not lie, or steal food, or bring gross animals into my pod in the middle of the night.

The opossum remained unmoving, and slowly my mind settled into the stillness of the night.

***

The next morning, I awoke to the scurrying of the opossum as it was trying to find a way out of the pod. When I sat up, its dark body became rigid. It didn't collapse onto its side as I thought it might, but it did silently watch me from behind the toilet. I shuddered at the thought of sharing this pod with an opossum. It was against the rules to touch a wild animal unless it was hurt. Even then, I was to call out to the AIs monitoring my band for assistance.

I could easily open the door and let it wander out before anyone knew it was there. But I did not. I quickly dressed and drank my sustenance powder. The opossum didn't move; even its eyes remained perfectly still.

I did my work as usual. I smiled at Hastings and kept my head bent low to the other members of his family unit. I felt no twinge of guilt for breaking rules and having an animal in my pod—behavior that in itself would warrant severe punishment. Oddly, I did not fear the punishment … I was even more broken than I realized.

"Be back this afternoon," Hastings whooped excitedly as he ran out toward the school transporter.

"Yes, sir. See you this afternoon," I called after him.

Salt came through the doorway. I stepped out of her way, but she didn't try to shove me. Her hair was matted, her red eyes accentuated by dark circles.

Against my better judgment, I spoke. "Are you feeling okay, Miss Salt?"

"What do you care," she replied.

I hesitated. "I do care, very much," I answered, surprised by the truthfulness of my words. She was cruel to me as often as she could be, but still, I didn't wish her to be unhappy.

She stared at me, the hardness gone. In its place was sadness. She didn't speak and neither did I. A moment later she was gone, making her way to the school transporter.

My shoulders relaxed. So many times I had envied Salt's life. We came from the same embryo storage facility, but she was selected to be a person—someone's child. And I was gestated to be a servant. How much I wished for that life, and yet I detected misery behind her altered eyes.

In the distance Mr. Northup was emerging from his back porch. I shrugged off whatever concern I may have had for Salt and went bravely toward him. I would no longer avoid him. I stopped at the banana leaves; I had no legitimate reason to go any closer. He was moving slowly, giving me time to cut off several yellow leaves. When he got closer, I gasped … the transformation was startling. The whites of his eyes were a pale yellow, his skin thin and waxy. The skin of his arms and neck hung loosely, signaling rapid weight loss. He smiled at me—the action seemed to exhaust him.

"It's nice to see you, Azalea Rose," he said, his voice strained.

My throat swelled as emotion overcame me. "Thank you, sir," I said with as little feeling as I could accomplish.

I was not allowed to feel emotions. Especially not for a vintage born who was in the process of being dissolved.

"Are you ready for this storm?" he asked.

"I believe so," I answered, not actually believing I was ready for anything that was about to happen. "I haven't heard any updates, sir. Is it still on course for this area?"

"The latest I heard was …." He stopped mid-sentence.

"Sir?" I asked.

"What was I saying? I forgot," he said with concern.

"You were telling me about the storm coming."

"It's a big one, supposed to be here in the middle of the night."

"Do you know what time, sir?" I asked. My timing would need to be perfect.

He rubbed his arms. "I'm not feeling well," he said, as if pleading with me to do something.

"May I help you into your house, sir? It's best you were inside."

"Yes, thank you."

"Did you receive your shipment of storm supplies, sir?" I asked as I put an arm around him, doing what I could to support his weight.

"Storm supplies? No," he said weakly.

"Let me help you into your house, sir, and then I will search for your shipment. I am sure you received them." In truth, I wasn't sure of anything.

"Thank you, Azalea Rose. I came outside to see you," he said, his voice difficult to understand.

I didn't respond to his kindness; I could not. Not while they were listening.

"Here you go, sir." I opened the door and entered his house for the second time. A stench of sickness hung in it.

I helped him sit at the table and then went swiftly and silently around his house. I glanced up in the corners. I focused. There were no cameras. I inhaled and exhaled … the feeling of freedom. I was not being watched. I quickly made my way around his house; it was even more beautiful than I realized. Everywhere was beauty and warmth … even with the smell of sickness, I wanted to stay in this place forever.

I didn't allow myself to stop or even slow my pace. I couldn't be here for long. I looked in the area of the front door, as I had told Mr. Northup I would do. He was right. Nothing there. Apparently, they didn't care if he even made it past the storm, though whatever they would've sent him would probably be poisoned anyway.

I returned to the table, where Mr. Northup sat, disoriented.

"I'm sorry, sir, I did not find your supplies. Perhaps they will arrive in a few hours. I must be going now," I said, keeping my voice as unaffected as possible. Keeping my voice as a gestate's voice should sound.

"Azalea Rose," he pleaded, his pale brown eyes begging me to help him.

"I must be going," I said, with as much unkindness as I could manage.

Out of the corner of my eye, I saw a set of keys on the counter. Of course, he was so old-fashioned he would not use an electronic locking system. I swiftly took the keys, placing them in my pocket.

"Azalea Rose," he called again.

This time I could not stop myself. I lifted a single finger to the front of my lips. A signal to tell him to be quiet. I could not hear his suffering … not now.

"I must go, sir, but I will try and check on you during the storm if my assigned family unit gives me permission," I said, pleading with my eyes that he not ask me more.

He was silent as I went out the door. Did he understand my silent plea or had his mind slipped so that he no longer remembered he was asking me for help?

Mr. Northup's keys pushed against my right thigh. They would open his back door, as well as, I guessed, operate his personal vehicle. He was one of the few around here that had one. I felt a surge of something I was unfamiliar with … it was the sense that maybe things would get better. Maybe with the help of his vehicle and this storm, I would not be caught before I was able to get him to safety. Though where safety was, I could not begin to guess.

The hushed words Mr. James had spoken entered my mind: in other places the gestates were causing problems. Perhaps in those places they did not dissolve the old so easily. Maybe Mr. Northup could live out his life somewhere. I didn't pretend to believe that I might live out my life with him—that was beyond the realm of possibility. I would eventually be caught. My death would be preceded by more pain than I was willing to imagine.

I gulped down the fear.

It didn't matter … I was property … I existed to serve. My death meant nothing more than the death of an obsolete machine.

Mr. Northup was a person. His death mattered, just as his life mattered.

Ten

The wind pushed hard against the narrow windows and concrete walls of the house. The houses were made with storms such as this in mind. The pods were not. I wondered how many gestates would die tonight … I wondered if I would be one of them.

"It won't be long now," Mr. James said between bites of sauteed tofu crumbled atop strands of pasta that was coated with a sauce made of preserved tomatoes from the spring garden.

He was focused on his screen, with his ear speakers in. I doubted he heard the storm outside of his house, preferring instead to watch it on a screen.

Salt was picking at her food. Her screen was on, with the same newscast her father was watching. She was looking in its direction but her glazed expression told me she wasn't watching it.

Hastings's screen was not on and he wasn't trying to eat. He was anxiously listening to the debris that was hitting the side of the house.

"Is Mother coming home?" he said.

I felt bad that he was worried about Ms. Parker. I was not allowed to tell him what his parents discussed in private and, so, could not tell him she was working through the storm.

Mr. James didn't respond.

Salt, who sat next to her father, tapped his tablet, making the screen go black.

"Why did you do that?" Mr. James said, glaring at her.

"Where's Mother?" She glowered at him.

"Working. I figured she told you," he said, refocusing on his screen.

There were messages popping up on the screen.

Salt saw them too and her eyes narrowed.

"Why is she working during a hurricane?" Hastings asked, sounding scared for his mother.

Mr. James smirked at the message on his screen, then looked up at his son, his expression becoming more solemn.

"That's her job. She works in the storm management department. Typically they have very little to do," he said in a sort of scoffing tone. "But in times like this, they have to work. She'll probably be there for a few days if the storm is as bad as they think."

"Is she safe?" Hastings asked. "She isn't outside in the storm, is she?"

"No, no, she'll be inside, overseeing operations. And let me see." He scrolled through many messages, until he found the one with her picture next to it. "She sent this about an hour ago, saying to be sure to keep you two inside. So yes, she's fine." He gave Hastings a satisfied expression.

Hastings slouched back in his chair.

Salt remained focused on her father's screen. "Who are all the other messages from?"

"I don't invade your privacy," he said sharply. "But if you must know, most are from my supervisor. I had to leave early today to be with you two. She wanted to make sure I made it home safely in this weather. She's aware I live close to the reclamation zone."

"Are all supervisors so engaged with their subordinates?" Salt asked in an accusing tone.

Mr. James gave her a placating smirk. "We have a good relationship," he said as his screen changed to the face of a woman closer to Salt's age than to his. A call was coming in.

"That's her, I have to take it," he said, standing abruptly.

"Hi," he said, his voice becoming kinder, softer.

His ear speakers were in, so we couldn't hear her response.

"No, it's a fine time. I was just finishing dinner with my kids. ...... Yeah, they're great kids. My youngest was worried that his mother isn't here. ...... I know, he's a really sweet kid. ...... She's great too. A teenager, though, so not the easiest time." ...... He laughed. "Yes, you're right, of course. If I had to do it all over again, I would select things a bit differently. Live and learn, I guess." ...... He laughed a second time. "That's true." His voice echoed from down the hallway. "Enough about that. How are you filling your time?"

The door to his personal room closed.

Hastings continued to pick at his food. It wasn't clear if he was thinking about his father's conversation or his mother's absence. Salt sat perfectly still, her face turning purple. She was so upset I could feel the anger rolling off her in waves. I stepped farther back, against the wall.

She stood abruptly and slammed her hands on the table.

Wide-eyed, Hastings stared at her, but before he dared to speak, she was gone, storming off toward her room. I let out a sigh of relief.

"What was that about?" Hastings asked when we were alone.

"I believe she was angry at Mr. James, sir."

"Oh," he said, sounding confused as to why she would be mad.

"You should finish your dinner, sir," I said as I took the two partially eaten meals into the preparation room.

I scooped Salt's mostly untouched food into the compost container. If only she didn't have a habit of spitting in her food when she thought I wasn't watching, I would've eaten much better these last few weeks. There were a few mouthfuls left on Mr. James's plate, which I hurriedly ate before wiping both plates and placing them into the sanitizer.

I returned to the dining area. Hastings had left the room. I took his plate away, finishing his meal. I cleaned the food preparation room and the dining area.

The storm had quieted down some. Maybe it wouldn't be as bad as they had predicted. Maybe it wouldn't take out the cameras. Maybe I would be caught. That was a foolish thought, of course. I would be caught. It was simply a matter of when, and if I could get Mr. Northup to safety first.

I used the broom to sweep the dining area and the hall leading to the personal rooms.

All the doors were shut and the rooms were quiet except for Mr. James's. The weather forecast was on. I slowed and listened at his door.

"Those nearest the ocean reclamation zones are extremely likely to lose power within the next few hours. There's no need to panic. The system will be up and running shortly. Go to sleep as you would any other night, and when you wake in the morning everything will be back to normal."

My face went pale at the word "normal." I would not be able to get Mr. Northup to safety with only a few hours of the cameras being down.

"The storm might be a tad deceiving, though, so please stay in your houses. There will be several strong bands that are expected to take out the power. After that, there will be calm. This is when the center of the storm will be passing over you. You may be tempted to venture outside during this time to assess damage or take pictures. Do not do this, I repeat, do not leave your house once the storm starts. The hurricane will get far worse after this brief time of calm. Remain inside. There is no need to panic. Your dwelling was built with storms such as this in mind. You and your loved ones will be perfectly safe. We have been asked by the gestation firms to remind you that your gestates must be allowed into your house if they ask for refuge. It is thought their pods will be damaged. We know this is an inconvenience, but think of how much more of an inconvenience it will be if your gestate is injured or killed and you must wait for a replacement. This is an example of a little bit of prevention saving you a lot of frustration later."

The broadcast changed topic, and I began sweeping again.

I hesitated at Salt's door. I shouldn't bother her, but it was unlike her to be so quiet. I tapped on the door.

"Come in," she said, with less irritation than I expected.

The room was dark. She was sitting on her bed, staring out the window. Everything about the scene startled me. Never had I known her to be in her room without her screen being on, or at least the lights on. She often slept with the lights on—against the rules, but she did it anyway.

"May I get you anything before I leave the house for the evening?" I said, my head bent low.

"You've never asked me that before," she said, her red eyes seeming to glow in the dim light.

"With the storm and everything, I wanted to ensure you were okay," I said, not daring to enter the threshold of the room.

She was silent, watching me. "You felt sorry for me. You recognized how angry I got at my father, and *you* felt sorry for *me*."

"No, Miss," I said. "Have a good night, Miss." I stepped back and closed the door.

"If you want to feel sorry for someone, feel sorry for yourself," she yelled through the closed door.

I stood there for the briefest of moments, hoping I would never see her again.

I made my way down the hall, stopping at the last closed door. Hastings's door. I knocked.

"Come in," he said, and I entered the room.

"Close the door. I'm watching the storm," he said.

I did as he'd instructed, and then joined him at his narrow window that faced the towering skeletons of the reclamation zone.

Lightning flashed across the thick clouds looming in the evening sky. The setting sun illuminated the clouds, vast and angry as they rolled in from the ocean, bringing with them lightning bolt after lightning bolt.

"Isn't it magnificent," he said.

"Yes," I whispered. He was right; it was more magnificent and terrifying than anything I'd ever seen.

"You should stay in my room tonight. You're allowed to. We were told in school about the law allowing gestates to seek refuge."

"No, sir, I cannot stay in your room. That isn't allowed, not now that you're so old. I will stay in my pod, as I am assigned to do," I said with a falter in my voice that he picked up on.

"Your pod will be destroyed," he said, watching me closely in the dim light.

I was grateful there were no cameras in personal rooms.

"I'm sure it will be fine, sir. If I'm in danger, I'll seek shelter. Please don't worry about me," I said, doing what I could to keep my voice cheerful.

"I don't worry much about you. You're very good at taking care of yourself," he said while continuing to watch the lightning.

"I'm glad you don't worry, sir," I said, wanting to reach out and pet his messy hair, but restraining myself.

"Do you think my mother is safe?" He sounded worried.

"Yes, I'm sure of it," I said confidently.

"I heard people in school saying how this is going to be the worst storm that's ever hit this area, *ever*," he said.

"I don't think so, sir. As I swept the hall, I heard the newscaster from your father's screen and he said nothing of the sort. Why would the weather forecasters lie?" I said, sure the government would never allow such false information to be distributed.

Hastings shrugged. "That's what some of the other vintage kids were saying."

"You shouldn't listen to such idle gossip. The information systems would tell you if you were in danger. You have nothing to worry about."

"Maybe you're right," he said.

"Of course I am. Now lie in bed and watch the storm from under your covers," I said, guiding him toward his bed.

I helped him in, pulling his soft blankets up to his chin.

"Do you remember when I used to do this every night?" I asked.

"Yes," he said, squishing his head against the fluffy pillow. "I was little then."

"You've gotten so big," I said.

"Not as big as the kids who are altered," he said, pouting.

"Maybe not, but plenty big for me," I said, smoothing out his blankets.

"Are you sure you'll be safe in your pod?" His wide brown eyes gazed up at me.

I touched the side of his face, pushing some reddish-brown hair away from his freckled skin. "I will do my very best to remain safe," I said, not wanting to lie to him.

"And you'll come into the house if the storm does get bad?" He made a serious face that nearly prompted a giggle.

"I promise I will not stay in my pod if the storm is bad," I said, smiling down at him.

"Okay, fine," he said, sounding as though he accepted that he'd done all he could.

A bright streak of lightning lit up the dusk. Hastings jumped when the thunder roared a moment later.

"That was close, sir. I had better get into my pod so I am not walking around in such weather," I said, my heart beating fast. I didn't want to say goodbye to him. I didn't want to leave him, but he was not my little brother. I was merely his servant. I had no claim to him … or anyone.

"Okay, but be careful," he said, sounding both nervous and sleepy.

"Yes, sir," I said, leaning over and gently kissing the top of his head. I had done this often when he was a tiny baby in my little seven-year-old arms.

"Good night, Zelie," he whispered as I rose from his bed.

"Good night, young sir," I said, and quickly left his room before he could notice my tears.

Eleven

The rain was pushing sideways when I made my way into my pod, the walls of which were already bending against the wind. The thin metal would not remain upright much longer. I turned on the light, hoping the power would go out before the pod collapsed. The cameras had to turn off before I could flee.

I stuffed the extra set of Salt's old clothes into the small bag I'd stolen from the storage closet in the Parker-James house. From the one shelf in the pod, I took the tin of sustenance powder. It would not be enough to last both Mr. Northup and me for more than a few days. I pushed that thought from my mind. It was pointless to worry about the future, especially since it was unlikely that I would survive the night.

I ran my fingers along the smooth metal water bottle I drank from. My water came from the rainwater catchment system. It was often dirty from the roof, but it wasn't poisoned. Gestates weren't worth poisoning. I filled the bottle at the sink as wind howled through every crack in the thin metal walls.

The walls shuddered and the lights flickered and then came back on. I scanned the room. The opossum had burrowed itself under my sleep mat. The lights flicked again and remained dark. My body began moving before my mind fully realized what was happening. Something inside me drove me forward, my body working as if on autopilot.

I lifted the mat and grabbed the opossum by its thin, rat-like tail. It didn't fight; it didn't move. I laid it down on the mat. I kept the band pressed against my skin as I loosened the strap. I quickly strapped it around the thin neck of the opossum.

My heart felt as if it would beat out of my chest as I released it. It didn't move. It wouldn't, for hours, until it woke up from its fake death. Hopefully, the AIs would think I was injured, even dying, and that was why my heart rate was barely detectable. They wouldn't send anyone out in this storm for an injured gestate—a runaway, maybe—but not an injured one.

I didn't stop to think about what I was about to do. I couldn't. None of it made sense. I opened the door, the wind pulling it from my grasp and causing it to bang loudly against the thin wall of the pod.

I didn't stop to latch it; the wind was stronger than I expected. But it was not fighting against me, it was pushing me forward toward Mr. Northup's. It made every step I took count for two, as I ran across the darkened yards. In what felt like seconds, I was on Mr. Northup's back porch, water streaming off my chin and a few loose strands of hair. I hesitated for the briefest of moments and then reached for the keys in my pocket. They were clumsy in my hands; I was unfamiliar with the old-fashioned metal. It took me several attempts to find the correct key; my hands were trembling by the time I finally inserted and twisted the correct key, unlocking the door.

I stepped inside. Water was pooling at my feet, but I couldn't stop to worry about the mess I was making. The house was silent, though the storm raged against it.

"Mr. Northup, sir," I called softly, and then my right hand flew to my left wrist.

I exhaled in relief. It was bare.

I heard a cough in the distance. I inched toward the sound.

"Mr. Northup?" I said more loudly.

The lightning streaked, bringing more visibility into the house.

He was sitting in a chair in what must've been his personal room.

"Mr. Northup, it's me. It's …." I hesitated. I'd never called myself anything. "It's Azalea Rose."

"Azalea Rose," he repeated, barely aware.

"I'm taking you away from here," I said, going toward him and pulling him from the chair. He didn't try to stop me.

"I don't feel well," he said, and then wretched all over his lovely wood floor.

"Your water is poisoned. They're trying to dissolve you."

He sat and wretched again. The smell of death overpowered the smell of the rain from my wet clothes and hair.

"Dissolve me?" he said, his voice barely audible.

"Can you stand, sir? I'm not sure I can carry you to your vehicle."

"They'll follow us," he said, wincing as I lifted him to his feet.

"No, sir, I took off my band."

He shook his head heavily from side to side. "Not you … me. My car, they'll follow it."

I sucked in air and immediately exhaled—the smell was so putrid. "We'll go on foot," I said with determination.

"I'm too weak," he said, flopping his head from side to side.

"We'll use your vehicle to get us away from here and let you get some strength back. Then we can go on foot," I said.

"Azalea Rose, I'm dying," he said, his voice brimming with tears.

"No. You're coming with me," I said, forcing him to walk forward. I would not listen to more of his distorted speech.

"We all die. I have lived. You have not. Run while you can," he said, collapsing into an ornate chair carved from wood and covered in parts with soft red fabric.

"No, sir, if you don't come, I will slip back into my pod. I will go on as I have always been, and in a few days you will be dead, and in a few weeks I will be transferred away from here, to someone who can pay the gestation firm more than the government subsidy. Do you want that life for me?"

His eyes locked on mine. "You promise that when I die you won't come back, you'll keep running," he said, breathing heavily, like it was difficult to speak and breathe at the same time.

I swallowed. "Yes, I promise," I said. I knew I wouldn't live even as long as he did. It was impossible for a gestate to escape.

In the distance a door banged open.

"Did you leave the door open?" he asked, his voice feeble.

"No, the storm must have pushed it open," I said.

He shook his head heavily from side to side. "No, stay here."

"It is the storm, sir, nothing else," but I kept my voice low as I spoke, kneeling beside him.

"You don't understand. They'll come for me," he said, his voice quivering as he found the strength to stand and shuffle toward the noise.

I remained kneeling by the chair, unsure of what to do. Mr. James said the toxins would dissolve his mind along with his body. Maybe Mr. Northup was becoming paranoid, making up danger in his mind. That must be it. We would take his vehicle and leave this place. If he was right and we were followed, so be it. It would give him a chance to live that he wouldn't have here. I doubted he would survive another twenty-four hours, drinking the poison they were forcing through the pipes of his house.

I stood, going toward the hallway he had made his way down. Once we made it to his vehicle, he could show me how to turn it on and drive it. He could not be so out of it he couldn't remember how to do that.

"Who's there?" I heard him call into the darkness.

I was close to him now and was going to answer him, to tell him there was no one else in the house, when I stopped, the blood draining from my face.

"It's me," a stranger's voice answered, and my heartbeat thumped in my ears.

Mr. Northup was not a crazy old man. Someone was there. Someone that must be a born, someone that, if I was discovered, would be paid a substantial bounty to turn me in.

Lightning flashed against my sun-browned skin. The pale ring around my wrist, from the band I'd worn for the last nine years, seemed to be glowing. I opened the bag I carried and pulled on the long-sleeved lavender shirt. It was as wet as the rest of me. That didn't matter. What mattered was it had originally been intended for Salt, who was taller, with longer arms. The lightweight sleeve hung low, easily covering the pale ring around my wrist.

I was shaking as I stepped into the hallway, determined to help Mr. Northup. He was too sick to protect himself.

His voice shaky, Mr. Northup asked, "Who are you?"

"Your grandson," the voice answered with emotion.

"Kolbe?" Mr. Northup said, unsure of himself.

It was a lie. Kolbe had died in an accident years ago. Whoever this person was must know that Mr. Northup was not in his right mind and was trying to take advantage of him. Stepping from the shadows now would mean no escape for me, but I was here to help Mr. Northup. If I didn't do that now, when he needed me most, what good was any of it?

"Mr. Northup, don't believe him. Your grandson died in an accident," I said, stepping to Mr. Northup's side.

"Who are you?" the man in front of me asked.

His body appeared tense, ready to attack. His eyes glared through the darkness, examining every inch of me.

I swallowed. "I'm his—his friend. You're a liar," I said, standing in front of Mr. Northup to block the man.

"Are you really Kolbe?" Mr. Northup said, leaning on me as he took a step closer to the stranger.

"I am," the man said, coming toward us.

Mr. Northup began to reach his hand out to touch the stranger's face.

"Mr. Northup, you told me yourself that your grandson is dead," I whispered harshly into Mr. Northup's ear.

He shook his head. "I told you what I had to … while we could be overheard. My grandson was alive, at least I hoped he was. Now I know he is."

He began to cry, his body and mind so exhausted as he reached out for the man. "My sweet little Kolbe, I never thought I'd see you again," Mr. Northup said, hugging the man.

The stranger held Mr. Northup. "I'm sorry I didn't come sooner. They would've known and that wouldn't have been good for Mom or the rest of the community."

"You're here, I can't believe you're here," Mr. Northup said, leaning heavily against Kolbe before beginning to slide downward.

I reached him in time to help guide Mr. Northup into a chair.

"What's wrong with him?" Kolbe said as he knelt beside his grandfather, a panicked expression on his face. A face that was not much older than my own.

"They are dissolving him," I said, kneeling beside him to ensure Mr. Northup didn't slip out of the chair. "His water is poisoned."

"They're what?" Kolbe said as if shouting, but his voice remained low.

"That is why I am here. I was going to take him away. Another day or so and he will be dead, but if we can get him away from the poison, he might … he might live."

"How could they … *why* would they dissolve him?" Kolbe asked.

"He entered the age of uselessness several years ago. It is surprising they let him live as long as they did."

Mr. Northup was valuable to me and apparently to Kolbe, but it was foolish to pretend he was valuable to anyone else. Mr. James and Ms. Parker were right—it was strange they allowed him to live as long as they did.

"I can't believe they would do that to him … we were wrong to stay gone," Kolbe said, focused on his grandfather.

"That doesn't matter right now," I said, needing Kolbe to act. "What matters is getting him away from here and giving him a chance to live."

"What about you?" he asked, turning his attention to me.

"What about me?"

"You were going to leave your … your family to help my grandfather?"

"Ye-yes," I said. "Mr. Northup means a great deal to me."

Kolbe hesitated as he noticed my sun-browned skin and my hair braided tightly in a bun at the base of my neck. He cautiously reached for the sleeve of my left arm. I didn't move, didn't breathe as he slid the loose fabric up beyond my wrist. His fingers grazed the pale ring around my wrist. He took his fingers away and lowered his gaze.

He could turn me in now, claim the sizable bounty that any born could claim when they helped locate a runaway gestate.

He lifted his eyes to mine. "Thank you for helping my grandfather. I understand now what you're risking."

A shiver went up my spine. "You are not going to turn me in?"

He stood, pulling me up with him. "I have no use for their blood money. Help me lift him," he ordered, with a confidence I wasn't used to. It wasn't inflated or cruel. There was a kindness to his demand, but it was a demand no less.

Mr. Northup groaned as we got him onto his feet.

"Azalea Rose, Azalea Rose," he mumbled, "my pictures. Get the pictures of my family off the table."

"Yes, sir," I said. "Hold him, I will be right back."

I ran into the food preparation room, to the framed photographs that were on the narrow table in front of the windows. Lightning streaked across the sky as I held the picture of Mr. Northup's son and his family. Even in the dim light, I could tell Kolbe looked almost exactly the same as the man in the picture—the man who was Mr. Northup's son. The stranger wasn't lying; the little boy in the picture had grown into a man and was now with Mr. Northup. I slipped the frames into my bag and ran back to the men.

"I have the pictures, sir," I said as I returned to Mr. Northup, who appeared unconscious in Kolbe's arms.

"Can you help me?" Kolbe asked.

I went to Mr. Northup's other side and helped support him, while Kolbe held Mr. Northup's left arm over his shoulder and looped his own right arm around his grandfather's waist. Together we carried him out of the house and into the room that held his vehicle. His house was the only one around here that had such a room.

"He told me they would follow his vehicle," I said.

"I'm sure," Kolbe said, moving us toward the side door that went out to where Mr. Northup's roses were.

"Where are we going?" I asked, not wanting to carry Mr. Northup through a hurricane—when there was a vehicle we could use.

"Outside, I have a truck they won't track."

Twelve

The rain poured in sheets from the roof, overpowering the gutters, pushing down on us like a waterfall. Mr. Northup gasped as water soaked through his clothes.

"It is okay, sir," I said, "the hurricane is here."

He groaned, yet began walking a little more on his own, allowing Kolbe to release Mr. Northup's waist.

The tall rose bushes that Mr. Northup loved so much whipped violently in the wind, their thorns snagging any clothes or skin they touched. He would hate leaving them, but they would be destroyed anyway; not much would survive this storm.

In the dark sky, something flew, hitting the house nearest Mr. Northup's, impaling the roof. A sheet of metal, maybe from one of the condominium skeletons or part of a gestate pod that had been destroyed. Maybe it was from my pod. I instinctively turned toward the property of the Parker-James family unit but could see nothing, my view blocked by Mr. Northup's house.

"Get in and help me pull him into the truck," Kolbe yelled above the cries of the storm.

I ran in front of them, studying the door for a moment, before waving my hand close to the side. This was the way most vehicles opened, but nothing happened.

Kolbe shouted, "Pull the handle on the side."

I noticed the vertical bulge on the side of the door, slipped my hand into it, and pulled. The door swung open, not up, as other private vehicle doors typically did. I climbed in, releasing the bag from my back.

I bent down, placing my hands beneath Mr. Northup's arms.

"Argh," I groaned, lifting as Kolbe pushed.

Mr. Northup was barely conscious. He needed rest. He needed clean water and healthy food. At least the rain had washed off whatever toxins may have been oozing from his skin. The metallic smell of death was replaced by the smell of a hurricane. The hurricane smelled better.

Once Mr. Northup was in the vehicle, Kolbe slammed the door and sprinted around the truck. A moment later he was in and the engine was alive.

There was movement behind me. I jumped when a girl popped up from the back seat.

"Is this Grandfather? What's wrong with him?"

"Talia!" Kolbe screamed. "I told you to stay home!"

"You know I never do what you tell me to," she said, her fingers clutching the back of Mr. Northup's seat as the vehicle spun backwards out of the yard, next to Mr. Northup's roses. The roses continued to whip violently in the light of the headlights. Already the red petals were gone, already the plants Mr. Northup loved so much were being destroyed.

"I can't believe you did this," Kolbe yelled over the noise of the hurricane. "Buckle up, all of you."

I twisted forward to pull the strap around Mr. Northup, who remained unconscious. I loosened his strap and then laid him down, placing his head on my bag. It was wet, but soft. I buckled my own strap as the truck jumped over the curb and onto the narrow street in front of the houses. Kolbe drove with headlights on. I wished he would turn them off. I wished we could disappear into the storm, but that wasn't safe. He had to be able to see the debris that was littering the streets.

"What's wrong with Grandfather?" Talia called over the storm. "That is Grandfather, isn't it?"

"No, I rescued some other old man," Kolbe said with biting sarcasm. "Mom was going to be mad enough, but now"—he shook his head—"she's going to be furious. She's going to blame me, even though I told you not to come." He scowled at his sister in the rearview mirror.

Talia yelled, "Mom won't be that mad."

"Maybe not at you," Kolbe screamed back, "but she's going to kill me."

"She doesn't believe in killing people. You know that."

"I didn't mean literally. Don't speak again—seriously, don't say another word!"

Talia leaned back in the seat. Kolbe concentrated on driving, his grip tight on the steering wheel. Today was no day for autopilot; the system would've been overwhelmed in the first few feet.

"Who are you?" Talia asked from behind me.

Her words startled me. She was speaking to me, and by her tone she had no idea I was a gestate. I felt the sleeve around my wrist; the mark from the band was covered. I glanced at the rearview mirror. Kolbe's eyes flashed to mine, but he didn't say anything. He could tell her who I was, but he didn't. His focus went back to the road as he swerved around something.

"I'm a-a friend of your grandfather's," I said, stumbling over the words.

"What's your name?" she asked.

I hesitated for longer than I should have.

"Her name is Azalea Rose," Kolbe called from the front, "and I told you not to speak."

"That's a very pretty name," Talia said, ignoring her brother's command.

"It's the name your grandfather gave me," I said, without thinking.

"Grandfather gave you your name?" Talia asked, confused.

My pulse quickened.

"She means that was his nickname for her," Kolbe answered.

"Oh, that was sweet of him. What's your real name?"

My mind raced. "Zelie," I answered. "My real name is Zelie."

"That's a very nice name. Why did Grandfather give you a different name?"

"He … he liked the wild azaleas and the roses he grew. And since Zelie and Azalea sound similar, I guess that's why," I said, trying to sound as if I had the right to speak to a vintage born.

There was enough light from lightning flashes to make out the shape of the Parker-James house and the empty space on the side where my pod should have been. I gasped and touched my fingers to the glass. I would've died anyway, probably impaled by rusted metal.

I closed my eyes. I would've died. My life would've ended.

"Why did you gasp? Is that your home? Do you want us to take you there?"

Her words startled me. She was watching me; she was paying attention to where I was looking. I wasn't used to anyone watching me—except for the cameras and Hastings. Would he think I died? My fingers touched the window. Would he let the memory of his gestate die?

"Zelie, are you okay?" Talia asked, her voice kind. Her fingertips touched my shoulder, and the touch made me jerk out of … fear. Yes, my response was fear; I was afraid she was going to hit me. My mind spun. I should've died. Hastings would think I died. I shook my head. No, he would search for me. He would realize my body wasn't there. Would he tell the others? Would anyone else look for me?

"Azalea Rose," Kolbe said gently, from the front.

His voice woke me from my thoughts.

"I-yes, that was where I lived. No, I-I don't want to go back."

"Won't your family miss you?" Talia said, concerned.

Tears burned my eyes. "My, my brother will, but he will understand why I … why I left," I said. I hoped these words were the truth … I hoped Hastings would forgive me for leaving him.

Thirteen

The storm worsened. We rode in silence, constantly bouncing over fallen debris and with walls of water sprayed up by the tires. A few times the wind was so strong Kolbe's hands jerked the wheel to keep the vehicle on what was left of the road. I held Mr. Northup in place as gently as possible. His body was so frail, I was sure every touch of my rough hands was bruising him, but it was all I could do to keep him from falling off the seat.

After an hour or so, the trees gradually stopped bending.

"The wind is dying down," Kolbe shouted over the thudding raindrops.

"This must be the calm part," I said, though I shouldn't have spoken without being spoken to first.

"What?" Kolbe said.

I swallowed. He was asking me to speak. "The forecaster said there would be a calm part over us a few hours after it started. He said it will be even worse after that part passes."

"Worse than this?" Talia said in disbelief.

"I told you not to come!" Kolbe yelled at her, for what seemed like the hundredth time.

"If you truly wanted me not to come, you shouldn't have told me your plan," she said with a huff.

"I told you my plan so that if I *died*, Mom would know what happened to me," he yelled.

"You didn't tell me that part," she said, her voice subdued.

"I didn't want to scare you."

"Maybe a little scaring would've been good," she said into the darkness.

Kolbe's shoulders relaxed a little. The winds were continuing to mellow. "It will be okay. I'll get you home."

Talia was quiet as Kolbe looked back at her in the mirror. Something about his expression reminded me of myself. It wasn't right for me to make such a comparison, but still, the way he looked at her reminded me of how I would look at Hastings when no one else was around.

Mr. Northup groaned and slowly pushed himself from my lap. Around us there were houses, but all were dark. There was no power here … no cameras.

"Azalea Rose?" he asked, his voice scratchy.

"Yes, sir, I am here," I said, unzipping my pack to remove the water bottle.

"Hello, Grandfather," Talia said, still buckled, yet sitting at the edge of her seat.

Mr. Northup turned to stare at her.

"I'm Talia. Do you remember me?"

"My granddaughter?" he asked with surprise.

"Yes, sir," I said. "And your grandson Kolbe is driving."

"You were at my house and so was he," Mr. Northup said.

"That is correct, sir."

He stared at me. "They were dissolving me."

"Yes, sir," I said softly.

"Dissolving?" Talia repeated with horror. "Oh, Grandfather, no wonder you're sick."

He turned to face her. His bony hand reached out for her. She held it.

"Is that really my little Talia?"

She nodded, her cheeks becoming wet with tears.

He released her hand and used his shaky hand to wipe away her tears. "Don't cry for me, child. My goodness, how you look like your grandmother."

"That's what Mom says too," Talia said, sniffing.

"Your mom, how is she?" Mr. Northup asked, his voice shaking.

"Here, sir, drink this," I said, handing him the water bottle.

He lifted it to his lips, using two hands to keep it steady.

"She's good," Talia said. "She probably would've come with us to get you if she'd known we were coming," Talia said, her voice fading as she realized she shouldn't have said that.

"She doesn't know where you are?" Mr. Northup's voice sounded stern.

"Talia wasn't supposed to be here," Kolbe said. "And she certainly wasn't supposed to tell you that," he mumbled.

"Does she know you're here?" Mr. Northup asked Kolbe.

Kolbe thumped his thumb on the steering wheel. "No."

"You left your community in the middle of a hurricane to come get an old man that you barely know? Nothing about that makes sense," Mr. Northup said.

Talia said, "You're our grandfather, and besides, there wasn't a hurricane when we left."

Kolbe looked back at his grandfather. "I promised Grandmother."

"Amelia?" Mr. Northup said, his voice changing as he spoke her name.

Kolbe nodded. "The night we left, she kissed me and made me promise not to let you die alone."

Emotion swelled within Mr. Northup as tears burst forth. "She shouldn't have made you promise that," he said, pinching the bridge of his nose as he tried but failed to stop the tears. "You're only a boy."

"I'm of age now, and it was like she sent this hurricane so I could come for you without it all being caught on camera."

"That sounds like something Grandmother would do," Talia said.

Mr. Northup took the water I offered him and sipped.

"Do you remember her?" he asked after he had drunk.

"Not really," Talia said, "but Mom and Kolbe tell stories of her and Father often. It sounds like something either one of them would do … maybe both." She said this with a bit of happiness at the thought.

I took the water bottle back from Mr. Northup. I was grateful he was drinking, even grateful for the tears that would help carry away the poison. He had to get it out whatever way he could. The night had become quiet, the rain a mere drizzle, and the wind was still.

"This is weird," Talia said, her fingertips touching the window. "It's like the hurricane stopped."

"It's probably good we can't see the clouds above us. Seeing the wall of that storm would be intense," Kolbe said, leaning forward and looking up into the darkness.

Beside me, Mr. Northup leaned his head against the seat and a minute later began to softly snore.

"He fell asleep so fast," Talia said with concern.

"His body is full of poison," I said, wishing there was something more I could do.

Talia was quiet as her eyes were locked on the side of her grandfather's face.

Kolbe said, "Isn't it illegal to interfere with a dissolution?"

"Yes," I answered, confirming the simple truth.

"You aren't afraid of going to jail?" Talia asked. "I mean, if Kolbe and I hadn't come, you probably would've been caught."

"We might all be caught," Kolbe said.

I thought briefly of her question. "No, I am not afraid of going to jail." My punishment would not be time in jail. My punishment would be such severe pain, I would beg for death.

"You're very brave," she said.

I wasn't brave; I was a gestate. I was created to serve, and not to allow a vintage born who had done everything he could to help me, to be dissolved. It was what I was created to do.

Aware she was waiting for a response, I said, "It was something I had to do."

"That's because you're brave and selfless. You sacrificed to save our grandfather," Talia said confidently.

"Talia's right. Thank you for saving our grandfather," Kolbe added.

"You saved him," I said. "If I had stayed in my … my house, you still would have come."

"I wouldn't have understood what was wrong with him, and he wouldn't have, either. I may have left him, thinking the risk was too great for me to take for a dying man, or the trip too dangerous for him. Or he may never have come with me. He knows you. He feels safe with you. He hasn't seen me for ten years."

"That's why I don't recognize him," Talia said, gazing down at her grandfather. "I was barely two when we left."

"You're twelve?" I asked, thinking it was impossible this young, caring child was the same age as Salt.

"Yes. He looks so different from the picture Mom has of him. I guess because it was taken before Dad died," Talia said.

"He has lost a great deal of weight in the last two weeks, and his eyes … his eyes are so faded," I said, allowing my hand to brush Mr. Northup's thin hair back from his damp forehead. "You may have recognized him, if you saw him before they started filling him with poison."

"How did they do it?" Talia asked, her voice low, as if she didn't really want to know the answer.

"They poisoned the water going into his house," I said.

"His water," Talia said, sounding heartbroken.

There was no way to avoid the water. It was an effective plan.

I said, "Often, they use gas in the air vents. That works faster. But Mr. Northup's house was older, so that would not work for his house. If it had, I suppose he would already be dead."

"Oh," she said, and I realized that a born or vintage born who felt a true attachment would not have said that so matter-of-factly.

"I suppose it's good his house was so old," she said softly.

"Yes," I said, thinking of the house with soft fabric furniture.

"Do you think the hurricane will destroy it?" Talia said.

"If it doesn't, they will," Kolbe said.

"Why?" Talia said in a gasp.

Kolbe gave a little scoff. "You know why. Because everything out here has to be exactly the same. If everyone can't have a house that spacious and well-built, then no one can."

"Oh yeah, I forgot," she said, slumping back.

I'd never thought about the possibility of things being any other way, but by the way he said *out here* it made me wonder. "Is it different where you live?"

"Yes," Talia said, the side of her face leaning against the middle of the seat as she peered down at her grandfather. "There, everything is different."

Fourteen

I leaned my head against the back of the seat. An image of Hastings entered my mind. When he saw my pod was destroyed and realized I was either dead or had run away, there would be tears, and for the first time in his life I wouldn't be there to wipe them away. I fought the thought. In truth, I would've been gone in a few weeks anyway, sent to another family unit … or anyone who could afford my price. Leaving now spared him the sorrow of anticipating my leaving later.

The night went from a dark, dreamless sleep to a hurricane in a single breath. The vehicle was being attacked, thrown from one edge of the asphalt to the other, the wind assailing us from every side.

"I can't keep us on the road," Kolbe yelled above the shriek of the winds.

To my surprise, it was Mr. Northup who answered. "We're near the beach reclamation zone. Turn toward it. We can find a house to weather the storm in."

"You want me to go toward the storm?" Kolbe yelled back to his grandfather.

"What choice do we have?" Mr. Northup answered calmly.

"I'm so glad Mom is safe at home," Talia yelled as her brother sharply turned the wheel, taking us down a side street.

The wind was slightly calmer now that we were facing due east.

"That's where you two should be," Mr. Northup groaned as we bounced in our seats.

"Without them, we never would have made it, sir," I said softly.

He shook his head. "Their mother has lost enough. She can't lose her children too."

"We aren't dead yet," Kolbe said, turning onto a driveway.

I gripped the back of Kolbe's seat and tried to keep myself steady. The headlights fell upon a thick forest of scrub oaks laced with vines. In the middle was a narrow drive, made even more narrow by the encroaching vines. We were going up, the land was rising; we were on a slight hill. An unusual thing for this part of the country. I gripped the seat tighter. Kolbe was taking us closer to the Atlantic Ocean and the raging hurricane.

In front of us, a wall of green appeared.

"What is that?" Kolbe asked, staring through the window. The windshield wipers swept as fast as they could and still the rain was so thick we could barely see.

"Vines," I said. "They have taken over."

"Is the house intact?" Mr. Northup asked, his voice sounding weak again.

"I think so," Kolbe said as he pulled up to the house.

Kolbe parked the vehicle. Above the beating of the rain, he yelled, "I'm going to check it out. Stay here."

Part of me wanted to offer to go in his place, but I obeyed. Mr. Northup, Talia, and I remained in our seats. A wall of rain surged inside when Kolbe opened the door, much of it flying into where Mr. Northup and I sat.

Kolbe bent his head low and fought against the wind that was trying to push him back. In a minute he was gone, disappeared into the hurricane. I placed a hand on the back of the soaking seat. I should have been the one to go, not him— never a vintage born.

A gust of wind pushed hard against the side of the vehicle.

"I've never seen so much rain," Talia said fearfully.

Mr. Northup said, "When I was a boy, we had a hurricane, the last direct hit in this area. It was like this, but I wasn't driving in it. I was safe in my house with my parents, where you should be."

"You know Dad is dead," she said sadly.

Mr. Northup's shoulders drooped even more. "I think … I think I forgot for a moment," he said, sounding confused.

"It is the poison, sir. You will recover more in a few days," I said.

Mr. Northup suddenly thrust open his door. The wind pulled it out of his hands as he wretched into the hurricane, the rain soaking through him. The wind was swirling into the vehicle, causing my breath to catch.

He tried to pull the door closed, but was too weak.

"Help him," Talia cried.

I climbed in front of him and pulled against the wind. Mr. Northup, breathing heavily, leaned against the seat. Slowly, I managed to shut the door.

"Just a few more days and this will all be over, sir. It will be okay," I said, my hair and shirt soaked through once more.

He grasped my hand, still breathing heavily. "Yes, a few more days," he said, holding on to me.

Next to me, the door opened, the rain rushing in again. Kolbe was there, water streaming from him. "Come help me," he said.

"Take care of him," I said to Talia as I released her grandfather's hand.

"Always," she said, placing her hands on his shoulders as his breath continued to come in short, ragged waves.

I stepped from the vehicle, the wind pushing me back, pulling me forward, pushing me back. I could barely stay upright. Kolbe was next to me, his hand holding my upper arm. It was the only way we could stay together or even know where the other was. The rain was so thick I could barely see the light Kolbe held. Slowly he led us forward … the wind struck us again and again. He pulled me forward and then stopped, our bodies pushed against a hard surface, the side of the house.

"Hold on to me," he yelled above the storm.

I reached out, grabbing part of his shirt and holding on as he pulled a door open. He braced his body against it, against the storm.

"Go in," he yelled.

I practically fell into the house, my body exhausted. He pulled the door shut.

"Quite a storm," he said, his hands on his thighs and his breathing as heavy as mine. The flashlight in his hand pointed at the cement floor.

"Yes," I said, panting.

Rain trickled from my face and braided hair. Kolbe reached his hand toward me. I winced, not knowing what to expect. He touched my hair and held up part of a green vine.

"This was stuck in your hair," he said, handing me the vine.

I took it.

"Did you think I was going to hurt you?" he asked.

"I-I did not know what to expect," I answered, feeling acutely how isolated we were. I wanted Mr. Northup. I wanted to not be alone with a stranger, even one with seemingly kind eyes.

"I'll never hurt you, unless maybe by accident. I'm a bit clumsy sometimes," he said with the beginning of laughter.

I giggled and quickly covered my mouth with my hands.

"It's okay to find me funny. Lots of people do," he said with a wink, the sort of wink Hastings always tried to do but never succeeded at.

"Come on, we need to try and break the garage door free. I undid the latches holding it down, but couldn't lift it. It might be rusted or the vines might be holding it down. I'm hoping you're stronger than you look," he said, going to the metal door that spanned the length of the room.

I copied his stance. Together we put our hands beneath the lip of metal that stretched the length of the garage door.

"Ready?" he asked.

I nodded.

"Okay, lift."

It wasn't easy. The vines fought hard against us, but in the end we were stronger, or perhaps the plants were tired from fighting the storm. Either way, they released their hold on the door and it went up, pieces of green vine falling all around us.

"I was right, you're stronger than you look," Kolbe said, breathing heavily again as the water fell in sheets in front of us.

"So are you," I said.

Kolbe nodded. "That's 'cause you're used to the borns," he said over the rushing wind. "They're all blown up like balloons," he called as he ran out into the storm.

Fifteen

A minute later the headlights were shining in my face. I moved quickly to the side as the vehicle pulled into the garage.

The vehicle turned off, but the lights remained on. Kolbe hopped out and went to the garage door.

"Help me," he called.

Together we pulled the metal door down, the wind and rain pelting us.

"Put the latch in so the wind doesn't lift up the door during the storm," he said.

He slid a rusted metal rod on the side of the door into a hole on the metal track. I copied his action. The rust made the metal hard to slide.

He wiped the rust from his hands, onto his wet pants. "We should be safe now," he said.

I gave him a questioning glance before catching myself and lowering my eyes.

He laughed. "Okay. Maybe not exactly safe, but safer. Definitely safer."

"Unless the house falls down on top of us," Talia said as she climbed out of the truck. She kept her hands behind her so her grandfather didn't fall out.

"This house has been here for at least sixty years. I'm sure it will last one more night," Kolbe said, reaching for his grandfather. He helped him scoot out of the high vehicle which reminded me of something the peacekeepers drove, only a little taller and broader.

When Mr. Northup's feet hit the concrete floor his legs buckled, but Kolbe and I held him upright.

"We've got you," Kolbe said, his face set hard with determination.

Mr. Northup nodded, his skin gray in the dim glow of the vehicle's interior lights.

"Take the flashlight from my back pocket," Kolbe said to his sister. "We need to get inside. Maybe there are dry clothes or a blanket for Grandfather."

"I'm fine," Mr. Northup said, his words thick but clear.

"Azalea Rose would probably appreciate some dry clothes," Kolbe said in a fake whisper to his grandfather.

Mr. Northup nodded. Beside us, Talia clicked on the light. Kolbe led his grandfather around the vehicle. I reached back into the vehicle and retrieved my pack. The clothes inside were soaked. I hoped the glass and metal frames were enough to keep the pictures dry.

I followed Talia, who used the light to scan the empty walls and then found a door to the inside of the house.

"Let me," I said, stepping in front of her. A vintage born child should not be the one to go first into an unknown situation.

I tried the door. The handle turned but the door didn't open. I pushed against it, falling forward a little when it gave way. Talia shone the tiny beam of light into the vast darkness of the house. The strong smell of mildew hit us.

"I do not think anyone has been in here for a long time," I whispered.

"No, not in the reclamation zone," Kolbe whispered back.

"Then why are you whispering?" Talia said. The loudness of her voice sounded as if she was shouting. She shone the beam of light on the walls on the west side of the building. The walls were green … glass covered with green.

"It looks like there's another layer of wall outside of the glass. Like there's concrete with lots of opening for light and then glass," Kolbe said as we studied the vines. "I bet it was pretty once."

"It's pretty now and way cooler. It's like we're in a giant terrarium," Talia said with an air of excitement.

Hastings would like her. She was as lively as he was.

"What's on the ocean side?" Kolbe asked.

She spun the light across a vast empty space: there was more glass, covered on the outside with metal.

"Hurricane shutters," Mr. Northup mumbled. "The people who owned this house probably hoped they'd be able to come back here someday."

"This was *one* house?" I asked in disbelief.

"Those who lived near the ocean were very wealthy," Mr. Northup said, his voice thick. "Their houses reflected their wealth."

"Those shutters really work," Talia said, moving the light up and down the edges of the glass, searching for cracks. "There aren't any cracks, or at least not any big ones. That's pretty amazing."

Beyond the glass, the storm attacked again and again, shaking the metal.

"My family unit's entire house could fit in this room," I said, astounded that this was *one* family unit's house.

Mr. Northup groaned. It was difficult for him to walk, to breathe, to live. He would be strong again in a few days; like the storm, the poison would pass.

"That was the evil—or what they called evil," Kolbe said. "It was unfair. If all could not have houses of this size next to the ocean, no one could."

"So they left them to rot," Talia said.

I gazed around at what once was probably as beautiful as Mr. Northup's house, maybe more, and felt a pain in my chest.

"All are the same," I said, more to myself than to the others.

"Once, it was all are *equal*," Kolbe said with a sort of longing, "but you're right. Now all must be the *same*."

His tone of sorrow didn't make sense. All are the same. All borns and vintage borns must have the same. They do not have to look the same, though the borns do—but they must have the same abilities, the same opportunities, the same houses, the same education, the same options for employment. Without sameness there is unfairness and that is what existed before the reset, before the age of systematic reason. That was why such a grand house was built for merely a few, not for all. It was not fair.

"Talia, search for a bedroom. Maybe there's a bed for Grandfather or something dry to put on," Kolbe said.

Talia nodded and moved quickly. I went with her, leaving Kolbe and Mr. Northup to follow slowly behind us. In front of us, Talia's light hit upon a giant food preparation room in the middle of the house, like Mr. Northup's house had.

"Why is the food preparation room in the middle?" I asked before I could stop the curiosity.

"It's called a kitchen," Talia said. "There were no gestates when this house was built. Those in the family prepared their own food."

"Borns cooked?" I asked in amazement.

She continued moving us forward. "Then, they were all vintage borns, or most were, anyway, and yes, they cooked and cleaned. It's the same where I'm from," she said.

"You serve each other?" I asked as her light shone on a gold-framed mirror in a small bathroom near the food preparation room ... the kitchen. I wondered briefly why there would be a bathroom, here in the middle of the house, instead of in the personal rooms.

Her dark eyes stared back at me from the mirror. Her skin and hair appeared light compared to my black hair and tanned skin.

"It's a gift to serve those you love," she said. "I mean, sometimes when it's your annoying brother, it's a pain. But when it's others you love, it's a gift—or at least that's what my mom always tells me. … Oh, look, stairs!" she squealed with excitement.

"Be careful," Kolbe called from behind us.

"Zelie and I will check them out. You two wait here," she called back to her brother.

She began to move quickly down the stairs that were made of the same reddish-brown tile covering the rest of the floors in the house. The air down here smelled damp. It was thick with mildew and the walls were dotted with dark splotches where it had grown.

A large empty room took up one whole side of the downstairs. There were no windows in this room, only a large table in its center.

Talia went to the table. "Do you know why there are holes in the corners and sides?" she asked.

I wanted to run my hand along the table, but the cloth on its top was mostly black mildew. "Maybe it held water bottles," I said.

"Maybe," she said, and moved on.

On the other side of the long room, we found several smaller rooms. I followed Talia into each: empty, without the slightest trace of furniture or clothing, and one window covered on the outside with metal. In these rooms the storm was loud. Not as loud as it had been upstairs, but loud enough to make me afraid for the Parker-James house and those inside it. The newscaster had assured those nearest the reclamation zone that they had nothing to worry about. But the sound of this storm … I'd never heard anything like it.

Talia went to the last door, the only one that was shut.

The knob wouldn't twist. "It's locked," she said.

I pushed against it. "It's solid wood," I said in amazement.

The doors at the Parker-James property were made of a thin metal, easily dented, as Salt had proven on more than one occasion, but this door was nothing like those.

I heaved my shoulder against the door. It didn't give, even a little. In some ways it reminded me of the thick metal doors at the gestation firm, but while those were sturdy, they were hollow. This was sturdy and solid. There was no give.

"We found a locked door," Talia yelled back.

That sudden noise above the storm made me jump. If anyone was on the other side of this door, they now knew exactly where we were.

A second later Kolbe came jogging toward us from upstairs, and Talia swung the flashlight to light his steps.

"Where's Grandfather?" she asked.

"He's waiting upstairs. I didn't want him coming down here if he didn't need to. What did you find?"

"Nothing, except maybe there's something in here, but the door's locked," she said.

He pushed against it and then studied it. "The door's solid, but maybe the frame can be loosened. It's been sitting for a long time, so maybe the wood has started to give. Move to the side," he said, gently pulling his sister away from the door.

I watched him, wondering what he was going to do. He stepped back and kicked it. The sound was as loud as the hurricane. He backed up and kicked again and again. The third time, the door creaked open. The door held, but the frame had been ripped free from the inside edge.

Kolbe was breathing hard as Talia pushed open the door.

"Wow," she said as she shone the light around the room overflowing with stuff.

My eyes grew wide. A tall bed was piled high with so many objects. There was other furniture made difficult to see by the many objects that covered it. The smell of mildew was equally strong here. I touched a book; I'd never seen one before, but I knew what it was. They were not explicitly forbidden, though no one had any. Instead, they read on their devices when it was mandated.

The edges of the pages had turned black from mildew. A sudden sadness came over me. Like something had been lost. Something that had once been known, no longer was. It was stupid to feel such emotion for an inanimate object, but still, the sadness remained and increased as my eyes scanned the room, along with the beam of the flashlight. So many things … so many treasures—gone.

I felt as if I would cry.

"Help me get Grandfather," Kolbe said, gently touching my arm. His voice revealed the same loss I felt.

I blinked away the tears that formed, despite my realizing how foolish such tears were. I followed them from the room, grateful Talia's light didn't shine on me.

At the top of the stairs, Mr. Northup lay curled on his side. He looked so small … so frail.

"Wake up, Grandfather," Talia said.

His eyes opened and he stared at her with a blank expression. He'd forgotten who she was. Behind her, he saw me.

"Azalea Rose?" he said feebly.

"Yes, I am here," I said, crouching beside him. "We are with your grandchildren. We found a soft place for you to sleep through the rest of this storm."

"Storm?" he said, wrapping his arms around my neck to allow me to lift him.

"Remember, there is a hurricane," I answered, helping him to his feet.

"Oh," he said without any real awareness.

"There is no need for you to worry about any of that. All you need is to sleep. You will feel much better after that," I said, my voice catching as I lifted his thin frame.

Kolbe helped me get Mr. Northup down the stairs. Talia went in front of us and made sure to carefully light every step, though Mr. Northup didn't appear to be looking at them. His eyes were lost, like he'd forgotten how to use them.

We were soon in the room. I held Mr. Northup while Kolbe cleared a spot on the bed for him to sit.

Mr. Northup sat there, the blank expression beginning to clear.

"I've never seen a room like this," Talia said with wonder.

Mr. Northup's eyes followed the light Talia shone, from one stack of objects to the next.

"It's a hope room," Mr. Northup said, his voice raspy.

"What does that mean?" Talia asked, sitting down beside her grandfather.

He cleared his throat. "That's what these rooms were called. The rooms where things were hidden. Things someone hoped to return to someday, when all of this was over. Only, it never ended," he said.

He was no longer lost, he was here … present, aware, and deeply troubled by what he saw.

"What were they hoping would be over?" I asked, as quietly as possible above the noise of the storm.

"I didn't understand it then," he said, more to himself. He sat a little taller, his attention turning to us. "The insanity that took everything from them … that took everything from all of us."

Sixteen

Talia shone the light onto the bed, near where her grandfather sat. She didn't shine the light directly at him, but it was close enough that I could see his expression. It remained unsettled, like he was fighting with himself.

"None of this is how it was supposed to be," he said, rubbing his shaking fingers against his thin, unwashed hair. "Everything is wrong, everything."

I looked at Kolbe and Talia. Their faces were concerned, but they held recognition. They understood what their grandfather was speaking about.

I hesitated until the curiosity could not be contained. "What's wrong? How are things supposed to be?"

Mr. Northup focused on me, his awareness full and present. "You think this is normal? ... Of course you do, you've known no other life," he said, his voice frail.

He reached his hand for mine. Some part of the gesture felt natural; standing beside him, I held his hand.

"It's a lie."

"What is?" I asked as the wind violently shook the metal covering the windows.

"Everything you've ever been told," he said, the attentiveness in his watery brown eyes already fading.

"Sir," I said, "what is a lie?" I squeezed his hand. "What is a lie?"

He didn't answer.

Talia said, "He's too tired."

She helped him lie back. His awareness slipped into the darkness of the poison.

"What did he mean, everything I have been told is a lie?" I asked.

"You're right," Talia said to her brother, "he has changed. Mom said she thought he would … with time."

"He's had lots of time," Kolbe said, exhaling loudly as he leaned against a tall pole connected to one of the corners of the bed.

"Yes," Talia said, moving the hair away from his forehead. "We should at least take off his wet shoes and socks." She began to unlace the black shoes from her grandfather's feet. Kolbe came beside her and helped.

"What did he mean?" I repeated.

Kolbe and Talia glanced at one another. Talia gave a faint nod to her brother.

"It's a dangerous belief outside of the settlements," Kolbe said, as if cautioning me.

I moved out of his way as he helped his sister get their grandfather settled.

Kolbe said, "Many believe that something is very wrong with the country."

"What is wrong with it?" I asked.

"So many things," Talia said, exasperated.

"Talia, be cautious," Kolbe said.

"What? How are things going to change if people don't talk about what's wrong?"

Outside, the wind cried, and the whole house seemed to shake. We each stared above us as if we could see the hurricane beyond the wood-paneled ceiling.

"I'm going upstairs to check things out," Kolbe said.

"Why?" Talia asked.

Kolbe started toward the door. "I want to make sure we're as secure here as I think we are. Want to come with me?" he asked, his voice becoming slightly softer as he spoke to me.

I hesitated. I didn't want to leave Mr. Northup or Talia, whom I thought might be willing to tell me more—especially if her brother wasn't there to tell her not to. But Kolbe wanted me to go with him and I couldn't deny a vintage born.

Kolbe didn't move as I went toward him.

"Only if you want to," he said, as if he could read my mind.

"I-I do," I said, unsettled by a vintage born saying I had a choice in what I did, when we both knew I did not.

"Here," Talia said, tossing her brother the flashlight and then opening something she pulled from the pile near her. A dim light filled the room. "I thought it would still work," she chirped, pleased with herself for finding a lantern.

"Nice work," Kolbe said, aiming the flashlight at the space outside the room.

I followed him up the stairs. On the main level of the house he used the flashlight to scan every part of the room in front of us—the kitchen, as Talia had called it.

"Let's open the cabinets in case there are some supplies we might use … or someone hiding," Kolbe said in a whisper to me.

My steps faltered; I hadn't thought of someone hiding. I swallowed hard. I opened first one cabinet and then another. He was right. In these large spaces, someone my size could easily be hiding.

"What's it like?" His voice was quiet, almost inaudible.

I lifted my head, a question in my eyes.

"Being a gestate," he said quietly, not daring to look at me. "What's it like?"

I allowed my hand to fall to my side. I had pulled open a drawer. It was empty.

"It … it is what it is. It is all I have ever known," I said. I ran an index finger along the dusty edge of the wooden drawer.

"You ran away. I've been told some don't want to leave," Kolbe said in an accusing tone.

"I left to help your grandfather. But there are many reasons one stays," I said, thinking first of Hastings and then of the gestates tortured in front of me during training. I shivered at the memory.

"Are you okay?" Kolbe asked, his focus on me.

It was unsettling to be watched … to be noticed. "I was remembering something," I said.

"It wasn't a good memory?" he said.

I was puzzled by the strangeness of his question. "I have very few of those," I answered.

"Oh," he said, as if my response startled him.

I continued searching the kitchen. All the while he was watching me.

"What was the memory?" he asked, as the hurricane shook the house.

I hesitated, but then said, "It was of a female gestate who tried to run. She was caught and we … we were made to watch her … punishment."

Kolbe's head fell forward as if my words affected him, as if he cared what I felt.

"I'm sorry," he said.

The kindness in his tone made emotions swirl.

"Are you okay?" Kolbe asked, standing inches from me. His expression was so concerned.

"You are different than other men."

Kolbe cocked his head. "Different, as in, I need an alteration to fix something?"

I studied him. "No, different like …" My hand moved toward his face, his strong jaw, his sharp nose. He was standing perfectly still. I stopped myself before my fingers reached his face. What was I doing, touching a grown vintage born? I quickly lowered my hand and took a step back.

"You are not hiding anything," I said, suddenly aware of what the difference was. He was who he appeared to be.

"Technically, I'm *in* hiding with you and my grandfather."

He started to smile at the joke as I continued to study his expression.

"I trust you," I said bluntly. "There is no deception."

His expression became serious. "No, there's no deception. I am who I am and I don't try to hide it."

"Is that common where you are from? In the settlement, I mean."

"It's probably more common, but no, just because someone is part of my settlement doesn't mean you should trust them."

"But I should trust you?"

"I won't hurt you," he said, echoing his words from earlier.

I tilted my head. "I do not believe you will."

"May I offer you a suggestion?" Kolbe asked, his gaze intense.

I lowered my eyes. "Yes."

"Use contractions."

I raised my eyes. "What?"

"When you speak, use contractions and don't be afraid to look at people. That's what a vintage born would do."

"But I am not a vintage born," I said. "You and I both know that."

"Talia doesn't, and it's better that way. Better if everyone you ever meet for the rest of your life believes you're a vintage born."

"That is not possible," I said.

"That *isn't* possible," he said, correcting me. "And I think it is. You look like one—well, you could if you acted like one. And if you started talking like one, that would go a long way."

"I-I will try," I said.

"Good," he said, still watching me instead of searching the house.

Around us the storm became louder, shaking us from our thoughts.

"I think this room is empty," he said, guiding the flashlight beam toward the large open room beyond the kitchen. His steps followed the light. In that room, he scanned the light over the walls and ceiling.

"Look at those beams," he said in awe. "I bet they're oak."

He was focused above our heads, at giant wooden beams that spanned the width of the ceiling.

"I've never seen beams that big. And to have so many of them," he said, using the light to follow them end to end.

"They're gorgeous," he said with more enthusiasm than I'd heard before.

I giggled at his excitement. "You really like wooden beams."

He grinned. "I'm a carpenter, I work with wood. Seeing beams like this is incredible. Oh wow, do you see the indentations there?"

I followed the ray of light. "Maybe," I said, squinting.

He came and put an arm around me, using the flashlight to guide my sight. "See there? It's a small hole."

"Yes," I said, able to see what he was showing me, though I wasn't thinking about it. I was thinking about his chest pressed to my back. Aside from when I was caring for Hastings or Mr. Northup, I'd never stood so close to anyone.

"I bet that's where it was attached to something else. This wood is ancient. One of the guys in the community told me his grandfather told him that people would take wood out of old buildings about to be torn down and use it in their houses. I bet that's what this is. I bet these beams had a life before this house." He was practically gushing.

"What is … I mean *what's* that?" I said, taking his hand and directing the flashlight to the corner where two beams connected.

It was rough and uneven.

I gasped. "It moved!"

We studied the spot longer.

"It's a bird's nest, with a little bird inside," Kolbe said, his voice sounding sweet.

"There are two of them," I said, realizing there was a bird behind the nest as well.

"Aww," he said, making a sighing sound.

I gave him a look of surprise.

"What?" he said. "I love birds. When I was a kid, I wished I could turn into one and fly around. I'm glad they're safe in here, where the storm can't reach them."

"Yes, it does seem safer in here than out there."

I jumped at the crash of thunder, sounding as if it was on the other side of the metal shutters.

"It's okay," he said, "just thun—"

Before he could finish his words, his arms were around me, pushing me down and away from the crashing.

"Get down," he shouted. He pushed me farther out of the way, his back above mine, protecting me from things falling around us.

A second later, the crashing sounds stopped, but the storm sounded as if it was a hundred times louder.

Kolbe groaned.

"Are you okay?" I asked, my heart racing, my hands trembling.

"I think so," he said. He moved and shards of glass fell from his back and head.

I took the light from his hands and examined his hair and back. In places, his shirt was ripped, but beneath, the skin had only shallow scratches.

"I don't see any serious damage," I said, running my hand along his back to make sure I wasn't missing anything. The muscles tensed beneath my touch as he stood straighter.

"That caught me off guard," he said, rubbing his fingers gingerly through his light brown hair. Pieces of glass fell to the floor.

The storm howled, no longer outside but inside.

"You protected me," I said, above the noise. I didn't bother to hide the shock in my voice.

"It was instinct," he said, breathing heavily, recovering from the fear we both felt. "I reacted without thinking."

"And your instinct was to protect me—*a gestate*?" I asked.

"My instinct was to protect you—*a woman*. It's what a man does," he said.

Glass crunched beneath his shoes.

"I hope the birds are okay," he said, taking my hand in his and rapidly scanning the ceiling with the light to find the nest. The bird in the nest had left. It was on another beam. The other bird had remained nearby.

"They'll come back," I said, more confused by his behavior than the birds'.

"The lightning must've hit that tree. The hurricane shutters were probably too rusted to keep it from crashing through," he said as I released the light into his hand.

He shone the beam on the shredded branches of a palm tree poking through the corner of the house.

"The storm is so loud," I said, fighting the urge to cover my ears.

"Makes you realize how well insulated this house is," he said, his voice raised against the storm. "It won't last long, now that the wind and water can get in so easily."

"I guess not," I said, my voice loud to match his. "I guess it doesn't matter anyway."

"Why not?"

Water poured down the inside of the glass, forming a puddle on the hardwood floor.

"Why would it? The ones who hoped to come back here are long gone," I said, feeling my own sense of hope fade.

Kolbe faced me. He shone the light at the floor beside us.

"Don't become one of them," Kolbe shouted above the storm.

"One of who?"

"One of the hopeless."

Seventeen

I opened my eyes, startled by what surrounded me. Around the edges of glass at the far end of the hope room, sunlight streamed in. It was enough to dimly light the room. I'd never woken up when the sun was already shining. True, we'd gone to sleep not long before my band would've woken me, but I could've been up all night at the Parker-James house and still, my band would wake me at five fifteen. This was the first day in almost nine years that I'd slept past that time. I felt an odd sense of guilt mixed with freedom as I sat up.

"Good morning," Mr. Northup said from the bed above me.

"Hello," I answered awkwardly.

I'd almost convinced myself that yesterday had been a dream, it all seemed so unreal. Me, tying my band to an opossum, leaving Hastings, fleeing with Mr. Northup and his previously thought-to-be-dead grandchildren. All of that while a hurricane fought against us or, perhaps, fought to free us.

"Typically, when someone says good morning," Mr. Northup said kindly, "you say good morning back to them."

"If you can correct my speech, you must be feeling better," I said, pulling my tangled hair back away from my face.

"Yes, better than yesterday, I think. I woke up an hour or so ago, and I've been trying to figure out if all I dreamed was real. When I noticed you on the floor beside me, I decided it must be real."

"I was thinking the same thing," I said.

Across the room, Talia groaned in her sleep.

"Why did you tell me your grandchildren were dead?"

"Their father is," he said, his stoic face lit by the dim light. "Their mother took them away after he died. I didn't know for sure what happened to them, but I couldn't tell you that when your band was on. I've done enough to hurt my daughter-in-law."

I wanted to ask what he meant. The thought of his hurting anyone struck me as unbelievable, but on the floor not far from me, Kolbe sat up. His hair stuck out straight in multiple places, reminding me of Hastings.

"Good morning," Kolbe said, with a smile to me as he stretched, his muscles pulling tight against his shirt.

"Good morning," Mr. Northup answered. "Did you sleep well?"

"Yeah, pretty good."

"To be young and have a body that didn't ache, even if it slept on the hard floor," Mr. Northup answered in a lighthearted voice.

"You sound much better," Kolbe said. "Do you feel like eating?"

"Yes, I think so."

Kolbe opened his pack. "It isn't much, but it's better than nothing," he said, pulling out a cloth bag.

He untied it to reveal nuts and dried fruit within. These were luxury items that I'd only ever tasted a few times. He handed it to his grandfather. Mr. Northup took a nut and slowly chewed it, the action exhausting him.

"I have some sustenance powder. It might be easier for you," I said.

Mr. Northup leaned his head against the ancient pillow. "That may be best," he said, his voice feeble again.

I opened my bag and took out the metal tin, along with the metal water bottle that was nearly empty.

"Here," Kolbe said, tossing me a personal water container from his pack.

I put two scoops of powder in the container and closed it, shaking it before I handed it to Mr. Northup.

He took a sip. "It tastes like water."

"Sustenance powder doesn't have a taste or texture," I said.

"The ones I always had did," Talia said, popping up from her spot. "My favorite is the cherry kind," she said, yawning and smoothing her knotted hair.

"I've never had that kind," I said.

Kolbe's expression became hard before he turned away.

Mr. Northup took another sip. "This is better. It's easier to drink water than chew nuts. Here, Azalea Rose, you take them," he said, forcing the cloth into my hand.

I wanted to object. They were more than I deserved, but it was too late; some of them spilled into my hand.

"Thank you," I said, slowly lifting a pecan to my lips.

"It's much better if you eat the nuts and dried fruit together," Talia said, coming beside me and taking a few of each from the cloth.

"Mmm, these are delicious," she said, closing her eyes as she chewed the food.

"Of course, you say that. You made them," Kolbe said with a wry smile.

"Yes, but sometimes I overdry the fruit, sometimes I don't dry it enough," she said, rocking her body rhythmically from side to side. "This time it's perfect," she said, twirling around in a display of what I could only understand to be happiness. I saw it sometimes in Hastings … never in anyone else in his family.

She was so unlike Salt; they were the same age, but were nothing alike. It was unusual for me to interact with people of such distinct personalities. I was not around many people—only when Ms. Parker told me to run an errand or if she brought me along to help her with something. Even during those outings, I'd always been struck by how similar everyone was. The different generations of borns look, speak, and act almost identical to one another. But in this room, there were three very distinct vintage borns, each of them unlike anyone else I'd ever met.

"We should be going as soon as you're ready, Grandfather," Kolbe said, reorganizing his pack.

"Have you been to the beach before?" Mr. Northup asked me.

"Me? No, sir. It is forbidden."

"Many things are forbidden," Mr. Northup said dismissively. "For instance, it's quite forbidden to interfere with a dissolution. Seems to me today is the perfect day for you to feel the sand beneath your toes."

I could hear the faintest sound of enjoyment in his voice. If he was stronger, I think he would be laughing.

"Have you been on the beach, Grandfather?" Talia asked, her eyes wide.

His eyes brightened. "Some of my best memories come from this ocean. I proposed to your grandmother on her shore. It was at dusk, dolphins jumped in the background, the breeze lifted her sun-streaked hair. That was the most enchanting day," he said with a mixture of joy and sorrow. "Not long after that, the beaches were forbidden."

We sat silently watching Mr. Northup. His eyes closed and then opened.

"Go, I'll rest. Then we'll leave," he said, and closed his eyes again.

"It would be a shame to come so close and not see the ocean," Kolbe said, rubbing his fingers across his lips in thought.

"Mmm-hmm," Mr. Northup said with a faint smile, his eyes remaining closed.

"Come on, let's go," Talia said with a squeal.

She pulled her brother and me up and out of the room.

"I forgot Grandfather was alive before the reclamation zones," Talia said as we walked around the table with holes in it.

"They began sixty years ago," Kolbe said. "So much has changed in his lifetime—reclamation zones, gestates, government controlling everything."

"If it changed that quickly, maybe it can unchange just as quickly," Talia said with a lightness to her voice her brother didn't have.

Kolbe said, "Lies always spread quicker than the truth."

"Yes, but at some point, good wins," Talia said cheerfully.

He exhaled in a sort of relieved acceptance. "Yes, at some point, good wins."

Faded light reached us as we turned the corner on the stairs. Further up, a muted green hue shone on everything, making the walls and floor appear green, though they weren't. It was the vines that covered the western wall of the house, a wall of glass for the house and, outside, a wall of concrete with slits throughout.

"I bet they had plants there between the glass and the concrete," Talia said, going toward the wall of glass-covered vines.

"I've never seen so many windows," Kolbe said in a hushed tone that told me he felt the same about this place as I did. It demanded respect; no, that wasn't the correct word. I searched my mind. There was a word for this feeling … reverence. It demanded reverence.

Kolbe and I followed Talia to the wall of vines. Against the glass, the tiny tendrils of the vines could be seen clinging to the glass. It was a thick mat that only the brightest sun could shine through.

"It's beautiful," I said, touching my fingertips gently to the smooth glass as if I could reach the delicate wisps of green.

"Yes," Kolbe said, his voice as reverent as my own.

"I have always hated vines, but these are so pretty. Maybe I was wrong to destroy the ones I did," I said, wondering if I'd been fighting against nature out of foolishness.

"It has to do with the right ordering of things. Vines in the right order or location can be majestic. In the wrong location they suffocate everything else," Kolbe said, his pale blue eyes on me instead of the vines.

"They'll take over this house," Talia said, pressing her face against the glass and gazing upward. "I bet they're already on the roof."

"Thanks to last night's storm, it won't be long until they're inside," Kolbe said, turning to face the eastern wall, which once had a view of the ocean but now looked out at rusted metal.

One large section of the window was broken, and a few strands of green palm were swiping into the room on a faint salty wind. On the ground beneath the splintered glass was a pool of water.

"This house lasted so long," Talia said with a sense of sadness. "I bet it's as old as Grandfather."

"I'm sure it's much older than him. No one would've built such a beautiful house so close to the age of insanity," Kolbe said with sarcasm.

"I've never heard of that age," I said. Above us the bird was watching us from her nest.

"He means the age of systematic reason. The age of insanity is what we call it," Talia explained.

"Because that's what it is," Kolbe added.

"Do you think the people knew?" Talia said, ignoring her brother's glib remarks. "Twenty years before, when Grandfather was a little boy, did his parents know that the world their son would grow up in would be totally different from the world they grew up in?"

"The world always changes," Kolbe said, "so they must've known it would be different."

"But so different that when their precious baby grew old, the establishment would poison his water because they decided he wasn't useful enough to have access to resources?" Talia demanded, her fists clenched.

Kolbe placed a hand on his sister's shoulder. "No one could've known such darkness would exist. You're right, maybe the house isn't that old. Maybe it's only as old as Grandfather. Maybe the people who built it had no idea of what was coming."

I listened to their words, emotion stirring in me. The same emotion I felt that night on Mr. Northup's porch. A longing for something … something different.

"Well," Talia said, straightening herself and clearing her throat, "I suppose there's no point in getting angry at people who aren't here. Let's go see the beach. Who knows if I'll ever get another chance."

"I suppose that's true," Kolbe said. "Who knows what will happen in our lives?"

Next to him, Talia shuddered.

"Come on, there's a door here." Kolbe led us toward a door not far from the splintered glass.

He unlocked it and then shoved hard against the swollen wood. The bright light was blinding for a moment, with no metal or palm fronds obscuring it. There were vines here too.

Kolbe pushed the door open farther, and they pulled away from the house. He started to reach for them, to get them out of the way.

"They have thorns," I said, and his hand fell back.

He used his foot to move them away from the door.

Talia stepped out. "It smells so different out here," she said.

I took a deep breath. It was the smell of the sea, the smell of the Parker-James property, the smell that always surrounded Hastings.

"Are you okay?" Kolbe said as he waited for me to step from the house.

"Yes," I lied.

The air was warm and heavy. The palm tree stretched in front of us, reaching into the top of the house. Others were nearby—most remained upright, but several others were down. The grass was taller than Kolbe. The tips of the grass held pods of grain.

"There's a break in the sea oats up this way," Talia said, leading the way.

In front of us, the tall grasses came to an abrupt end. Beyond that lay sand packed hard from last night's storm, and beyond that, gray water constantly pushing itself forward and quickly retreating. There was no end to it and no beginning; it stretched farther than the eye could see.

"It's beautiful," Talia said, her voice low.

"Yes," I said, in a whisper that was drowned out by the waves.

Kolbe hopped down onto the precious sand. "Looks like last night's storm caused a lot of erosion."

His sister followed him, jumping off the three-foot cliff we stood on. Her feet sank deep into the sand, causing craters in the pink, gold-hued surface.

"Come on, you've got to feel this," Talia said with a joyful grin up at me.

Kolbe held his hand out for me. I hesitated.

"I won't hurt you," he said, his eyes on mine.

Cautiously I took his hand. His fingers felt rough and calloused, like mine. I stepped down as gently as possible, but still, my leading foot sank deep into the sand. Kolbe held my hand for one more moment and then released it.

"It is so squishy," I said.

"It's amazing," Talia said, quickly sitting and slipping off her shoes and socks.

"What're you doing?" Kolbe asked.

"Don't you remember what Grandfather said? He said we should feel the sand between our toes." She grinned up at her brother.

She stuffed her socks into her shoes. "It feels cool," she said.

Kolbe slipped off his own shoes and socks.

"This is a once-in-a-lifetime opportunity," he said, grinning at me.

"It feels amazing," Talia said. "So much better than dirt or mud or anything else."

I giggled at Talia's exuberance; I couldn't help it.

"It's okay, we won't tell," Kolbe said.

I hesitated, but then leaned against the low cliff of sand and sea oats. I slipped off my right shoe and lifted my foot to remove the sock. I was grateful I had Salt's old clothes; Talia never would've believed I was a vintage born if my toes stuck out of my socks.

My right foot went into the sand. "You are right. It's much nicer than dirt," I said, causing Kolbe to laugh.

Standing barefoot in the sand was a feeling like none other. Even the earth at the Parker-James property was so very different. Walking on the sand was soothing to my calloused feet. Feet, that if anyone paid close attention to, would clearly reveal I was not a vintage born; they were too rough, too scarred from all the times I walked in shoes with holes in the soles.

I stared out at the ocean. Heavy clouds hung above us. The storm was over, but the clouds remained thick and gray.

"Can you imagine how terrifying it would've been out here last night," Kolbe said.

I closed my eyes. The warm air pushed strands of hair away from my humid skin. "I don't know if terrifying is a strong enough word," I said.

"If I'd seen this before, I definitely would've watched the storm. I bet it was amazing!" Talia said as she went leaping toward the water.

Kolbe and I followed her, going more slowly, more cautiously. With each step, I felt the sand on my feet. If I walked on this beach long enough, I was sure my hard, calloused feet would be changed, they would become soft. If I walked on this beach long enough, I would be changed. I felt so much of the pain I carried slip away. I didn't think it would stay gone, but even to have it leave for a few minutes—it was a gift.

"You look happy," Kolbe said.

"I feel happy," I said, surprised by how I was feeling and that I shared it with him.

He took a step closer; his eyes were so kind. "I've been told people used to take vacations to the beach. They would drive and fly for hours, sometimes days, just to watch the waves." He was watching his sister approach the water.

Ms. Parker and Mr. James each took a one-week vacation every year. She typically went to the capital. I wasn't sure where he went; he never discussed it in my presence. I was always grateful for that.

"Why *aren't* people allowed to come here?" I asked, stumbling a bit over the words.

"Nice contraction," Kolbe said with a grin, and then became more serious. "The official response is that people cause too much damage and the health of the ocean is too important to life on the planet for us to disturb it."

I was familiar with this answer. It was the one Hastings told me after he learned about it from one of his assigned viewing videos.

"That was the answer I was taught. I never questioned it until now," I said.

Kolbe laughed. "I was taught to question every official answer, so I never believed it. My father told me the reclamation zones were created to take from the financially wealthy, to knock them down, take away a place they loved. He said it helped also to make those who were financially poor falsely believe officials cared about them. Now that I'm here, I think there's something more to the zones, or at least the beach ones. Something about how majestic it is," he said like he was trying to solve a mystery.

"It is beautiful," I said, though what that had to do with the creation of the reclamation zones, I didn't know.

Kolbe was silent for a long time. The sound of Talia giggling, muted by the waves, carried on the breeze.

"It is," he said in the same mystery-solving tone. "I think that's the answer."

"What?"

"Beauty … beauty will solve this. Beauty will help people see through the lies."

He stared out at the sun streaking through the gray clouds. Streams of light hit the sand and water. Talia was dancing in one of the rays.

"I wish I understood what you mean," I said.

"It's not your fault, I'm the one not making sense. I told you I was raised to question everything. When you're raised that way, by parents like mine, you look around the world that you and Grandfather came from, and all you see is lies."

"What sort of lies?" I asked, still so unsure of what he was saying.

"Everything. The reclamation zones, the once incredible and now crumbling houses, the lifeless government housing everyone lives in, everything exactly the same, even the people. And then there's the gestates …"

I lowered my head.

He bent his head so he could see my downcast eyes. "I didn't mean it was their fault. I meant the fact that they're considered any less than anyone else—that's the lie."

"You think I'm equal to you?" I whispered above the waves.

He stepped closer. "I think you're far better than me."

I gazed at him in confusion. How could he think that? How could any true vintage born believe I was anywhere close to equal to them? The thought was disturbing. A thin film of water touched the tips of my toes, startling me from my thoughts.

A second later Kolbe's eyes became wide. Mine must have done the same as we turned our heads to the west—the sound of giant helicopters droned in the distance. We couldn't see them yet, but that didn't matter. They were coming. They would be here soon. There was no excuse for being in the reclamation zone. Kolbe and Talia would be punished. I would be killed.

I froze, unable to think or feel.

"Move, you have to move," Kolbe said, shoving me toward the gray waves.

"What is it?" I faintly heard Talia ask, startled as her brother came charging toward her.

"Helicopters! Get in the water!"

He pulled her, she followed, tripping after him.

The cool water was a shock to my skin, a shock that woke my mind and body.

"Dive," Kolbe shouted, pulling me down with one hand and shoving his sister down with the other as the tip of a blade appeared above the house.

Eighteen

I couldn't swim, but that didn't matter; the water was shallow enough for me to stand if I needed to. I held my breath and allowed the waves to roll above me. Kolbe's hand held my hand down against the sand. The water was dark, too dark to see Kolbe, Talia, or any other creature that might be nearby. I felt a fish nibble my toe, not in a painful way, but it made me flinch all the same.

The waves came and went above me. I could hold my breath no longer, but I did not lift my head, not yet. Seconds passed and my mind began to blur, so I pushed my face to the surface. My darkened skin and black hair should blend with the dark water. I spit out salty water, quickly inhaled, and dropped back below the surface. The sound of the helicopter blades could be heard above the pounding waves; they must be right above us. I allowed my body to sink lower, toward the sand, as if I was drowning. For an instant, panic surged, but I pushed the feeling away.

I could stand … if I needed to, I could stand. I would not be killed by the ocean; perhaps by those who hovered above it, but not by the sea itself.

More time passed and my lungs began to burn again. How long would we have to stay like this? As long as it took.

Discovery of any of us would be the end. Not even a vintage born could explain being in the ocean.

As my face neared the surface for another breath, I forced my eyes open. The sunlight blurred with the stinging saltwater. I didn't see a helicopter, nor did I hear one. Slowly, I raised my head. My lips reached the surface. I breathed greedily. Far to the north there were three large military helicopters. I stayed low in the water, allowing the waves to wash over my head. Finally, I could see them no more.

"We've got to go," Kolbe said from somewhere beside me.

"Did they see us?" I asked.

"I don't think so," he answered, making his way back toward the shore. "But even if they didn't see us, they would've seen our prints and shoes."

"If they were looking," Talia said.

"Of course they were looking," Kolbe said. "Why else would they have been here, if they weren't searching for violators?"

"Maybe they wanted to see the beach," Talia said as she wrung out her long brown hair.

Kolbe thought for a moment. "Maybe," he said, sounding mildly hopeful, "but we still need to get out of here."

Each of us raced through the sand, the fine grains sticking to our wet bodies and clothes. We picked up our shoes at the edge of the bluff and clambered up to the area of sea oats.

"Oww," Talia cried, "I need to put my shoes on."

"We don't have time for that," Kolbe said, hoisting his sister onto his shoulders.

"Lead the way," he said, following me through the tall grass. My feet were calloused, so the blades of grass didn't cut them. I doubted the same was true for Kolbe, but he didn't complain. Once we were near the house, he sat his sister down and ran inside. Talia and I followed.

"You're okay," Mr. Northup said from somewhere in the dim room.

"Grandfather," Talia called, "where are you?"

Our eyes were struggling to adjust from the bright sunlight to the dark room.

"I was afraid they got you," he said, beginning to weep.

He was so weak, the fear brought on by the helicopters and then the rapid climb up the stairs, it was too much for him.

I went to him, not wanting to touch him in my soaking clothes. "We are okay, sir, they didn't see us."

He continued to sob softly. "I thought I lost you, all of you," he said, his face contorted with fear.

"We hid in the water, but now we have to go," Kolbe said. "They could've seen our shoes, or us below the waves. We have to get our things and get out of here."

Mr. Northup sniffed.

Talia said, "You two get our packs. I'll go with Grandfather to the truck." She helped her grandfather stand. He latched onto her.

"I was so afraid," he said as he clung to her.

"I was too, a little bit, but we're okay. Now come on and walk with me to the truck."

Kolbe and I sprinted away and down the stairs, chunks of sand falling from my clothes and skin. The saltwater was so sticky.

I went into the hope room and collected my bag, stuffing my shoes and socks inside. Kolbe wasn't moving; he was standing idly over a clear plastic storage container.

"We've got to go," I said, my voice sounding desperate.

"Do you know what these are?" he said in a hushed tone.

"Books," I said, panting.

"We can't leave them here to rot," he said.

"They've lasted this long," I said.

"The storm broke the window. Everything in here will be destroyed soon." He slipped his bag around his shoulders. He hesitated and then lifted the plastic container and started for the door.

"You're taking it?" I said, following him.

"We can't leave them here," he said, moving as quickly as possible up the stairs.

"They left them here for a reason," I said, sure these were books that people were not allowed to possess.

"And I'm taking them for the same reason," he said with determination.

Together we sprinted up the stairs and ran through the upstairs; every second I expected to hear the helicopters return and the peacekeepers descend upon the house.

The door was open to the garage, the door we had used to first enter this sanctuary. Above us the birds chirped to one another. Emotion caught in my throat when an image of Hastings entered my mind. There wasn't time to think about anything, about what this place had been, of all that used to exist here.

The garage was dark. Kolbe opened the back of the vehicle and shoved the container of books inside. He threw his pack on top and the blanket his sister had used to conceal herself from him. I wondered what the penalty was for having these books. My head swam as Kolbe slammed the back of the vehicle shut. Together we lifted the garage door.

We stared in front of us. Our world had dissolved.

Nineteen

I blinked and blinked again. Around us, nothing was left. The trees were uprooted, twisted around one another.

"We have to go," Kolbe said, pulling me from the garage opening, back toward the vehicle where Mr. Northup and Talia waited.

I did as he instructed, fastening my seatbelt in silence as the engine roared to life and Kolbe spun us out of the garage. The truck's chassis sat high, and the truck had strong, thick tires made for rough terrain, but even with such a vehicle we couldn't drive over the trunks of fallen trees.

"What happened?" Talia said, eyes wide.

"A hurricane," Kolbe answered.

Every tree of any size was down, each facing west, toward the end of the reclamation zone and the borns beyond. The trees lay on either side of the driveway, but because they all fell due west only some of the tops extended into the drive. There was enough space for Kolbe to maneuver around them. I exhaled with relief when we were out of the driveway and on the main road.

Being on the broken asphalt of the reclamation zone border would be easier to explain than being in the actual reclamation zone. Though I was still barefoot and covered in sand. I took the socks from my pack and used them to brush off as much of the sand as possible, and then put my socks and shoes on.

We were on the reclamation zone dividing road, which was already cracked from decades of neglect but it was wide enough that trees could not completely cover it. Kolbe drove along the western edge, the side that put us closest to the borns' houses. The trees that had surrounded these houses were down … many of the houses were destroyed.

"So many houses are fallen in," Talia said with a gasp, "and none of them have roofs."

"It was a strong storm," Kolbe said solemnly.

"The roof of the house we were in wasn't blown away," she said from her spot on the other side of her grandfather.

Mr. Northup said, "The government housing isn't built to the same building codes that were once mandatory for houses so close to the sea. Those codes were deemed an unnecessary expense a few decades ago."

My fingers pressed against the glass of the window as if I could somehow reach out to the wrecked houses, as if I could do something. "The broadcast said the houses were strong. They told everyone not to worry."

"They lied," Talia said, staring out the window.

House after crumbled house blurred by. Sometimes there were people outside … sometimes not.

I swallowed; my throat was tight. "How could they not tell them? How could they not tell everyone to evacuate?"

Mr. Northup placed his bony hand on my leg. "Hastings is okay. That boy is smart, smarter than the rest of his family. He would've hidden under something."

"Who is Hastings?" Talia asked.

Kolbe watched me from the rearview mirror.

"Her brother," Mr. Hastings responded.

"It isn't nice to say he's the smartest," Talia said. "Zelie is very smart too."

"Yes, she is," Mr. Northup said. "I only meant that if there was a way to survive, Hastings would've done it."

"The walls were poured concrete. Nothing in that house could have supported the weight of a wall if it collapsed on top of him." My words came out more like a sob.

"It *was* foolish to build weaker houses," Talia said, her voice like that of a gestate telling a young born that they shouldn't have reached for the hot stove or played with fire ants.

"It was not their fault," I said forcefully. "They were told the houses were strong."

"Maybe they didn't know the houses were weak, but they went along with a government that lies about everything else. Why wouldn't they lie about the houses? It's foolish to do everything to create an outcome and then complain when that outcome happens," she said, her voice forceful, like she was accustomed to being right.

"My … my parents did not know the government lied. They believed every word they were told. My m-mother worked for the storm division. Even she believed her children were safe. They didn't know. No one did." My anger was clear, I didn't try to hide it.

"They may not have known, but they should have," Talia said.

"That's not fair, Talia," Kolbe said, glancing into the rearview mirror.

"Life isn't fair," she shot back at him. "No matter how much they try and pretend it is, it isn't."

He looked away from the mirror.

"Hastings is a smart boy," Mr. Northup said, his voice beginning to fade. His grip on my leg had weakened.

Kolbe still watched from the mirror. "Perhaps the damage there wasn't as bad as here," he offered.

All around us as we drove, the houses had crumbled. Not all; some stood, though all had lost their roof.

I didn't speak; I couldn't disagree with any of them. Though I did. I disagreed with each of them, Talia most of all. It was not Hastings's fault if the house he had to live in fell on top of him. She wouldn't say it was. He was only a child. He had not voted in the elections. But she blamed his parents. I did not. I didn't blame any of them; they were told their house was safe. They were told to stay there, there was no need to evacuate. Why then would they not believe that? Why would any of them have left?

My fingertips went again to the smooth glass. On the rubble of what had been a house stood a girl, more accurately a young female gestate. She was dressed in old clothing; she was probably no older than eight or nine. She crouched, lifting broken concrete. Beside the house, a giant oak stood, its leaves stripped bare, branches broken, but it stood. Around the trunk of the oak, on one side was a sheet of metal—her pod. The wind must have wrapped it around the tree trunk. Had she hidden against the trunk? Had she escaped her pod and taken refuge against the trunk of the tree? How had she not been blown away? Perhaps she tied herself to it or perhaps there was a hole in the trunk that her small form could fit in.

"Why is she alone?" I said out loud to no one in particular.

"Who?" Talia asked, turning to look out the window beside me.

"Why are there no peacekeepers helping her search through the rubble?" I said, pushing my fingertips harder against the window as Kolbe drove us past her.

She did not look up when we passed. She was trained not to look up.

"I don't think they expected this," Kolbe said, his voice low. "I don't think any of them expected this."

Talia didn't respond, and neither did I. He was right. No one expected this.

Twenty

The vehicle bounced as Kolbe swerved around the largest obstacles and rolled over the others. This vehicle was built for this, with large, wide tires.

My legs reverberated to the truck's movements while I tried to quiet my mind. A world without Hastings was unimaginable, and yet that was my world now. Even if he still lived, I would never know that and I would never see him again. Even if I had stayed there, I wouldn't have seen him again after I was transferred. But I could've helped him survive the storm. I shook my head. I didn't know … I didn't know any of this. I leaned my head against the seat. The sun was sinking in the sky. We hadn't traveled far—much farther than we would've if we'd been walking—but not nearly as far as transports would've taken us in the same amount of time. Kolbe couldn't drive fast if he wanted to avoid punctured tires or a destroyed vehicle.

"Are they fighting?" Talia asked.

I turned, following her gaze. Near the remains of a house were three men, two moving closer to the third. The two were gestates, the third a born. My heart beat faster as one of the gestates used the limb of a tree and swung it at the born. The born held his hands up in self-defense, but it was useless. The limb caught him on the side of his shoulder and head. He was thrown against the concrete wall and slid to the ground. The other gestate went to him. I forced my eyes shut when the gestate lifted his foot above the born's head.

Mr. Northup squeezed my hand as I turned away. "A day of reckoning," he said with quiet intensity.

"A day of evil," Talia said forcefully.

"Much evil had been done to those men," Kolbe said, glancing at me in the rearview mirror.

My stomach churned, my head spun. He thought it was okay. He thought the violence done to them deserved death for its payment. He was wrong.

I said, "Murdering a born won't make their lives better."

"There will be many deaths today, and they will continue for as long as the gestation firms and peace keepers remain blinded by no cameras," Mr. Northup said.

"It's wrong for a gestate to kill and pointless to run," I said, swallowing hard. "They'll always be caught."

Kolbe stared back at me through the mirror.

"Those men were gestates?" Talia said, turning to stare out the window. "How do you know?"

I felt the hard callouses on the palms of my hands. "They are easy to recognize, if you know what you're looking for," I said. I wondered what her life must've been like for her not to have known from the first moment she saw me, what I was. I was so far below a person—like a robot in a human's body, without the ability to think freely or attach at any meaningful level.

I thought then of Hastings, of his likely death. The air felt thin; my lungs couldn't get enough of it. I was grateful in this moment to be less than a person; I couldn't handle more feelings of attachment to the boy who was no longer mine.

"What's that?" Talia said, pointing at the horizon, where an orange glow illuminated the sky. Dark billowing plumes of smoke rose from the orange glow and tried to cover the sun.

"A fire," Kolbe said.

Talia climbed past her grandfather, in the middle of the seat, and moved into the front seat.

"What're you doing?" Kolbe asked.

"I wanted to check something," Talia said as she removed an inconspicuous screen from the dash of the vehicle.

She clicked it a few times. "That's a large city," she said.

He nodded like he already knew that.

"More reckonings," Mr. Northup said solemnly.

I held my stomach, which continued to churn.

"Use that to help figure out how to get us home," Kolbe said to his sister, who continued to hold the screen. "Keep us as far away from populated areas as possible."

Talia did as she was instructed, telling her brother where to turn and keeping us away from areas where large numbers of people would be. Often, when we drove past an area, there were people outside of what remained of the houses. The borns were easy to notice, with their bright hair and sometimes luminescent skin—an odd alteration even in the born world.

Talia shrieked, "Stop!" She whispered, "Back up."

Kolbe turned his body to steer the vehicle backward, along a narrow street. His face was not far from mine, but he looked past me, out the back window. In front of him the headlights shone on the body of a man lying in the street. The asphalt glimmered near his head.

"That's blood," Talia said, her voice quivering.

"He was a gestate," Kolbe said.

"That doesn't make it any better," Talia said, sounding as if she was going to cry.

"I didn't mean that it did," Kolbe replied, his voice heavy.

"This is not how we intended it," Mr. Northup said solemnly.

"How who intended what?" Talia asked with concern in her voice.

"Everything was done to end chaos," he said, his voice weak. "Now there's even more."

"You can't alter human nature," Kolbe said, his eyes reflecting in the rearview mirror. "People are broken, and with brokenness comes chaos."

Mr. Northup was silent. He turned to stare out the window closest to him.

Dusk was falling. It was as if the sun didn't know that on a day like today, a day of reckoning, it should stop. Time should stop. The world should end. But it didn't. The planets continued on their courses and the darkness of night slowly surrounded us.

Twenty-One

We were near the center of the state, far from the beach reclamation zones and even those of the Intracoastal Waterway. We were farther west than I'd ever been—farther from my gestation firm than I'd ever been. The distance brought a feeling of safety, as did the darkness.

Talia had done a good job navigating; she'd kept us away from houses, as much as possible, and we never saw anything that came close to a town.

A few hours after the sun had disappeared below the bleak horizon, we reached an area that Kolbe was familiar with, so Talia switched off the screen. Now the inside of the vehicle was dark and silent. Mr. Northup had been asleep for hours, and if Talia didn't occasionally point out something to her brother, I would've thought she was asleep too.

They didn't tell me and I didn't ask, but from what I could tell from their sporadic conversation, we were close to their settlement. The area was rural … with more trees than I was used to, even as far out of town as the Parker-James family unit was. No debris covered these roads. Kolbe was driving fast, with only trees and the occasional open field illuminated by the headlights. We saw no more storm damage, which meant if there were cameras, they were working. I made sure to keep my face away from the windows.

"Do you see the light?" Talia asked, her worried voice breaking the silence.

Far in front of us, a glowing light rose above the horizon. We couldn't see the source, but Talia must've known where it was coming from.

Kolbe instantly flipped off the vehicle's headlights, plunging us into darkness. "A warning?"

She nodded. "They must be watching."

Kolbe kept the vehicle steady. "The cameras must be on near here."

"They may have never gone out," Talia said. "The storm didn't do much this far inland."

"We'll go in through the side gate."

"If the cameras never turned off, how will you explain being gone?" she asked, holding her bottom lip between her fingers.

"Maybe they didn't notice. Besides, if they've noticed I'm missing, they'll know you are too," he said, turning the vehicle toward the south.

Trees were thick along this road. Kolbe knew the area well; he must have, because he drove us perfectly along the twisty road, with only the light of the moon to guide him.

"I'm not of age," Talia said. "They don't care about me."

"Once we're safe, I'll worry about where I was. Though I'm pretty sure I've been here the whole time," he said, with a wink to his sister.

Talia shook her head. "If they saw you leave, they saw you leave. I was hidden, but you were driving."

Kolbe was silent for a brief moment. "I wanted to watch the hurricane. It was a foolish thing to do, but I drove east until I could see the edge of the storm. Now hop out and open the gate."

The truck lurched to a stop in the middle of a muddy stream surrounded on either side by massive live oaks.

She groaned. "Ugh, I hate this part."

She opened her door and splashed down into the dirty water. I leaned forward to watch her swing a part of a metal fence back that had appeared to be stationary.

"This is one of our back doors," Kolbe explained. "You'd never know it was an entrance. The ground around here is perfect for it. We keep the area mulched so we don't leave tracks, and the fence is in the middle of water that's pretty deep everywhere but this spot."

Talia hopped back into the vehicle. "My shoes were perfectly dry until then," she complained.

"It can't be helped, not if they're watching the main entrance. It's one thing if I entered alone—though that wouldn't be good either—but to have you three in here. That would be impossible to explain."

"None of that makes my feet any dryer," she said.

Kolbe drove a short distance and then reached the hard asphalt of an old road. This time he jumped out and quickly sprayed the outside of the vehicle with a water hose.

"We spray it off here so it has time to dry before we park it in the garage," Talia said with a sly grin.

I asked, "Do you do this often?"

"No, but enough to know the drill. We learn pretty young," she said as Kolbe got back in the vehicle. "You should tell them you were hunting. You'll still get in trouble, but not as bad as interfering with a dissolution."

"I don't have any game to show them," he said.

"Just because you went doesn't mean you were successful," she said.

"Maybe, but I'm covered in salt and sand," he said.

"Change clothes in the garage. We can hide these," she said.

"Yeah, maybe."

Around us were many houses. "These houses are all different," I said with surprise.

"The people who built them are different and so are the people who live in them. Makes sense for them to be different," Kolbe said as he drove along the dark street to an industrial-sized building.

Talia touched a button on the dash and one of the smaller bay doors opened. Kolbe pulled inside. In a second, he and Talia were out of the vehicle. She came around to the back door and pulled out the mats, taking them outside and shaking off the sand that had covered them.

"Wake up, sir," I said, gently rubbing the side of Mr. Northup's arm.

"Where are we?" he asked.

"In the place where your grandchildren live," I answered. I couldn't explain any more than that.

In front of the vehicle, Kolbe was connecting a long cord to the bottom of the bumper, reaching up and plugging it in.

"Cooling the engine?" Talia asked as a wall unit connected to the cord showed a charge of one hundred percent.

Kolbe gave a nod to his sister and then ran to the side of the car, where I was helping Mr. Northup scoot from the high seat.

"It isn't electric?" I asked.

"It's a combination of electric, solar, and combustion. What I plugged in is an engine cooler that shows a full charge, no matter what. I'll come back after the peacekeepers leave, and connect the actual charger."

He stepped in front of me. "Here, Grandfather, grab onto me," Kolbe said gently, helping Mr. Northup get out of the vehicle. "Talia's going to take you and Azalea Rose to a friend's house while I figure out what's going on. But don't worry, you're safe now."

Mr. Northup placed his hand on the side of Kolbe's face.

The skin of his fingers was purple from the numerous broken blood vessels beneath his paper-thin skin.

He said, "I wish I could believe that."

Kolbe hugged his grandfather. "Go with Talia. We can talk later."

"Where should I take them?" she asked.

He appraised his grandfather. "Aunt Viv is the closest."

Talia nodded. Kolbe stripped off his shirt, tossing it in a barrel. His back muscles tensed when he opened the pack he carried. He pulled out clean clothes and placed them on the hood of the truck. He pulled a short-sleeved shirt over his head, the thin material covering the muscles of his chest and torso. He began to unfasten his pants, then stopped when he realized I was watching him.

"Come on," Talia said, pulling me away, "he's not that cute."

My face reddened. "Wait," I said, leaving Mr. Northup's side and going to Kolbe.

He stared at me in surprise, his fingers unmoving at the waist of his pants.

I whispered, "What about the books?"

His expression relaxed. "I'll hide them in here for now. It isn't safe to get them out while the peacekeepers are on the property."

I quickly returned to Mr. Northup's side and took his hand.

"If you ask me," Mr. Northup said with a lightness to his voice that didn't fit the situation, "I think my grandson is quite cute."

Talia snorted with laughter, and if Mr. Northup had the energy he would've snorted right along with her.

Twenty-Two

Beyond the darkened garage a few lights could be seen in scattered houses.

"The sun will be up soon," I said to Mr. Northup as I helped him hobble along. The feel of the humid air was nice, yet different so far away from the ocean … slightly cooler and lighter.

"Where are the pictures you took from my home?" he said to me, his voice ragged.

"In my bag."

"If anything … happens to me … give them to … my daughter-in-law," he said in exhausted breaths.

"You're going to get better now that you aren't drinking poison," I said. I supported him as we followed Talia through the deserted streets.

"Perhaps," he said.

Talia ran in front of us, leading us to the back of a house with a faint light glowing in a window. She tapped lightly on the wooden door which encased a large glass window. The shades were closed. Immediately, a shadow appeared at the door. It opened. An older woman in a long sleeping gown stood before us. Her hair was pulled back from her round face. Her skin looked even darker than Mr. James's. Her eyes were fearful, until they saw Talia.

"Where have you been? Where's your brother? You've put us through … oh, how could you do this to us?" she said as she pulled Talia into her, enveloping her.

The scene was strange. I wasn't used to such displays of affection and yet Talia treated it as nothing unusual.

Talia stepped out of the embrace. "We rescued Grandfather," she said, sounding proud. "And we brought his friend Zelie with us. I think she may have needed rescuing too, but I'm not sure."

I kept my face turned toward the worn floor as Ms. Vivian shifted her confused expression from Mr. Northup to me, and back to Talia.

"Your grandfather?" Ms. Vivian asked with startled concern.

"Yes, you know Kolbe has wanted to go after him for years. That promise he made to Grandmother meant so much to him, even though he was only a boy when he made it. He loved her so much. I wish I could remember her. I wish I could remember Dad too," Talia said with a longing sigh. "But he does remember them and nothing could make him forget that promise. He told me the hurricane was the perfect chance. He didn't want me to go, but I snuck into the truck."

"He drove into a hurricane—you both did?" Her voice was growing in pitch and concern.

"Actually, we spent the night in an old house in the reclamation zone. It was beautiful. This morning we went out on the beach and ended up hiding from helicopters. But it was beautiful. I wish you could've seen it."

Ms. Vivian's eyes grew angry. "You put your mother, and all of us, through too much. None of us deserve for the children we love to risk their lives like that. To go toward a hurricane, to seek refuge in an old house that could've crumbled on top of them, to set foot on the sand—it was foolish and selfish."

Talia asked, her voice solemn, "Did you see the crumbled houses?"

Ms. Vivian's anger faded. She nodded slowly.

"It's horrible," Talia said.

"It's a natural consequence, but yes, it's horrible."

"That's what I said too, but we shouldn't talk about that. Zelie's family lived near Grandfather. She's worried for them."

Their eyes shifted to us. Mine stay trained on the floor.

"Can you hide us?" Talia said. "Grandfather's too weak to go much farther … they were dissolving him."

Ms. Vivian gasped. "Come this way," she said, flipping off the lights and locking the door behind us. It was not electronic; she turned a metal knob, the same sort that had been on Mr. Northup's house.

"Come with me," she said. "Now watch your step, don't trip on my kitchen chairs."

The house was dark, with the least bit of ambient light coming in from the windows. Outside, in the front, there was more light. I wondered if that was where Kolbe had gone. I wondered if he would be able to explain his absence. ... I wondered if I would be caught.

Ms. Vivian led us into a personal room, the outline of two single beds visible in the dim light. She opened two wooden slotted doors, folding them back on themselves. These were similar to the closet doors in Salt and Hastings's rooms, except their doors were metal.

Inside the closet, she pulled a chain which turned on a dim light. She pulled the clothes from one end, toward the center, and stood at the narrow end of the closet. She slipped her fingertips beneath something, releasing a door.

"You know the drill. Stay silent. And try not to get sand everywhere." Ms. Vivian tsked at Talia.

"We won't," Talia said.

"You're lucky you were a cute kid," Ms. Vivian said with narrowed eyes.

"Am I not cute now?" Talia fluttered her eyelashes.

"Get in there and take care of your grandfather and his friend. Feed them some of my preserves. They're too thin," Ms. Vivian said, shooing us into the narrow room.

"Thank you," Mr. Northup said as we passed Ms. Vivian.

Her expression became more serious. "Never thought I'd see you here."

"I never thought I'd be here," Mr. Northup said, his voice tired.

In spite of herself, she laughed. "I don't suppose you did. Neither of you." She studied my ragged hair and downcast eyes. "Lock the door and be quiet."

"I do have common sense, you know," Talia said.

"I'm not so sure," Ms. Vivian said, swinging the door shut behind her.

Talia flipped on a lantern and guided a heavy latch across the door. A second later we heard the muffled sound of clothes hangers being dragged across the wooden bar in the closet.

"Here, Grandfather, lie down," Talia said, unrolling a thin mat onto an elevated cot.

"Thank you," he said, sounding exhausted.

It had been a short walk for Talia and me, but for Mr. Northup it must've felt like miles.

I sat on the concrete floor, next to the cot. The room was no wider than the cot and my body, but it was long enough to hold two cots. The walls were made of concrete blocks; they would not crumble. At one end of the narrow room were canned foods and jugs of water.

Talia went to the shelves and selected a jar with something orange inside, along with a package.

"Aunt Viv's safe room is the best place to hide. She makes the best preserves of anyone in the settlement. The mango passion fruit is my favorite." Talia sat at the foot of the cot her grandfather was lying on.

"You're so calm," I said.

Talia twisted open the jar. "How else should I be?" She opened the pack of what appeared to be thin dried bread and used a knife from one of the shelves to spread the thick orange goop onto a piece.

"Here, Grandfather, try this. There's no way you can stay sick after you've had some of Aunt Viv's preserves."

I helped him sit up a little.

"Thank you," he said, taking the food from her. He took a small bite and then brought his hands to his lap while he chewed.

"Very good," he said, forcing his voice to sound better.

She spread another piece of dried bread with the fruit preserves and handed it to me. I felt too anxious to eat, but I accepted it anyway. If I was about to be taken back to the gestation firm, I may as well eat before they began starving me.

I took a bite. Talia was right—this was probably the best thing I'd ever eaten. Once my piece was gone and Talia had given us each a cup of water, I again thought of where we were and what was happening outside.

"I don't understand how you can be so calm," I said as Talia helped her grandfather take a sip of water.

"We do this often," she said.

"You hide people from the outside often?" I questioned, shocked by the thought.

She giggled. "No, we hide in safe rooms. As soon as we're old enough to walk we begin learning how to hide. And once we get a little older, we begin learning how to tell convincing stories about where we've been or where others have been. We're inspected fairly often. Sometimes we don't want the inspectors to know what's going on, so we learn how to keep that information from them. It's part of life here."

"You practice hiding and lying? What kind of life is that?" I said, realizing how different her upbringing had been from that of Salt and Hastings. Gestates learned to lie, but we lied to the borns. Here were vintage borns—brought down to the level of gestates.

Talia looked thoughtful and said, "It's an honest life."

***

After I helped Mr. Northup lie down, Talia clicked off the light. He'd eaten half of his bread with preserves, giving me the rest. I ate it quickly. Talia ate her piece slowly. Eating slowly was a luxury I'd never had. If I didn't eat fast, I'd be caught. That was lying. I did it often, as often as I could, but I never pretended I was being honest. I never pretended I was living the way I was supposed to. I was simply too weak not to eat. How Talia believed she was living an honest life … that didn't make sense.

I finally whispered, "How is hiding and lying being honest?"

Talia's head jerked up. She must've been falling asleep.

She yawned, and then said, "Because we know we aren't free and we don't pretend like we are, not like those outside of here. We might lie to the peacekeepers, but we don't lie to ourselves or each other. We live freely within our community and we do what we need to do to keep that freedom."

"Is this freedom?" I said into the darkness. "You have secret gates, secret rooms, secret signals. You aren't supposed to leave. It's like you live in a giant jail."

She yawned again. "I think that's what the government thought too, a way to keep the rebels contained and controlled. I guess they're right, sort of, but inside this four-hundred-acre jail, as you call it, we live free. No one watching, no one listening, no one telling us what to think."

"No one controls the thoughts of borns and vintage borns outside of here," I argued.

She giggled. "You're funny," she said, and yawned again.

"I'm serious," I said while doubting myself.

"There's no freedom where we're from," Mr. Northup said, his voice hoarse.

I was startled by his words; I thought he was asleep.

"How can you say that, sir? The borns and vintage borns had complete freedom," I said.

"Do you believe that because I was allowed to stay in my house and grow my roses, I was free? Or that your … parents were free because they left the house and went to a job? Do you forget that there were cameras everywhere and bands on all the gestates?"

"You didn't have cameras in your house," I said.

"Not having cameras in your house, is that how you rate freedom?" he asked, his voice becoming choked, as if he might cry. "You have no idea what has been lost, no idea of how beautiful the homes and the families were that once surrounded me. The laughing, the playing, the love … there was love. Good, true, beautiful love between husbands and wives, parents and children. No, Azalea Rose, what you witnessed was not freedom. It was … it was a valley of tears, though no tears were shed." Covering his face, he began to cry.

"It's okay, Grandfather," Talia said, rubbing his legs.

"I didn't understand," he said, weeping harder.

"Sir, please, you mustn't waste your strength on tears," I pleaded from my spot beside him.

"Tears are not a waste."

For the first time ever, he sounded angry with me.

"A life where nothing is treasured enough to shed tears when it is lost, that is the waste. The lives you witnessed in the house where you lived were a waste."

"Hastings's life was not a waste," I said in quiet defiance.

"It will be," Mr. Northup said, still angry. "If he grows to become his parents, to live the same meaningless life—void of love, as they live—it will be."

"Shhh," Talia said.

Somewhere in the distance a door slammed. Heavy boots echoed off the floor, the vibration making its way to the floor I sat upon. My heart raced, the terror causing my throat to become so dry I couldn't swallow. I heard the muffled voices, angry but bored at the same time. Next to theirs, the calm female voice of Ms. Vivian. The steps came closer. The blood pulsed so loud in my ears I couldn't have heard their words even if there wasn't concrete between us. Next to me, Mr. Northup remained perfectly still, his breath shallow; the anger had faded. His granddaughter sat at his feet. I couldn't hear or see her, but I could feel that she was not afraid. There was nothing unusual about this to her. Yet she and Mr. Northup believed this was freedom … this place of physical captivity.

After ten or fifteen minutes, the outside door slammed. We listened to silence for several minutes, and then padded steps came toward us … we heard a light tapping on the safe room door. Keeping the light off, Talia stood and unlatched the door.

Ms. Vivian was there, holding a flashlight at her feet. "You'd better get home," she said to Talia. "I expect they'll be at your house soon."

"Right. Be back soon," she whispered. A moment later she was gone.

"Is that really Josiah Northup?" Ms. Vivian whispered to me.

Mr. Northup was already falling asleep beside me.

"Yes," I said.

"I guess it's true what they say. No one is safe when they make a deal with the devil," she mumbled.

I blinked up at her, not understanding her meaning.

"Wait here until the peacekeepers finish their rounds. They should be gone in an hour or so," she said, closing the door.

After her footsteps were far enough away, I quietly rose and latched the door. I sat down. Mr. Northup's heavy breathing was all I could hear. I was grateful for the darkness, grateful to be alone with Mr. Northup. I felt secure in this hidden room, more secure than I ever had felt in my pod.

I lay my head down on my pack, but moved it away; it was still damp. I scooted down toward the center of the room and leaned my head against the cot, near Mr. Northup's feet.

There were so many things I didn't understand that I should try and understand, but in the quiet of this dark concrete box, all I thought of was the opossum I had left in my pod. I hoped it had escaped the destruction of the hurricane and wandered off deep into the woods or even into the inland swamps. Anywhere that would make it difficult for them to search for me. Maybe they wouldn't bother. With all the destruction caused by the hurricane, they might decide to leave one young gestate alone. Maybe I could be free.

Twenty-Three

"Azalea Rose."

I was startled awake, jerking up from the floor.

"Azalea Rose, open up. It's me, Kolbe," I heard again as I frantically twisted my neck in the pitch-black room.

"Can you unlatch the door?"

That was Mr. Northup's voice. His face was right behind mine.

The memories of the last two days returned. I understood where I was.

I lifted the latch and the door swung open, light pouring in around Kolbe.

"Sorry we left you two in here so long. We had to be sure they were gone. Though by the looks of it, you didn't seem to mind." He grinned as he offered me his hand.

I stood on my own. "I guess I was more tired than I realized."

Mr. Northup groaned as he pushed himself into a sitting position.

Kolbe said, "I can't imagine why you would be tired. It's not like a harrowing escape in the middle of the largest hurricane to hit our coast in a hundred years was any big deal. No reason to be tired after that."

"Talia was here in this room with us," Mr. Northup said, rubbing his thin, greasy hair. He needed to bathe.

I felt the stickiness of my skin and the tangle of my hair. We both needed to bathe.

"She was, but she needed to get home before the peacekeepers inspected our house. Thankfully, they always go in the same assigned order. Their lack of creativity is a great help," Kolbe said, his voice light, his skin clean.

Unlike us, he had bathed. He no longer smelled of the ocean; he smelled of oranges and rosemary. It was an inviting scent … everything about him was inviting. I shook away the thought.

Mr. Northup lifted his hand, a signal that he was ready to stand but needed help. Kolbe helped lift him.

"Are you okay, sir?" I asked, reaching my hands toward his unsteady form.

"Yes, yes, don't worry," he said, dismissing my concern.

Kolbe caught my eye. He had no idea how healthy his grandfather had been even two weeks ago, how far he'd fallen in such a short time. Perhaps that was good, perhaps that meant he could rebound just as quickly.

"Come on, let's get out of Aunt Viv's hair. Mom's cooking breakfast for us," he said as he helped his grandfather.

I put my damp pack onto my back.

Kolbe's free hand came toward me. I stood, frozen, as his hand touched the sleeve of my shirt, pulling the fabric up around my wrist. His fingers grazed my skin, sending a shiver through my body.

"You may want to keep your arm down," he said, his lips close to my ear.

I quickly lowered my arm. I was foolish not to have realized that with my arm around the string of my bag, the pale ring left from the missing band was clearly visible.

"Thank you," I said, keeping my eyes trained to the scuffed wood of the floor.

His hand moved closer to my face and then quickly pulled away. He stood straighter, his voice not as close. "The fewer who know, the better," he said, and then helped his grandfather leave the room.

I kept my eyes lowered. How foolish I was to forget, even for a second, who I was. Anyone in this place could turn me in and get a year's salary as my bounty. I needed to be more careful. I must not forget who I was just because I no longer wore the gestate band and a boy with pale blue eyes was nice to me.

"Thank you, Aunt Viv," Kolbe said as he helped his grandfather down the steps that led out of the house.

"Don't you dare put your mother through anything like that again," she said, drying her hands on a dishtowel.

"I'll try," Kolbe said in a teasing tone.

He and Mr. Northup stepped carefully down the concrete steps.

"You'd better do more than try," she said sternly.

I started out the door. Her hand went to my shoulder. I stopped, keeping my eyes low.

"Be careful," she said.

I could feel her rich brown eyes staring at my face.

"Have Carolyn cut your hair, first thing, and use a pumice stone to see if you can smooth down some of those calluses on your hands. You can sit in their backyard with your sleeve up. It's secluded. Once you get some sun on it, that line around your wrist will go away quickly."

"Ye-yes, ma'am," I said, my voice shaking. She'd been around me only a few minutes and yet she saw my secret so clearly.

She stepped closer. "The ones who were born here will be easy enough to fool. It's the old ones, like me, you need to be careful around. Mimic how Talia acts. Practice." Her hand went to my chin and lifted my face. "And look up, child. Remember, you're a person. You always have been. Don't let them tell you any different."

"You know what I am and believe I am equal to a person?" I asked, my mouth dry, my mind confused. Kolbe had said something similar, but I never thought anyone else shared his odd belief.

"You *are* a person. That is the first step, believing the truth of who you are. You've been told a lie that you're less than others. A lie that you deserve only to serve. You deserve anything and everything this life has to offer."

"I am a gestate. I am property," I stated.

Her arms went around me, holding me in a gentle embrace. "Fight back, Zelie. Don't let them control your mind. Be the person you were made to be."

My arms remained at my side as I felt tears form—tears I did not understand.

She squeezed me and then released her hold on me. "It'll be all right. Carolyn will get you fixed up. And if you need me, I'm here."

I raised my eyes to hers. I felt a tear run down my cheek.

She used her thumb to wipe away the tear. "There now, better already." She gave me an encouraging smile before yelling after Kolbe, "Don't you dare do that to your momma again!"

"Never again," Kolbe called back to her.

The lightness of his voice told me he was not taking his promise seriously.

I exhaled more easily in the humid outside air. The concrete room I'd spent the last many hours in had made me feel secure, but the air had been suffocating. Now I could take large, deep breaths without the feeling of walls shrinking toward me.

I walked closely beside Mr. Northup, who was being guided by Kolbe. My hands were positioned to help support him should he trip. The path we walked along was dirt, lined with wildflowers. There was no asphalt, not even old broken bits beneath the dirt. Around us I saw houses of different sizes, shapes, and colors. So many different houses.

It was not the outside of the houses that were the most remarkable, it was the inside. People were inside, which didn't make sense, given that based on the sun it was at least 9:00 a.m.

I hesitated. I should not ask questions and yet I wanted to know why there were faces watching us from the windows.

"Wh-why are there so many people in the houses?"

"Where else should people be?" Kolbe said.

The simplicity of his response made me feel stupid for asking such a question, or any question.

"She's not used to people not being at work or school," Mr. Northup responded.

"Oh," Kolbe answered. "It's Saturday."

I'd lost track of the days, but what difference did that make?

"She has no concept of weekends," Mr. Northup said.

Kolbe paused before saying, "Of course not. I'd forgotten how people live out there. Here, we don't typically work or go to school on Saturday or Sunday. Some people do, occasionally, and at harvest time we all work regardless of the day or time. Otherwise, most of us are off on the weekends.

And we don't have an official school. Parents of similarly aged kids co-teach."

"Parents teach?" I said, stunned by the thought.

"Not all parents," Kolbe said. "They tend to take turns."

A young girl waved at me from an open door. She wore a loose-fitting sleep dress, and her uncombed hair stuck out from her head, reminding me of how Hastings looked when he first woke up. But this was hours after she should have woken up, and still she wore a sleep dress and her hair was unbrushed. What was she doing on the porch? In her hand she held a doll. Was she playing? Did young children play outside when they should've been at school and their parents at work?

Kolbe waved at the girl when we passed.

"If people don't work on Saturday, what do they do?" I asked.

We were going by a house with a man sitting on the porch. He watched Mr. Northup and me with suspicion, but when Kolbe nodded a greeting to him, he returned the gesture and took a sip from the mug he held in his hands.

"They do whatever they want," Kolbe said.

"What does that mean?"

Kolbe laughed. "What do you mean, what does that mean? People do whatever they want. Sleep in, go for a walk, tend their garden, visit with friends, cook an elaborate meal— whatever they want. Why is that hard to understand?"

I stared at the dirt path in front of me.

"How easily you forget," Mr. Northup said in a reproving tone.

We neared a large planted area. Half a dozen people were tending numerous vegetable plants. Tall pecan trees dotted the western edge of the garden.

Kolbe stepped toward me while his grandfather took a seat on a wooden bench.

"I'm sorry," Kolbe said. "I forget how lucky I am. Here we're governed by ourselves and the others in our community, though that's rarely needed. There's no larger governing body telling us what to do, what to watch, what to eat. It's an entirely different way of life than the one you're used to."

"No one tells you what to eat?" I asked, tilting my head.

He started to laugh, but became more serious when he saw my expression. "No, we decide that ourselves. We decide everything ourselves."

The muscles in my jaw flinched. Him laughing at me was what I got for asking so many questions. Gestates were not to ask questions for a reason; we were not as smart as others, clearly. Kolbe understood that.

"I'm sorry," Kolbe said, stepping even closer. "You can ask me anything. I won't laugh anymore, I promise."

He didn't understand it was wrong for gestates to ask questions, wrong for us to think. I would stop being so foolish. I would stop forgetting who I was.

"Is this the community garden?" Mr. Northup asked.

Silently I thanked him for taking Kolbe's attention away from me.

Kolbe stepped back, no longer focusing on me, but on the garden in front of us. "Yes, it's the largest one, but we have others. Every lane has their own. This is enough veggies to feed us. But not enough for us to make preserves—which you could tell from Aunt Viv's safe room, is important to us. We also plant larger fields, with different grains and corn, but we keep the more tender vegetables close to our homes so we can watch for pests."

"Do you have refrigeration?" Mr. Northup asked.

Kolbe nodded. "And freezers, but no drones delivering food from a warehouse. If we don't grow it or forage for it, we don't eat it."

"So you work in the garden?" I asked, before I realized I was speaking. Why could I not behave?

"Sometimes," Kolbe said. "My main job is carpentry, but we all work where needed and the garden often needs us. The fields definitely do from time to time."

I touched the wooden post in front of me. "Vintage borns working outside," I said to myself. I'd never heard of such a thing. There were some that oversaw large government farming operations, but none actually worked in a field or a garden.

"There are no slaves here. We each do our fair share," Kolbe said, his voice even, though I could tell he was working hard to make it sound that way.

Near my feet I saw the scat of a deer, a week or so old. I bit my lip, but it didn't stop me from speaking. "How do you keep the deer and rabbits from eating the plants?"

Keeping them out of the Parker-James garden had always been a challenge, one that sometimes led me to be behind on my housework because I was spending so much time outside guarding the garden.

Kolbe grinned. "To be honest, we're grateful when they come in. When we find a rabbit, we catch it and typically add it to our colony. The deer, we shoot, unless it's a fawn, and then we let one of our dogs run it out. They don't tend to come back. We sometimes have an issue with birds and squirrels, but there are usually a number of cats hanging around the garden. They control what we don't."

"You shoot deer?" I asked, my voice showing the repulsion I felt.

"That's the quickest way to kill them," Kolbe answered.

I stared at him in disbelief.

"She doesn't understand that you eat animals," Mr. Northup said.

My stomach heaved. "You eat animals?"

"It used to be the way," Mr. Northup said. "It wasn't always believed to be as bad as you've been taught."

My stomach and head were spinning. I held onto the rough wood of the fence to keep from falling.

"We believe in balance, and if we don't kill some of the animals there's no balance. Besides, meat tastes better than you might imagine," Kolbe said.

I clung to the fence post, breathing deeply to try and keep from vomiting.

"Are you okay?" Kolbe asked with concern.

"I can't imagine being so cruel," I said. The words sounded harsh in my attempt not to be sick.

"I can't imagine owning slaves or killing old people," Kolbe said, his voice matching mine.

"Kolbe!" his grandfather admonished quietly.

I stared down at the blossoming passion fruit vine.

"I'm sorry," Kolbe said. "We were raised very differently."

I inhaled, my stomach no longer spinning. "I wasn't *raised*, I was *trained*," I said numbly.

The breeze lifted the ragged ends of my hair. I pulled it back, embarrassed by how disgusting I must look.

"I'm sorry," Kolbe said from beside me. "I didn't mean to hurt you. We don't eat animals to be cruel. We do it because we believe it leads to balance, both for the land and our bodies. Perhaps we're wrong."

I squeezed the fence post to keep from crying. I was unworthy of such kindness. Why should he care what I believed? My thoughts didn't matter. I didn't matter.

"Will you forgive me?" he said, his body close to mine.

I nodded because I couldn't speak.

"There, now," Mr. Northup said. "We must all learn to accept apologies and to give them," he said, his voice ragged.

I mumbled, "I do not deserve to be apologized to."

I was so far beneath them I did not deserve for them to speak to me with any form of kindness. I knew this, Mr. Northup knew this, and Kolbe was from our world, so he knew it too.

They were silent for a moment, until Kolbe stepped so close his chest touched my arm. "When a man's actions upset a woman, it's right for him to apologize."

"I am not a woman, I am not even a person," I said so only the three of us could hear.

Kolbe's hand went to my face, gently turning and lifting my chin. "You're very much a person," he said.

I looked up. He was staring down at me, his thumb caressing my cheek. I leaned into his touch; it was like a reflex. A reflex I never knew existed.

Kolbe didn't move and neither did I. I was afraid to. Afraid he would realize how inappropriate I was being and have me punished.

Kolbe's head bent toward mine … my heart beat faster.

"It's too soon, Kolbe," Mr. Northup said, pulling on his grandson to get himself into a standing position.

The action caused Kolbe to move his hand from my face, though his eyes remained fixed on mine.

Kolbe blinked. "Too soon for what?"

"She has to learn to choose dinner before she can learn to choose you."

"I-I don't know what you mean," Kolbe said, though his face was turning red.

Mr. Northup scoffed. "You know exactly what I mean. You see a gorgeous woman, and she is. But she's also a beautiful little girl who has never chosen anything freely in her life." He took a breath; the short walk had already made him tired. He continued speaking, though he should be resting. "If she doesn't choose you freely, it means nothing."

Kolbe stepped back. His expression thoughtful, as if Mr. Northup's words affected him deeply. I went to Mr. Northup. I didn't understand what he meant or what I was supposed to be choosing or how anyone could ever consider me even remotely pretty. I was sure Kolbe didn't share that view of me. He couldn't. But none of that mattered, nothing about me mattered.

"Are you ready to go to your grandson's house, sir?"

Mr. Northup held my arm as I led him away from the lovely garden. "I'm ready to stop walking. I'm not so ready to see my daughter-in-law."

I wanted to ask him why, but I'd asked more than my share of questions for the day. Besides, something about the way he spoke told me he wouldn't have answered anyway.

Twenty-Four

The door in front of us swung open as Talia burst out of the bright blue house onto the porch. "Good morning, Grandfather," Talia squealed, running out to meet us.

She gave me a quick hug. It startled me, but before I could even understand what was happening, she moved on to her grandfather, forcing me away so she could help him.

"Good morning," he said, his steps becoming quicker with her by his side. "You smell good, child."

"I took a shower while we were waiting for you. Mom wouldn't let me leave the house. Otherwise, I would've gone with Kolbe to bring you back."

"That's right, you won't be leaving this house for a very long time," said a slender woman that could have been Talia's older twin. Though her hair and eyes were light, the same as Kolbe's.

Mr. Northup stopped and stared up at her as she came down the porch steps.

"Hello, Josiah," she said, her voice heavy with meaning. Streaks of silver reflected from her mostly sandy-blonde hair.

"Carolyn," he said, his voice faltering.

"It's been a long time." She hesitated and then stepped closer to him.

He nodded. Tears began to slip through the wrinkles of his sunken cheeks.

She wrapped her arms around him, and his crying increased so that his body rocked.

"He forgives you," she whispered as she held him in her strong arms. "And so do I."

Mr. Northup fell against her, holding her with all the strength he had left.

I felt tears stream down my face, though I didn't know why. … I was exhausted and when I was exhausted, tears came more easily. That must have been why. Why else would watching Mr. Northup cry cause me to do the same?

Talia embraced her mother and her grandfather. "It's okay, Grandfather, we forgive you."

Mr. Northup cried harder and his tears brought more of mine.

"Let's get them inside," Kolbe said. "No need for the whole settlement to watch our emotional reunion." He ushered everyone toward the porch.

"Grandfather needs to sit down," Talia said, helping to support Mr. Northup.

Kolbe helped his grandfather up the two steps and then came back to me. "Come on, you'll feel better once you've eaten and showered," he said, placing a gentle hand on my back to guide me toward the house.

He was right; I didn't feel well. My mind was spinning. Everything here was different; everything made emotions come so easily. I wasn't used to feeling so much … or anything. It felt unnatural and natural at the same time.

As Talia helped her grandfather cross the airy porch, Carolyn came toward Kolbe and me.

"You must be Zelie," she said.

Her tone of intense kindness startled me. I sniffed. I should not be crying. I could not look at her. None of these things were allowed. I jerked my head down and nodded.

Her fingers gently touched the skin beneath my chin. "You must learn to look up," she whispered, her thumb brushing my chin before she took her hand away.

Her eyes were so … tender. Never before had I seen eyes like that. They showed so much caring, so much understanding.

"It will get easier," she said. Her dark green eyes, the color of the rounded oak leaves, bore into mine as if she was trying to speak through them instead of using words.

"What will?" I asked, my voice cracking.

"Everything," she replied, pulling a thin strand of hair away from my damp face.

She turned her attention briefly to her son. She placed her hand on the side of his face. "Proud of you," she said before removing her hand and leaving us.

"Watch your step, Josiah. That rug can be a little tricky," Carolyn cautioned, placing her hand gingerly on Mr. Northup's back as he stepped through the vibrant blue doorway into the house.

The floor of the house reminded me of Mr. Northup's house: wood the color of honey, except this floor was more worn out than his. Around the edges of the room, it remained shiny, but the areas that were most walked on were dull, the finish worn away.

They were in the middle of the room. Kolbe and I stood on the oval-shaped rug made of many different colored cloths braided and wrapped together. It was simple and may have been made of rags, and yet it was one of the prettiest things I'd ever seen.

"I like the rug," Mr. Northup said as they continued moving him toward the dining table at the far end of the room.

"I made it with Aunt Viv," Talia said proudly.

"Your grandmother used to make them too," Mr. Northup said with an air of longing.

"I know. That's how Aunt Viv and I learned. Mom taught us, but we made that one on our own," Talia said, beaming.

"I'm glad you remembered," Mr. Northup said, making an effort to face Carolyn.

"I remember everything Ms. Amelia taught me," Carolyn said quietly.

Mr. Northup didn't respond, though his head moved a little like he was trying to nod. Next to us were several pieces of furniture, all made of wood, and beyond that a brick structure. I knew they were bricks because the gestation firm had an ancient walkway made of them at the far end of the grounds. Rumors were that once, long ago, something else had been there before the gestation firm. Those bricks led some foolish gestates to believe the rumors that the gestation firm had not always existed and so it might someday no longer exist.

Kolbe saw me staring at the brick structure, which had blackened walls.

"It's a fireplace," he said.

"What is that?"

"It's how we stay warm in the winter."

I went toward it, bending low to see inside. "It's open at the top," I said, not understanding how that could help create heat.

"Yes, to let the smoke out. We burn wood in it. The fire creates heat and warms the house."

"You burn wood inside of your house?"

"Mostly parts of the thick limbs that come from the trees we harvest for lumber. The fire's nice. When it's cold outside and the night is long, the fire is warm and brightens the whole house."

"I've never heard of such a thing."

"I suppose not. Outside of the settlements, you have electric heat, at least in the south."

"Not in the gestate pods," Carolyn called from deeper into the room. "There's no comfort in them."

For some reason, her words caused my face to burn with embarrassment. She was right, of course, but I felt shame at their truth.

"We don't have air cooling either," Talia said. "Aunt Viv does, but not us."

"She only has it in her bedroom," Carolyn said. "We're lucky our house has so many trees around it. Their shade helps keep us cool."

"It's not luck," Talia said. "Dad picked out the best for us. If only he had picked it out a little sooner. Maybe he would've lived."

"We stayed on purpose," Carolyn said as she helped support Mr. Northup, who was now softly weeping. "You know that, but now is not the time."

Mr. Northup was weeping in her arms.

"I'm sorry, Grandfather. I didn't mean to upset you. Sit down. I'll get you some hash browns. Mom kept them warm in the oven."

Carolyn helped Mr. Northup onto a wooden chair while Talia used bright blue quilted oven mitts to remove a ceramic plate from the oven and carry it to the table.

"Mom said these are your favorite," Talia said, taking her hand away and removing the oven mitt.

"Come on," Kolbe said to me, "I think he'd do better with you beside him."

I left the fireplace and followed Kolbe past a rocking chair and a wooden bench with a bright blue cushion on it. On the floor in front of the fireplace was a large cushion made of the same blue as the fabric on either side of the window.

"You shouldn't have cooked for me. What would Joshua say?" Mr. Northup said, staring down at the hash browns.

Carolyn sat beside him and leaned her face against her hand, her elbow on the table. "He would be grateful we're together. It's been a long time. … A lot has changed. Zelie is proof of that," she said, watching him. "Besides it's a gift to serve you."

He sniffed, his feeble right hand resting on the table, fork between his fingers.

She placed her hand on his and said tenderly, "We all make mistakes."

"Mine cost you everything," he said, his face contorting into deep lines of sorrow.

Talia came and stood beside her mother.

Carolyn put an arm around her daughter's hip, leaning her head against Talia's waist. "Not everything," Carolyn said.

Twenty-Five

After I'd eaten two platefuls in the same time it took the others to eat half of their first serving, Carolyn said, "Kolbe, show Zelie where the shower is. If she eats any more right now, I'm afraid she'll be sick."

I lowered my eyes. The only way I ever ate anything was by doing so as fast as possible. It hadn't occurred to me that would be another way I acted differently from the borns and vintage borns.

"Sure. Come on," Kolbe said.

I went toward the sink with my plate. "May I put this in your sanitizer?" I asked as politely as I knew how.

"We don't have one," Carolyn said. "We wash our dishes the old-fashioned way."

"Leave it there. It's Talia's day to do the dishes," Kolbe said as he took the plate from my hand.

"Thanks," Talia said sarcastically.

"If you show me how, I will do it," I suggested.

Carolyn said, "There will be plenty of time for dishes. Go get clean. You'll feel better with some fresh clothes. I left some for you in the bathroom."

Beside her, Mr. Northup nodded, encouraging me to go.

I took my bag from the floor and followed Kolbe.

He stopped in the hallway, opened a narrow door, and removed a pale green towel. He closed the door and continued down the hall, past an open door.

"That's my room," he said, pausing for a moment for me to see inside the room. A wooden desk and chair sat under an open window, next to a bed with a faded blue quilt spread across it.

"That quilt is very pretty," I said, wishing I could touch it. It looked soft and worn.

"It was my dad's. Blue was his favorite color. My grandmother made this for him when he was a boy. It's one of the few things we brought with us," he said.

"Was it hard coming here?" I asked.

"It was a hard time," he said, picking at a fleck of dirt on the frame of the door. "But we made it through."

He continued past two other personal rooms with doors partially open and then stopped at the bathroom. He set the towel next to a pile of folded clothes on the carved wooden cabinet that held a white porcelain sink.

"I made this," he said, rubbing his hand along the polished wood of the cabinet.

"You did?" I ran my fingers across the smooth surface.

"It was my mom's birthday present last year."

"It's incredible," I said as I admired the natural grains of the wood that he'd somehow made more vibrant.

"That's what she said."

His eyes sparkled back at mine through the mirror. I watched him for longer than I should have, forgetting myself in the beauty surrounding me.

"I can show you the woodshop … someday … if you're interested."

"I would like that very much," I said sincerely.

His tanned face darkened a little, with red beneath it. He was embarrassed, for some reason.

Kolbe turned toward the shower. "This is how you turn the water on. The more you turn it in this direction, the hotter the water gets."

"Hot water," I said out loud, before I could stop myself.

"Yes, and it gets really hot, so don't turn it all the way or you'll get burned."

I nodded slightly while staring at the red *H* on the knob. I'd never bathed with hot water.

He left the bathroom, closing the door behind him. I stood for a moment, staring at the closed door.

I bent and touched the cool white material that formed the bathtub. Hastings's bathroom had something similar, but it was bare metal. There was always one bathtub in each born house, to allow for the possibility of a child needing to take a bath. Above this tub was a curtain of tightly woven white fabric. I pulled the curtain across the tub. Slowly, I stripped away the clothes I wore, trying and failing to keep sand from falling to the floor. There was already sand beneath my feet, probably from Talia and Kolbe. I would clean this room after Mr. Northup had bathed.

With my clothes off, I turned on the water, my hand shaking as I moved the nozzle to the place where the blue and red met. It was wrong of me to waste resources to make water hot for someone like me.

I pulled the curtain aside and stepped into the shower. Small bumps formed on my skin where the cold water hit it. I allowed myself to stand in the water, washing away the salt and sand from my skin.

I saw a bar of soap. I reached for it, but stopped. I could not use the same soap as vintage borns; it was against the law. As I lowered my hand, the water began to feel different; it began to warm up. I hadn't put the knob onto the red, only not on the coldest setting. I hadn't meant for it to be warm, but now it was. I felt it wash over me, warm, gentle water. Never had I felt such a thing. The bumps on my body went away; I was no longer being pelted with cold water. I stood unmoving, unthinking.

Finally, my hand moved toward the bar of soap. Without permission, my fingers grasped the slippery bar and ran it across my body. The soap smelled of orange and rosemary. After I washed myself, I saw two containers with pumps. One read "shampoo" and another read "conditioner." I'd never used such things, only a bar of soap. I didn't allow myself to think. I quickly squirted shampoo into my hand and ran it through my knotted hair. I felt the strands snapping, but I didn't stop. I allowed the warm water to wash away the soap in my hair and on my body. Then I squirted the conditioner into my hand and ran it through my hair. It felt smooth and soft. Some of the knots came out as my fingers raked through them. I quickly rinsed it from my hair and turned off the water. I stood, breathing heavily, water dripping from my body. I had used warm water—warm water, shampoo, conditioner, and the same bar of soap vintage borns had used. My heart was racing and my hands shaking as I opened the curtain. For some reason I expected someone to be there. Someone who would immediately take me to the gestation firm to be beaten for the multitude of infractions I had committed. But only my foggy reflection stared back at me from the mirror. Foggy from the heated water that dripped from my body.

I reached, taking the towel from the vanity. The towel was softer than any towel I'd ever used. It dried my body so well and did not leave a dirty smell behind.

In my pod I washed my towel often, but was not allowed to hang any of my items outside to dry, as I did with the items used by Hastings and his family. Without the sun's rays for a thorough drying, the towel was still damp when I used it the next day. It always had an odor I didn't like but could never fully get rid of. I hung up the towel and examined the stack of clean clothes. A wooden hairbrush with soft black bristles sat on top of the clothes. Carolyn left it here for me to use, as she'd left these clothes for me. I touched the brush. I didn't deserve to use such a fine brush. As if my hand was rebelling, my trembling fingers grasped it and quickly, as I had with the shampoo, ran it through my thin, broken hair.

Before I stopped myself, I took the clothes she'd laid out, undergarments and all, and put them on. When they were on, I grasped the edge of the wooden vanity and sank to the floor. I lowered my head to my knees. My arms pulled my body into a tight ball. My heart was beating so fast it felt as if I was running a race … a race against myself … a race against time.

***

I carried my dirty clothes from the bathroom. I was grateful for something to hold so that my trembling hands were hidden.

"Why are you wearing a long-sleeved shirt again? It's so hot," Talia said as I neared her at the end of the hall.

"I gave it to her," her mother answered from the kitchen in an insinuating tone directed at her daughter. "So many of my other shirts are dirty."

"I'm getting ready to start laundry," Talia said. "I was waiting for Zelie's clothes." She was holding out her arms for my dirty clothes.

My head low, I held tight to them. Talia came closer and tried to take them.

"I'll do my own washing," I said softly, not daring to release my dirty things to be washed by a vintage born.

From where he sat beside Mr. Northup, Kolbe called out, "No way, it's Talia's week to wash clothes."

Carolyn came beside me. "Let me have the clothes," she said in a tone that meant to convey her words were intended to be both kind and stern. Like she didn't mean to upset me, but she couldn't be argued with.

I reluctantly released my grip on the sand-and-salt-soaked bundle.

"We each do our part here—Talia included," Carolyn said to me as she removed the clothes from my hands.

"Here you go, Talia. Zelie, we will add you to the chore rotation. You may do all of our laundry in four weeks, when it's your turn."

"Yes, ma'am, thank you," I said.

Talia took the clothes from her mother and went to the end of the hall, where a large machine sat. It did not resemble the clothes sanitizing machines I was used to.

"Now that that's settled …. Kolbe, take your grandfather to the bathroom. Help him get cleaned up," Carolyn said.

She removed an empty plate in front of Mr. Northup. He didn't respond; he stared blankly out the open window.

"Come on, Grandfather," Kolbe said, helping his grandfather stand.

Mr. Northup's body obeyed, but his mind appeared absent. As he stood, his legs started to quiver. I ran over and helped support him.

"Could you help me get him into the bathroom?" Kolbe said, as together we kept his grandfather from falling.

"Yes," I said, adjusting my grip on Mr. Northup.

"Azalea Rose?" Mr. Northup said.

His voice sounded scared.

"It's me, sir," I said.

"Where are we?" he asked, clutching me.

I exchanged a worried glance with Carolyn and Kolbe.

"We're here with your family, sir. Remember, your grandchildren came for you, and we're here now, in their home, with their mother."

"Their mother?" he asked.

"I'm here, Josiah," Carolyn said, stepping toward us.

He released me and lunged for her. "They'll come for you," he said, panicked. "If I'm here, they'll come for you."

"We're safe here," Carolyn said, holding Mr. Northup.

He shook his head. "They'll come. If I'm here, they'll come."

"Why do you think they'll come for you?" Carolyn said as she and her son helped support Mr. Northup.

He shook his head again. "I shouldn't have left. I didn't think," he said with panicked urgency.

Carolyn pressed, remaining calm. "Why would they come?"

"I wasn't supposed to leave."

Kolbe said, "They were trying to dissolve you."

Mr. Northup became still. "Dissolve me?" His gaze became blank, the memories fading.

We were silent for a moment as we watched his awareness fade.

Carolyn's eyes became clouded with the beginning of tears. "Oh, Josiah," she whispered, though he didn't respond.

"He'll be okay," Kolbe said to his mom. "He'll feel better once he's bathed and more of the poison is washed away."

She bit her bottom lip as tears brimmed in her eyes; she nodded to her son. She wanted to believe him, but didn't. Her doubt spilled over to me, but I refused to accept it. Mr. James said he would be fine once the poison was out. Sitting in a bath would help. The healthy food and water, the clean clothes and air ... he would be better in a few days.

I took Carolyn's place, helping Kolbe get Mr. Northup to the bathroom at the end of the hall.

"Do you want me to help you?" I asked as the three of us stood together at the door of the bathroom.

"I think he'd want privacy," Kolbe said, with the same heaviness his mom felt.

I nodded and released Mr. Northup to his grandson.

I shut the door behind me, moving aimlessly down the hallway. At the sight of the open door to Kolbe's personal room, I went in. It smelled of him—the smell of the orange-rosemary soap with the hint of fresh-cut timber.

My fingers went to the worn blue quilt. It was as soft as I had imagined.

"Are you all right?" Carolyn asked from the doorway. She held a pair of scissors.

I quickly released the quilt. "I-I don't know why I came in here," I said, suddenly aware that I was in the personal room of a vintage born, a vintage born I was not assigned to serve, and so I had no right to be in his room.

"You're not in trouble. Something in here must have felt comforting to you."

"The quilt," I said, my gaze focused on the scuffed pine floor. "I wanted to touch it. That was very wrong of me."

"I'm sure Kolbe doesn't mind a beautiful girl in his room," she said with a forced lightness to her tone. "And that quilt has a lot of meaning. You must be able to feel the love within it."

I didn't respond; there were too many emotions for me to begin to understand them.

"It's a lot, what you've been through these last few days. Your world has completely changed. It must be overwhelming. Not to mention the state of my father-in-law.

You must be concerned for the man you've served these last many years."

I stared at her. She knew a lot, but not everything. "I was not Mr. Northup's gestate."

"No?" she said, surprised.

I shook my head. "I served his neighbors."

"Then, why were you in his house when my children arrived?"

I swallowed. "I found out he was being dissolved. I thought I could get him away during the hurricane."

"You were not his gestate and yet you risked your life for his," she said.

"My life is meaningless. Mr. Northup has never had a gestate. He refuses them," I said.

She focused on the open window behind me. "Neither of those statements is true." She rubbed the silver scissors in her hands, and her eyes became red. "Come with me," she said as she exited the room.

"Where are we going?" I asked, obediently following.

"To the backyard. You need a haircut."

Twenty-Six

"Bring out a chair," Carolyn said, gesturing to one of the kitchen chairs.

I picked up the low-backed wooden chair and traced her steps out the door. Ms. Vivian was right. This area was private, with no other houses looking out on the area. Farther behind us was an open field dotted with live oaks. Closer to the house, a small fenced area sprouted well-tended herbs.

"Sit down, please," Carolyn said, gesturing toward the chair.

I did as she instructed. She wrapped part of an old sheet around my neck.

"I'll have to cut it pretty short to make it remotely even," she said, fingering my hair, her touch sending a shiver through me.

"I don't care," I said.

She stood in front of me, tapping the scissors against her open palm. "You must care. You are free now, and if you don't care about yourself, no one else will. This haircut will be about getting your hair even and healthy. In the future you will choose the length and style. Roll up your sleeves. Back here, no one will see the tan line, and the sooner it's gone, the sooner you can wear short sleeves."

I didn't move. She pulled up my sleeve and then moved behind me. She began running her fingers through my hair.

"I never knew I was good at cutting hair until we moved here. Turns out I'm not too bad at it, so, hopefully, you'll be happy. It has so much breakage. Didn't you wear it braided in a bun? That should've protected your hair better," she said. She began by cutting away the longer strands.

How did she know so much about my life?

I swallowed hard and said, "The clip I had to hold it in place was rusty."

"Sticks would've worked equally well. The gestation firm never would've known unless they did an inspection," she said.

"I-I never thought of that."

She moved to my side, pulling the hair out and snipping it away. "That's because you never knew you could think," Carolyn said. "But you can and you must. Here no one will tell you what to do or how to live. You must decide that on your own. You will make choices every moment of every day. Some will matter a great deal, others not as much, but each will be yours to make."

"Gestates were not created to think, we were created to serve," I said.

I felt her posture become more rigid.

"You were created for more than you will probably ever understand."

I didn't respond; I couldn't. She was wrong, but to disagree with her was not allowed. I knew who I was and why I existed; those were the only things in my life that I have ever truly known.

"Do you see those live oaks?" Carolyn asked as she continued to cut my hair.

In the distance, not far from where the grass became long, were two rows of sprawling live oaks that went to the horizon.

"Yes."

"This land has been owned by the same family for over three hundred years. There are a few oaks left from that time, but for the most part what you see is the second planting of those trees. The first planting marked the edge of the driveway that led to the original home on the property. Based on the ruins, it was quite spectacular. After that first set of trees began to die off a hundred years or so ago, the new generation of owners planted new live oaks to mark the same path, even though the house was no longer lived in and this community was already forming."

I asked, "Why did they create a path to something that was no longer used?"

"It was a path to history, a path to where they began. But they weren't afraid to move beyond that path. Origins matter, but they don't dictate where you go. It matters how you were created, but that doesn't define who you are. That family went beyond what those that came before them believed was possible. They expanded the path and created a sanctuary for freedom in a world that lost its past … and its future. If you were to fly up like the birds do and look down on us, you would see that around us, on every side, is a row of live oaks. The family kept the path to the old homestead and they expanded it to include all of us."

In the distance, children shrieked in delight. Behind me, scissors cut away the damaged hair.

"Is that why this community was allowed to exist in such a strange way? Because the family owned the land, like Mr. Northup was able to keep his home because his parents owned it?"

"No, though I have no doubt that's what he told you or what you heard," she said flatly. "Those taking land didn't care about ownership. That's what made the people here so smart. If it had been just one family here, they would've lost it. It would've been stripped from them like everyone else's land was stripped from them. Part of their brilliance was they saw what was happening and they preemptively invited like-minded families to move onto their property. By the time the world fell apart, dozens of families lived here and they were willing to fight. The country is dotted with places similar to this, some larger, some smaller. Ultimately, it was decided to allow the people to keep what they had. It wasn't worth the fight, not so long as those on the land stayed on the land. Those who took control weren't concerned about the land, they were concerned about the ideas spreading … allowing those who wanted to live in settlements such as this to do so keeps the ideas contained. In many ways, those in charge couldn't have asked for a better situation. They allowed those who had already isolated themselves the ability to remain isolated. Works perfectly," she concluded with the slightest contempt.

"You don't agree with people staying here?" I asked, not understanding her meaning.

"There's no choice now," she said, exhaling audibly, "but before all of this … if they would've tried to make a change … if they'd spoken out, maybe things would be different." She stood, unmoving, for several seconds. "Move your wrist to the sun, Zelie. It does no good having your sleeve rolled up when it's in the shade."

I did as she instructed. I studied her while she studied my hair … parting it one way and then the other, snipping off long ends. By the feel of the scissors against my scalp, the hair was no longer than my ears.

I asked, "Is that why you didn't want to move out here when your husband asked you to? You didn't want to isolate your ideas?"

She scoffed. "It was far too late by then and my ideas certainly didn't matter. How does that feel?"

I ran my fingers through my hair, stopping almost immediately. My hair hadn't been so short since I was a very young child. I had committed yet another crime—cutting my hair.

"It feels lighter."

She took the sheet carefully from around me, throwing the loose hairs into the wind. "You actually have pretty thick hair, but because of the breakage it looked ragged and thin. Once it gets longer, you can use cloth or strips of leather to tie it back. Or you can keep it short if you prefer. The cut is cute on you."

"Thank you," I said, nervously rubbing the callouses on the palm of my left hand. "Why was Mr. Northup allowed to keep his house if it wasn't because his parents bought it?"

She held the sheet crumpled against her stomach. "That's the mystery, a mystery I've been curious about since I was a child." She caught my eye and then turned away. "I'm going to go in and check on Josiah. Kolbe should be done bathing him by now." She started toward the door off the kitchen.

"Ms. Carolyn," I said, my throat going dry.

"Yes," she answered while wiping the scissors on the sheet.

My heart beating wildly, I asked, "How did you meet Mr. Northup's son?"

She lowered the scissors, her eyes serious. "It's best not to ask questions you already know the answer to," she instructed, her voice disciplined.

"You were his gestate," I said, with wide eyes.

A subtle smile formed. "I knew you could think for yourself."

***

The breeze picked up. My mind spun as I studied Carolyn, who was casually sitting on the sheet she'd been carrying. We were in the shade of a mulberry tree in her backyard.

She'd been a gestate and yet, now she was free and raising children—her children. She'd married. Not partnered, as the borns did to create family units, but married—the ancient form of union. I could tell the union still meant a great deal to her even though her partner, her husband, had died eleven years ago. If Mr. James died, I couldn't imagine Ms. Parker being upset for more than a few weeks at the most, and yet Carolyn was a gestate. She was altered, as we all were, to be compliant and not to be able to care for anyone with any true depth. How had a vintage born developed feelings for a gestate? We were disgusting to them, so far below humans that they found us repulsive. Yet Mr. Northup was a vintage born; there was no doubt about that and no doubt his son had also been one.

"You seem lost in thought," Carolyn said with some degree of amusement.

"You broke every law there is," I said, staring at her in awe.

She laughed. "So says the runaway gestate with short hair."

I lowered my head.

She continued. "It wasn't a criticism, it was more an instance of the pot calling the kettle black."

I didn't respond.

"You don't know what that means … it doesn't matter. We've both broken laws. We've freed ourselves from the slavery forced on us."

"But you … you've created a life. I didn't even know places like this existed."

She leaned back and said, "It was Joshua who wanted to move here. As soon as we got married, he begged me to come to this place. I don't even remember how he first found out about it." She drifted off for a moment.

"I refused. I couldn't take him away from his mom, and then Kolbe was born and then Talia, and I couldn't take away her grandkids. She loved them so much. Not like those we were trained to serve. She wanted to be with them every second and she practically was, since we lived with them."

"You lived with them?" I said, mouth open wide.

"We had nowhere else to go. I wasn't allowed to work, which means we were excluded from government housing. Josiah and Amelia were our only option, but it was the option I preferred anyway. I never had a family, and with them I did. A real family. At least with her. Josiah was often angry with me, but he was always kind to the children. That's all that mattered.

"I thought we were safe. It'd been so long. Joshua paid my existence fee before we got married. I couldn't work, but I could exist—the gestation firm no longer owned me. I thought we would be okay, but he never did. He asked me all the time if we could move here. I thought he was overreacting or that if one of us would be punished it would be me. I never thought it would be him and I never thought he would be killed." Carolyn stared into the empty space between us. "The kids and I came here that night," she shuddered. "I had to protect them. Joshua already had everything arranged. He was only waiting for me to agree."

There was silence for a long time as I absently watched ants carrying seeds across the ground between us.

"My kids don't know of my past. We thought it was easier for them … the less they knew. Actually, that was my husband's preference. I thought it would be best, in the long run, to tell them."

"Do others here know?"

"Vivian, whom you've met. She's my closest friend, so I told her. Plus, she guessed. So, in truth, I simply didn't lie to her. And of course, Josiah, and now you."

"I'm sorry I guessed. I shouldn't have," I said.

"I wanted you to."

"Why?"

She tapped her lips with a finger. "I wanted you to know what your life could be."

Twenty-Seven

A hawk landed on the garden fence post. Carolyn and I watched it as Talia emerged from the house carrying a basket of wet clothes.

"You cut her hair," she said to her mother.

"I did. What do you think? Did I do a good job?" Carolyn said, her voice light.

Talia came closer to examine me. "Will you cut mine that way?" she asked.

"You have your father's hair, lots of wavy curls. It wouldn't be as straight and smooth as Zelie's."

Talia sighed. "I wish I had her hair."

"You must never wish for that," her mom said. "You must wish to be the best version of you."

"I'm pretty sure straight hair would make me the best version of me," Talia teased back.

Her mom laughed. "Go hang up the clothes. You're beautiful and you know it."

Talia twirled in the loose sand of the path to the clothesline. She was beautiful and it was clear by her dancing to the clothesline that she did know it. How different she was from Salt. Talia's features were distinct: a sharply pointed nose, large eyes, and soft brown hair that flew everywhere. She didn't look like all the other girls her age, with their delicate rounded noses, perfectly proportioned eyes, and hair that was never out of place. Yet, she was beautiful and she believed she was beautiful. How strange this place was. How strange this family was.

"Grandfather is asking for you," Kolbe said as he too emerged from the house.

It was overwhelming how much these three interacted with one another, though perhaps that was because Mr. Northup and I were here and we were requiring more of their time.

"Which one of us?" Carolyn asked as she stood, brushing off the dirt from her shorts.

"For you," he said quietly.

Together they disappeared into the house while I remained in the chair. So much … there was so much to think through.

"You're hanging up everyone's washing?" I said, realizing what Talia was doing.

"We find it dries better that way," Talia said in a teasing tone.

I jumped to my feet. "Let me finish. You shouldn't be doing that," I said, taking Salt's old shirt from her.

"Why not?" she said as she lifted another shirt from the basket and shook it out.

"You're a—" I stopped.

"I'm a vintage born, is that what you were going to say?" she asked, hanging the shirt Kolbe wore during the hurricane.

I nodded.

"So are you, and so is almost everyone here. The Jacobs, who live closer to the main garden, do have a son who's a born. He's odd, for sure. His hair is teal and there's a purple hue to his skin, but even he does his part. We don't have gestates to do things for us," she said.

I averted my eyes as I picked up Salt's old shorts from the basket. "Do you want gestates?" I asked, feeling nervous about asking such a question.

"Why would I?" she asked.

"Life is easier with them," I answered, not sure why any vintage born would not have a gestate.

"So?" she said as she hung the shirt she'd been wearing the day before.

"Don't you want an easy life?"

"I want a fulfilling life, not an easy one," she said.

"Is it fulfilling to wash and hang clothes?" I asked.

"Yes," she said. "Anytime you serve someone you love and you do it with the right spirit, there's honor in the work. And if you allow it to be, it's quite fulfilling." She started to twirl her way back to the house with the empty basket.

"You seem so sure of yourself and so ... wise," I said, wondering if I was right. Her words struck me as wise, but could I judge wisdom?

She bowed. "I totally agree," she said with a broad grin.

Kolbe came out of the house. "Mom wants me to go get Dr. Maggie. She thought you might like to walk with me," he said to me.

I went obediently to him.

He was taken off guard at the immediacy of my reaction. "You don't have to come. She just thought you might want to," he said.

I thought for a moment. "Would you like for me to join you?"

"Yes," he said without reservation. "If you would like to."

I twisted my foot in the dirt. "I would like to go," I said.

"I'm glad," he said, taking a step toward me.

"You two are weird. You make so much out of the littlest stuff," Talia said.

"Go inside," Kolbe said, irritated with his sister. "And take that chair."

"You should say please," Talia said, lifting the chair I'd been sitting in up over her head.

"Please," he said, stepping around the side of the house.

I trailed him as we reached the front and cut through the wildflowers to get to the walking path.

"Your hair is pretty," he said, once we were on the main path.

"It's the first haircut I've ever had," I said, pushing a chunk of straight black hair back behind my right ear. Carolyn was right; it felt much thicker now that it was short.

"Do you prefer it long?" he asked.

"No, it's illegal for female gestates to cut their hair," I answered.

Kolbe didn't respond. He put his hands in his pockets, his shoulders falling forward. Every few houses, he waved to people. But no one came toward us. I could tell that was unusual and it was because of me.

He slowed his pace to match mine. I hadn't realized I was walking behind him. It's what I was trained to do, but I hadn't meant to do it.

"This all must be so strange for you," he said as the birds called to one another in the distance.

"It-it is," I said, surprised he would say such a thing. No one ever cared what I thought or felt before, and it was such a focus for these people.

"I remember when I came here, it was a shock. It was a difficult time, anyway. I lost my father and then we left my grandparents. Leaving Grandfather wasn't such a big deal. He'd been kind enough to me and Talia, but he wasn't great to either of my parents or even my grandmother. But leaving her … that was like cutting off an arm or something. And then to be in such a strange place, it took some time."

"I'm sorry about your father and grandmother," I said.

"Thanks," he said as he kicked a clump of dirt. "I'm sorry you left Hastings. I could tell by the way you spoke of him you care deeply for him." His voice was tenuous, like it hurt him to say that.

"I'm not capable of caring deeply for anyone. Not like you and Hastings are," I said with a catch of emotion. "But I care for him more than I care for any others."

Kolbe stepped back; it was a subtle movement but I saw it. "He must be very special," he said, continuing his slow pace forward.

"Yes," I said.

"Why did you leave him?" he asked, his voice kind but faint.

"My year turns sixteen in a few weeks. I would be taken from him then anyway, and placed with someone who could pay more for me."

Kolbe shuddered. "You'll be tortured, won't you, if they ever find you? Which they never will," he said with quiet determination.

A ball rolled in front of my feet. Kolbe kicked it back to the children.

I wasn't sure what to tell him. It was clear the truth would upset him, and yet I didn't want to lie to him. I took a deep breath and said, "I would be tortured for running away. But I also revealed what my born masters said in front of me to a vintage born. Then I helped that same vintage born escape dissolution. For those crimes, I would be killed … after I was tortured.”

His pace slowed even more. “I didn't realize that.”

“I'm grateful Mr. Northup is safe. That was my only goal, to give him more time to live.”

Kolbe stopped. So did I.

He locked his eyes on mine and said, “I'm grateful you have *both* been given the chance to live.”

He began walking again, but I waited. The intensity of his gaze, the meaning of his words, his belief that my life mattered. That I mattered. It was all too much for me to understand.

Up ahead of me, Kolbe stopped at a white house with black trim. He waved me to him. I obediently went. Together we stood on the porch. He knocked loudly on the wooden door behind the screen and then allowed the screen door to fall back into place with a squeaky thud.

From inside, the sounds of chaos echoed. Children screamed, a dog barked.

“Hush,” a woman's voice called.

“Be quiet,” a man's voice said when the uproar didn't stop.

A second later, the door opened. A man stood before us. His brown hair and beard were cut short and his dark eyes looked tired. Kolbe opened the door as a woman with brown and gray-streaked hair joined the man in the doorway.

She didn't appear as tired as the man. In her arms was a tiny baby, only a few months old. I hadn't seen such a young infant since Hastings was a baby. Some urge within me wanted to reach for it, to hold it in my arms, but I kept my hands at my side. I forced my head up. I did not look the people in the eyes, but I did not stare at their feet either.

From behind the man and the woman, a dog burst out of the door.

"Hi there, Ashley," Kolbe said, petting the dog.

She came next to me. I wasn't trained to interact with large dogs. I moved to get out of her way and bumped Kolbe, who put his arms around me to keep me from falling.

"Are you afraid of dogs?" He was clearly entertained by my behavior.

"I … I've never been around one so large," I said, standing upright and using him as a shield to block the dog.

Kolbe laughed. "She's one of the smaller dogs in our community."

"Ashley, sit," the man said, but the dog ignored him, continuing to jump up on me while I tried to hide behind Kolbe.

He continued to laugh. Finally, Kolbe bent down and stopped the jumping dog. My hands were on Kolbe's back as the man bent and grasped the dog's collar.

"I'm sorry," the woman said, "she never gets to meet new people."

The door was thrust open and young children, all with light brown skin and clear blue eyes, spilled out of the house onto the porch. They weren't interested in us. One was yelling at the dog to behave and two others were chasing one another. Another young child toddled up to the woman and clung to her leg.

"Kids, stop!" the man bellowed, grabbing the two chasing each other. "You can play tag, but not around Kolbe and his friend. Take Ashley around back and chase each other there."

"Okay," the oldest boy said, and then hit the younger boy and ran off with the dog, the other boy running after him.

"Samantha, go with your brothers, please. Make sure they don't chase Ashley too far into the Diaz's yard. We don't want her disturbing their sunflowers," the woman said.

"When I get back, will you tell me who that girl is?" the young girl asked, eyeing me with interest.

"Her name is Zelie," Kolbe said. "She's a friend of mine and Talia's."

"Where did she come from?" the girl asked.

"Out in the world," Kolbe said in a spooky tone.

The girl gasped.

"Go, Samantha," the man said, and she went slowly around the porch after her brothers.

"You woke up my kids at three in the morning to bring back a beautiful girl," the man said in a chiding tone to Kolbe.

"Benjamin," the woman said playfully.

"You were thinking the same thing," he said, putting his arm around the woman's shoulder.

She wrapped her free arm around his waist, the other holding the baby who was staring at me as intensely as Kolbe had only moments ago.

"Perhaps, but it isn't polite to comment on a person's beauty," the woman said, shifting the baby onto her shoulder.

"That's a weird rule. I always thought it was you weren't supposed to comment on a person's *lack* of beauty," Benjamin said, making a pretend thoughtful face.

Kolbe chuckled. "I brought back my grandfather last night. Zelie is a friend of his who was trying to help him. Actually, that's why I'm here," he said, his tone becoming serious. "Mom asked if you could come to the house."

"Is he sick?" Benjamin asked, no longer leaning against the door frame.

"They were dissolving him," Kolbe said.

The woman gasped in much the same way the little girl had done a few minutes before. Then she handed the baby to the man. "I just fed her, so she'll be fine for a bit. Send one of the kids for me if she starts to get hungry," the woman said as she pried the toddler from her leg and wrapped her around Benjamin's leg. "Ruth, stay here with Daddy. Be a good girl and take a nap."

The woman disappeared into the house and a second later returned carrying a bag slung over her shoulder.

"Good luck," Benjamin said.

She placed a hand behind his neck and lifted her face to his, their lips pressing against one another.

"I'll miss you," she said, and kissed him again.

"I'll miss you too," he said, "and not just because you left me with the kids."

She laughed. "I'll be back soon."

"You'd better, or I'm sending them to you," the man said with exasperated amusement as the toddler and the baby began to wail.

Twenty-Eight

Kolbe and I had to practically run to keep up with the woman. After a few minutes, Kolbe slowed his pace and I did the same.

"Dr. Maggie knows where she's going," he said, waving her off as he slowed down to a more normal walking pace.

"What was that place?" I asked, slowing my steps to match his.

"What place?"

"Where Dr. Maggie was. Was it a school or training center or something?"

"It was her home. That was her husband, Benjamin, and their kids."

I stopped. He stopped and stared at me, clearly confused as to why I stood still.

"All of those children were hers and his?"

"Actually, they have an older son too. He's a little older than Talia. He must've been inside. They had him, and then moved here several years later and began having more."

I counted on my fingers. "They have six children?"

"They do," he said with a grin as he resumed walking.

"And she birthed them?"

"She did."

"I didn't know that was physically possible. I mean, I knew it was for the gestates selected for carrying born babies, but I didn't know it was for vintage borns."

"For some couples it is, for others it's not. Some here have more, some have fewer, some have none. Every family is different."

I thought of the place I knew: there, every family unit looked and acted very much the same. A few did have two children, but most had only one. Once that family unit was dissolved, either adult could get another child if they wanted to pay the fees and select one with their new partner. Though that was fairly rare; typically, one child was considered enough of a burden. The size of the Parker-James family unit and the fact that two borns conceived and birthed a vintage born made them quite unusual.

"Before Dr. Maggie left, she kissed her husband," I said, though it was more of a question.

"Yes, it's common here for married couples to do that. It's probably why some have so many children," he teased.

I ignored the implication. "I'd never witnessed a kiss like that … not in real life, I mean. Sometimes on a screen that Mr. James or Ms. Parker was viewing, but never in real life."

"Maggie and Benjamin are particularly affectionate," Kolbe said.

In the distance, I heard the happy shrieks of children.

"Everything is so different here. The family units, the children, the … the marriages. There aren't marriages where I'm from, only contracts."

"Contracts that dissolve fairly quickly, if I remember correctly," Kolbe said.

"Three years, if they have a born, ten if they have a vintage born, but that's pretty rare," I said, my tone implying those were not short durations.

"Here they last for life," he said.

"I can't imagine Mr. James and Ms. Parker being together for life," I said, amused by the thought.

"And people here could never imagine ending a marriage after three years. Most say life isn't long enough and they hope to be together after death if that's possible," he said. "But I remember that from before we came here."

"Is that why there's a heaviness to you that your sister doesn't have? You remember things about your life before." I immediately wished I hadn't been so nosey.

Kolbe turned his head toward me, his hands remaining in the front pockets of his pants while we walked. "Probably," he said. "Talia is different. As far as she can remember, she's only ever existed here. She doesn't remember Dad or Grandmother, and that's a loss for her, but it's a gift that she doesn't know that world."

"But you brought that world to her," I said.

He studied me for a moment before speaking. "I intended to only bring one small part of the world. I never expected you, nor did I expect her to go into it with me."

"Why did you bring me here? You know what I am. You know I could destroy everything, either by who I am, or by my gestation firm searching for me, or by others turning me in for the bounty."

His facial expression lightened. "No one here cares about government money. What good would that do us? And the hurricane was larger than we realized. I doubt your gestation firm will search for you."

"Still, bringing me here … it could ruin everything for your sister, for everyone. It was a risk, probably one that most here are angry that you made," I said, realizing that people were keeping their distance not because I was some random stranger, but because they knew exactly what I was.

He watched a bee buzzing from flower to flower. The sun warmed our backs as we started toward his house. "You were scared—you were trying so hard to be brave. And you were being brave … but you were terrified. I couldn't leave you there."

I stumbled. How had he realized so much so quickly? "I was afraid you'd turn me in for the bounty."

He glanced at me and then away. "It was more than that. It was like you'd always been scared. I …"—he swallowed—"there was something inside of me, something that wouldn't let me leave you there. Something that made me think you needed me."

"How could I have needed someone I'd never met?" I asked in barely a whisper. His words were true; I didn't understand how, but they were.

He was no longer walking, no longer paying attention to happy children down the lane or the birds hopping on the green grass around us. He was focused entirely on me. "I don't know, but that's what I felt—like you were crying out to me even more loudly than my grandfather was."

"I-I was trained not to feel, not to think … but I-I felt something at your grandfather's house. A longing for something."

"For what?" he asked.

I heard the happy cries in the background—the sound of the children coupled with the songs of the birds—the two in balance.

"I didn't know anything else existed, but when I took your grandfather to his house before the hurricane, I felt it … all of it. A longing for something I never knew could exist, but I wanted it. I needed it. It was what I was made for," I said, startled by the truth of my words.

"I thought you were made to serve," he said, his eyes heavy yet hopeful.

I shook my head, my heart racing. "I was made for more. I was made to serve, but out of kindness or … or caring, if I'm capable of it. I was made to make my own decisions and choose what to cook and who to cook it for. To work hard, and to rest, as well. I was made for this life, not the one that was forced on me."

A broad grin crossed his face.

"Most don't know this life exists," I said, thinking of Hastings and then even of Salt. It wasn't fair that their lives should be what they were, rather than filled with joy.

"People out there have stopped listening to their hearts. If they hadn't, the world would never be what it's become."

"Maybe they could listen again?" I said, hoping that at least Hastings, if he was alive, could have a different life.

Kolbe bent down and picked a purple wildflower. "Maybe they could," he said, handing it to me.

Our fingers touched as he slowly released the flower. His touch caused my heart to beat faster. It was a reaction I wasn't familiar with … feeling afraid, but not afraid. I was grateful.

Twenty-Nine

From the direction of Kolbe's house, Talia raced toward us, calling, "Mom needs you."

"Which one of us?" Kolbe asked.

"Zelie. Grandfather's confused. He doesn't recognize us and he's scared," Talia said, her voice worried.

I ran to their house, leaving Talia behind, but Kolbe kept up. Together we bounded up the steps, past the porch, and into the house.

Mr. Northup lay upon the bed in Kolbe's personal room. Talia was right. He looked like a scared child—with yellow-tinged, waxy skin. Carolyn and Dr. Maggie stood near him.

"Mr. Northup, it's Azalea Rose," I said, rushing to him.

"Azalea Rose." He grasped at me, pulling me down to a sitting position next to him. "Where are we—are we captured?" he said, his voice even more terrified than his eyes.

"No, sir, we're safe. I'm sorry I left you. I'll never do that again," I said, holding on to him, trying to comfort his shaking body.

He held me so tight, the action reminded me of Hastings on the last night, when the lightning burst and he begged me to stay with him. The memory brought tears: tears for the boy I left and for the man I feared would leave me.

"It's okay, sir," I said, doing what I could to steady my voice. "I'm here. We're with your family. They're helping you to heal. You'll be better soon." More tears spilled—I didn't believe my own words.

"I don't have a family," he said, sounding more distraught.

"Yes, you do. Remember your grandchildren and your daughter-in-law, Carolyn," I said.

"Carolyn?"

"It's me," she said, stepping a little closer.

"Me too, Grandfather."

I said, "That's your grandson, Kolbe. And your granddaughter, Talia, is beside him."

"I'm older now, Grandfather. I'm twelve," Talia said.

"Twelve?"

"We left a long time ago," Carolyn said. "After … well, after we had to."

"Joshua, you left because of Joshua," Mr. Northup said, his face contorting in pain. "It's my fault. It's all my fault," he murmured, his expression becoming panicked.

Carolyn knelt beside us. "Shh, it's okay. Don't think about any of that. Get better. That's all you need to think about," she said.

He sobbed, grasping her. It was difficult to watch this man who had once been so strong, crying like a child.

"It's okay, Josiah, I forgive you. Joshua forgives you," she said.

His sobs lessened as he became more exhausted. "Protect her, protect Azalea Rose. Don't let them get her," he begged.

Carolyn glanced at me, and I lowered my eyes. I should not be a concern for this man, or for anyone. A tear seeped into my partially open mouth.

"She's safe here," Carolyn told him.

He shook his head. "There are so many lies, but … not in the pictures. The pictures are the truth," he said, gripping her arms tightly with what strength he had left.

"What pictures?" Carolyn asked. She tilted her head, trying to understand his meaning.

"My pictures," he said, his voice groggy.

Dr. Maggie spoke. "Let him sleep. The medicine I gave him should be working now. He needs to sleep and drink as much as possible."

She was right; his eyes had closed, his body relaxed. Carolyn laid him back onto his pillow that was stained with a yellowish tinge from the poison seeping from his body. I doubted these sheets would ever return to their white color, even if they were left in the sunlight for days.

"He'll sleep now," Dr. Maggie said, "but every time he wakes up, he needs to drink water and chicken broth."

"So, you think he'll improve?" Carolyn asked her, sounding hopeful.

Dr. Maggie came closer, using a body scanner over his chest and abdomen. "There's been a change even since I arrived."

"He's improved?" Kolbe asked.

Dr. Maggie shook her head. "The toxins would be too much for anyone, let alone someone of his age. A few days, maybe would've been okay, but weeks …. His organs are saturated with the poison. Unless a miracle happens, which I never rule out, I don't believe he'll recover."

"No," I said. "That's not true. Once the exposure stopped, he was supposed to get better."

"That's what they tell people," Dr. Maggie said. "It makes the public feel better, and I suppose it's true if the exposure is a day or two, maybe three. But after that … the damage is too extensive to ever fully recover. Some can live a little longer, maybe even a year or two, but the damage can't be undone unless new organs are transplanted. And, of course, those who were in the process of being dissolved are not eligible for healthy organs."

I rushed to her. "Take my organs," I said, clutching her arm.

Dr. Maggie offered a kind smile. "That would kill you. I won't kill one person to save another."

"I'm not a person," I argued. Some gestates were created specifically for their organs. Why could they not take mine now?

Talia whispered, "What does she mean?"

I felt Kolbe's hands on my shoulders.

"Azalea Rose, please," he said, his lips next to my ear.

His tenderness caused me to fall against his chest, to allow his arms to hold me upright.

Dr. Maggie took my hand. "You very much are a person, and I will not end one life to save another. But in truth, I don't think it would help. Everything is saturated, his blood, his skin—"

"Please don't let him die," I begged.

"You witnessed his confusion," Dr. Maggie said, clasping my hands. "The toxins have entered his brain. That's how I know there's nothing we can do, not at this stage. I'm very sorry."

"No," I whispered as tears choked me.

"How much time does he have?" Carolyn asked, lovingly stroking Mr. Northup's hair from her spot beside him.

"A few days, at the most," Dr. Maggie replied.

A sob rocked my body. Kolbe kept me from crumbling to the ground.

Talia clung to her mother.

"It's a gift to be able to say goodbye. I haven't been given that gift before," Carolyn said, her eyes becoming red as tears filled them.

Thirty

The light outside grew dim and then darkness overtook it. A storm had blown in, causing dusk to be black as a moonless night. I didn't mind the dark. I never had. Perhaps because it was in the darkness of my gestate pod that I could be me—no one watching, no one listening. The storm, too, brought me peace. The house felt secure and I felt safe. No one would come for me in a storm. I didn't need to fear the effects of the wind and rain. There was no reclamation zone throwing shards of metal at my flimsy pod. Here I was safe and dry, and would remain so … at least until morning.

After we spent some time in the dark, lightning began to accompany the wind and rain. The room would go from dark to light and back to dark again. The navy-blue drapes were closed, so I couldn't watch the storm like Hastings and I had done the night of the hurricane. Instead, I listened. Listened to Mr. Northup's unsteady breathing above the sound of the rain rolling from the eaves of the roof.

Most of the water was being collected. Each house had a rainwater catchment system like at the houses of borns, though here the water was used for the houses and the people in them, not only for the plants and the gestates. Before, I thought it was because the rainwater was not considered clean enough for the borns. Listening to Mr. Northup's ragged breath, I realized that was a lie—like so many others I'd believed.

Those in charge wanted control of the water—and all it contained—going into the houses and the people. It was still hard for me to believe this—that the borns had been lied to and controlled. That they were not as free as they and I believed. But here, in this place of truth, it was difficult not to see the lies.

I lay on the floor next to the bed where Mr. Northup slept. I was given blankets to sleep on and one to wrap around me, along with a pillow for my head. Never had I slept in such luxury. Throughout the early part of the night, others came in. In whispered voices so as not to wake him, they asked how Mr. Northup was doing. I told them he was sleeping, or no change, or he was back to sleep after waking up confused. They asked if they could relieve me—a question that didn't make sense to me. It was my job to be beside him … it was where I wanted to be. None of them could convince me to leave him. I was the only one who could get him to drink the clean water or sip broth made from chicken and vegetables. It was me he recognized. I brought him comfort.

There were many moments during the darkness of night that I didn't believe Dr. Maggie. The moments when Mr. Northup woke up clearheaded, with full awareness of where he was. His body remained weak, his breathing ragged, but his mind was clear. During those moments he told me stories of when he was younger, when he met his wife, or when their son was born. Memories that meant a great deal to him. He told me too of the day the gestation firm transporter brought me to the Parker-James family unit. It was a Sunday and he, unlike most of the others, had never worked on Sundays and rarely on Saturdays. He remembered how soon after I'd arrived I was sent outside with Hastings because he wouldn't stop crying. He noticed that I was crying too and so came over to help, and he had. Hastings had stopped crying. The mention of Hastings made me want to cry. Mr. Northup had drifted back off to sleep. The next time he woke he didn't know where we were. I could barely contain my tears, until he fell asleep. To witness such stark changes … sometimes he seemed himself … other times it was difficult to doubt Dr. Maggie.

I wondered, as I tried to rid my mind and body of this sorrow, why it even existed. Gestates were altered not to care, or at least not to care in any real way, with any real depth, and yet I couldn't imagine more sadness than I felt as I thought of Mr. Northup's garbled mind. Occasionally, when the lightning flashed, I thought, too, of Hastings, of the last time I'd seen him, the loss I felt at not being with him. The loss I feared I'd soon have with Mr. Northup made my stomach and chest so tight there were moments I had to gasp for breath.

When morning finally arrived, I woke to the sight of Kolbe sitting near us, studying us both as we slept: Mr. Northup on the bed, me on the floor beside him.

"Did you sleep much?" he asked, sounding concerned.

"Yes," I whispered back so as not to wake Mr. Northup.

"You should've let us take shifts," he said, sensing I was lying.

I shook my head. "I can't leave him," I answered.

Kolbe's eyes were filled with compassion as he gazed from me to his grandfather; the compassion was not only for Mr. Northup but also for me.

"I'll be right back," Kolbe said, hurrying from the room.

I ran my fingers through my hair, forgetting for a moment how short it was now. I folded each blanket I'd used and carefully placed them on the edge of Kolbe's desk, and the fluffy pillow on top of them. Then I sat in the desk chair, leaving open the kitchen chair someone had brought in.

Kolbe returned. "Here, this is for you," he said, handing me a bowl of chilled oats and fruit. "Hot oatmeal is too warm for summer mornings. This is one of my specialties. I made it last night when I couldn't sleep."

"Thank you," I said, grateful once again to have the luxury of eating food. "It's very good."

"I'm hoping Grandfather will enjoy it."

"I'm sure he will," I said, taking another bite. In truth, I doubted Mr. Northup would be able to chew even something as soft as oatmeal.

"Pictures," Mr. Northup groaned from the bed. "Where are the pictures?"

"Right here, sir," I said, pointing to the framed photographs slightly above his head.

At the sight of them, Mr. Northup calmed down. "They're the truth," Mr. Northup said.

"Yes, sir," I said as he settled into a light sleep.

I slunk back in my chair, the bowl of oatmeal on my lap. Every part of my body felt the exhaustion of a sleepless night.

"What was that about?" Kolbe asked.

"He did it several times during the night," I said. "At some point I figured out he wanted the pictures from his house, so I got them from my pack and put them up here so he could see them."

"What did he mean by 'They're the truth'?" He scrunched his eyebrows together as he studied the pictures.

Holding the bowl close to my mouth, I swallowed my last spoonful of oatmeal. I felt too tired to eat, but to pass up food was foolish.

"I don't know. He never explained that part. I thought maybe he was trying to tell me that the families here, like yours in the picture, are the way families are supposed to be."

Kolbe didn't answer, only stared at the pictures.

"How is he?" Carolyn whispered from the doorway.

"He slept off and on," I said. "Several times he woke up and wasn't scared or confused. Other times he was, but there were times when I woke up and couldn't remember where I was, so that didn't seem too odd," I said, wishing I believed it was that simple.

She went to him and placed a hand on his waxy forehead. "He's cool to the touch. I wish he had a fever or something … I wish his body was fighting."

I set the bowl of oatmeal on my lap. I was no longer able to eat.

"Oh, his pictures," she said, eyeing them on the desk. "I wasn't sure what he was talking about when Dr. Maggie was here. I haven't seen these in years. The frames are different—Amelia never would've had metal frames in her house—but the photos are the same." Carolyn gazed lovingly at the framed picture she held in her hand.

"He asked me to bring them from his house," I said. "He was asking for them last night, so I put them up where he could see them. It calmed him down."

"This is the man I knew," Carolyn said, holding the picture of Mr. Northup and his wife when their son was young. "He was always so hard, so callous."

"That's how all the born and vintage born men look where I'm from, except Mr. Northup. I never saw the hardness before. Only in that picture," I said.

"That's who he was," she said. "You can see the contrast between him and Amelia … and then there's Joshua, caught in between. Thankfully, his mother's side won out."

"He was always kind to me," I said, defending Mr. Northup.

"You met him soon after my mother-in-law passed away," she said, focusing again on the picture in her hands. "He lost everyone … he lost everyone, and he cared. I never thought he would. I begged Amelia to come with us, but she wouldn't leave him. She wouldn't give up on him. She said he'd been good once … he could be good again."

Carolyn's fingers rubbed against the frame and her eyes showed how deeply she felt the loss of Mr. Northup's wife. "Amelia was right," she said, still rubbing the frame as if its cold metal brought her closer to those she'd lost.

Her expression changed.

"What?" Kolbe said.

She stared down at the side of the frame. "There's a compartment," she said, handing the frame to her son.

He examined it. "There's a microchip inside," he said, eyes focused on a narrow slit in the side of the frame.

Carolyn stepped back, her fingertips touching her lips, her gaze on Mr. Northup's sleeping form.

"They're the truth," I said, speaking the words Mr. Northup kept repeating during the night.

"What does that mean?" Carolyn asked.

"It's what Grandfather said during the night about the pictures," Kolbe said, still examining the frame.

"I thought he meant that the families like yours in the picture, like the ones here, were the truth," I said while nervously watching Carolyn, whose expression was becoming more concerned with each passing second.

She took the frame back from her son, closed the slit, and placed it beside the others on the desk. She ran her fingers through her gray-streaked hair. "You brought your secrets into my house!" she said angrily at the sleeping man. "I guess you haven't changed as much as I thought." Her voice had become higher pitched.

Kolbe asked cautiously, "Secrets about what?"

"So many …" she said fearfully. "He was never honest, never. Amelia said he'd change, and believed he would turn back into the man she'd married. I wonder if she ever really knew that man. Why did you bring your secrets here!" Carolyn crossed her arms in anger, her face flushing. "Even his job was a secret. He couldn't tell us the truth about something as simple as that!"

"What department was he in?" I asked as she unfolded and folded her arms.

"He didn't work for the state. He worked for the firms."

My body began to shake. "For the firms?" I whispered.

"Amelia hated that he worked there," she said. "She begged him to quit. He never would, never even entertained the idea. How this man won her heart, I'll never understand. He told us his work was basic, focused on training gestates."

Her voice quivered. "Joshua believed that was a lie and so did I."

"What did Dad think he did?" Kolbe asked, his eyebrows pulled together in concern.

Carolyn rubbed her hands together, breathing deeply to still the anger. "Genetics," she said, practically spitting the word. "He confronted Josiah, Josiah denied it, Joshua didn't believe him. Joshua was dead a few weeks later," she said in a quivering voice.

His words slow and deliberate, Kolbe asked, "You think the two are related?"

"I don't want to," Carolyn said.

"But you do," Kolbe said, staring down at his grandfather with a look of muted disgust.

"The timing is too close. Joshua said someone told him what Josiah really did. He worked in genetics, something Amelia would never have accepted. She put up with a lot from him, but that would've been the end. She would've agreed then to come with us, and we all would've come here."

"Dad would still be alive," Kolbe said.

Carolyn slumped against the desk, staring down at Mr. Northup. After a few minutes, she exhaled and said, "Your father would've been alive if I'd agreed to come here sooner. I don't think we can blame Josiah for his death ... I hope not, anyway."

Thirty-One

The morning passed quickly. I slept while Mr. Northup slept, ate when he ate, and listened when he spoke—which was mostly to his granddaughter because Kolbe and his mom were doing everything they could to avoid him. I didn't blame them. I didn't know the man they remembered, the man of lies and hardness that was nothing like the man who'd spent the last eight years watching over me, protecting me as much as he dared.

By now the entire community knew of our arrival and of Carolyn's aged father-in-law who was being dissolved. It was clear from the voices that came from the kitchen and front room that the people in this community could never condone dissolution, no matter how useless someone was. They never spoke of my presence, except for Ms. Vivian, who asked about me. Instead they expressed their concern for Mr. Northup and support for Carolyn and her kids, and completely ignored my existence. This felt more natural—to be ignored in actions and thoughts. It was Kolbe's family that was odd, in how much they focused on me, thought of me … cared about me.

From what I could tell, it was a custom for neighbors to offer whatever baked goods, preserves, fresh cheese, or dried fruit they had when one in their community was in need. It was strange to observe this: that neighbors did what the government should do. I supposed, in the absence of a government, the individual people had to step in. In some ways, this felt right. People helping other people, but mostly it seemed odd.

After one of the visitors left, Carolyn brought in various pieces of paper that had been decorated by Dr. Maggie's children and several others. There were drawings of flowers, sunshine, butterflies things children thought were beautiful in an effort to cheer Mr. Northup. When he saw them, he wept. He said he hadn't seen anything like that since Kolbe was a young child and his Amelia helped Kolbe make pictures to celebrate special days. Something about the way he cried told me he had not appreciated them as much then as he did now. I wondered if Mr. James would weep if given such decorated paper by his children; the answer was no. He would show gratitude because it was clear one should show gratitude when given a gift, but that would be all.

By late afternoon I was no longer tired, so as Mr. Northup slept, I stared absently at the picture frames and the secrets they contained. Since he first spoke to Kolbe and me in the early morning, he hadn't mentioned them again.

"He's doing better," Carolyn said as she led Dr. Maggie into the room to check on him.

I stood, moving out of the way. Dr. Maggie barely noticed me as she focused on Mr. Northup. She touched his forehead and began opening her bag.

"How long have you been in here?" she asked, startling me.

Carolyn answered for me. "Since yesterday. She's only left to use the restroom. We've tried to get her to take a break, but she won't leave him."

"That's too long. Go outside and get some fresh air," Dr. Maggie said.

I didn't move.

Dr. Maggie said forcefully, "That's not a request, that's a command."

I hesitated for a second and then left the room. My head felt dizzy and my legs weak. I stayed near the wall as I walked toward the front door, a wave of nausea crashing over me.

Dr. Maggie was right; I needed fresh air.

Beyond the front door, I saw Kolbe sitting. I went to him, breathing deeply when I reached the outside. The air here was fresh and clean, different from the air near Mr. Northup. The poison was leaving him, creating a strong smell around him which I only noticed when I was away from it. My head was throbbing and my stomach churning. I took deep breaths through my mouth.

Kolbe stood when I approached him. "You don't look good," he said, gingerly helping me into a rocking chair on the porch.

"I don't feel good," I said, rubbing my head as he sat cautiously in the matching chair next to mine.

"Did Dr. Maggie send you out?"

"Yes," I replied, feeling feeble.

"I'll be back." He went into the house and returned with a glass of water. "Here, drink this. I was wondering how you were able to be around that odor. It's so strong. That's why I'm outside and Talia's at a friend's."

"I didn't realize how bad the smell was until I came outside," I said, my head throbbing.

"I had no idea it would hurt anyone," he said with concern. "It was so strong I couldn't stand it." He placed his hand on my forehead. "I think you have a fever."

"You think the smell did that?" I asked, leaning my head against the wooden rocker.

"It must have."

"I thought he was doing better," I said weakly. I felt my stomach settling some after the water soothed it.

"Maybe he is," Kolbe said. "Maybe the worsening smell is his body fighting—pushing it out."

"Maybe," I said feebly. My head was hurting less.

I finished the water and placed the glass on a small table that sat between the two rocking chairs. I ran my hands along the smooth arms of the chair. "Did you make these?" I asked, my voice a little stronger.

"Yes, with some help," he answered. "They were a combined Christmas and birthday present for my mom."

"What's Christmas?" I asked, turning my head to the side as I leaned it against the back of the chair.

"The real name for X-mas or, I guess, the actual real name is Christ's Mass."

I nodded a little. That holiday I knew. It was the biggest one of the year, when people were expected to think of gifts for the members of their family units, even their extended family units, on their own, with only suggestions, not directives, from government shoppers. It always frustrated Mr. James. He said it was a way for stores to make more money, though he always said it in a hushed tone—like he wasn't supposed to say such a thing.

"I'm sure your mom appreciated the gift," I said, running my fingertips along the smooth grain.

"She did, and so did my sister. Truthfully, I wanted the rockers too," he said with a grin.

"You do good work," I said.

"I've been fortunate to have good teachers," he said.

"Hastings and Salt hated their teachers," I said, taking a sip of water.

Kolbe rocked. "Teachers here are different. They help us learn what our specific gifts are and how we can best use them to serve our families and the community. Our parents do that too, but since I don't have a dad, others have stepped in to help."

"That is very different."

"I was fortunate—I knew almost as soon as we arrived that I wanted to go into woodworking. Talia, on the other hand … she's a bit of a wild card."

"She's only twelve."

"True, but since no one tells you what job you're going to do, it's best to start figuring it out as early as possible. Of course you can always change later, but it's good to begin focusing on a direction you think you'd like to go. She's started trying different things. She knows she doesn't want to cut hair, like Mom does, or work with wood, like me. Aunt Viv helped her create some rugs. That's not what Aunt Viv does, but she was trying to help Talia. She didn't care for that, either."

"What does Ms. Vivian do?" I asked. "Make preserves?"

"She makes the best preserves, but that's more of a hobby. She doesn't do it for the whole community. Aunt Viv's job is more technical. She works with computers. Doing things I barely understand. She's one of the few who monitor what's going on in the rest of the world, communicates with other settlements, and generally manages our security."

"That sounds like something Hastings would enjoy," I said, smiling at the thought of Hastings being in this place, where he could run and play with other children.

Kolbe nodded. "We don't talk much about her work. We don't want the young ones to know. If they did, they might accidentally tell a peace officer. Technically we aren't supposed to use technology in that way, but it's in her blood. She can't not do it. It's the same with the other two who do similar work for us. Talia has no interest in Aunt Viv's work, though Aunt Viv has tried several times to get her interested."

I rocked for a moment, trying to clarify my thoughts.

"Could she … if we brought her the picture frames, could she read what's on the microchips?" I asked, keeping my voice low even though no one was nearby.

"Frames?" Kolbe said, raising an eyebrow. "You think there's something in the other one too."

"I know there is. I checked when no one was around," I said.

Kolbe stopped rocking. "I'm sure she could. As soon as Maggie leaves, I'll grab them."

The wind gusted, bringing with it the sweet scent of southern jasmine blossoms. The afternoon sun warmed my wrist … the pale band was nearly gone. It had faded quickly, like the memories of my past life. I didn't forget them, but they didn't haunt me as they had when I first arrived. In just a few days, something about this place made me forget. It was the peace, the happiness—the safety.

Carolyn came out and held the door open for Dr. Maggie. Kolbe and I stood when Dr. Maggie stepped from behind the screen door.

"Thank you," Carolyn said, her arms folded across her chest.

"I wish things were different," Dr. Maggie said to Carolyn, before turning her attention to me. "How are you feeling?" She first stared into my left eye and then my right.

"I felt sick when I left the room, but I'm better now."

Dr. Maggie gave Carolyn a meaningful glance. "I'm glad the effects faded so quickly. It would be best if no one spent more than a few minutes at a time in the room."

"A few minutes?" I asked, concerned for Mr. Northup.

"Even sitting at the doorway would be better. The gas is heavy, it doesn't go far. Your sleeping on the floor next to the bed was the worst possible place to sleep. Don't do that again," Dr. Maggie said in her commanding voice.

"Yes, ma'am," I responded.

Dr. Maggie's tone softened. "I'm glad you're feeling better. I want you to remain that way. Please maintain a good distance for the next several hours. Your body needs a break."

"Yes, ma'am," I said, though I wished I could disagree.

"Send for me if anything changes," Dr. Maggie said as she started down the walkway.

Carolyn leaned against the door frame. "You heard her, go for a walk or something."

"What about Mr. Northup? If no one can be with him …."

"We set up an electric fan. It's blowing the gas out the open window. I'll step into the room every few minutes to check on him. But Maggie's right. If you were feeling the effects, you need to stay away."

"I don't want to be away from him," I said, trying not to cry. Tears came so easily now. It was frustrating.

"He's sleeping soundly. He won't know you're gone," Carolyn said.

Kolbe disappeared into the house as the breeze picked up. I inhaled the fragrant jasmine. The direction of the wind shifted. I coughed. It was the smell of the poison. I gagged. Dr. Maggie was right. I couldn't be around that smell right now. Not if I wanted to be healthy … an unhealthy gestate was a waste of resources.

Kolbe returned, awkwardly hiding something behind his back.

"What are you trying to hide?" Carolyn asked as he went past her.

He held out the frames. Carolyn stepped back as if her son held rattlesnakes.

"I'm taking them to Aunt Viv's," he said.

"No, you can't bring her into this. You can't bring anyone into this," Carolyn said, stepping forward to take the frames.

Kolbe moved the frames from her reach. "They're the truth. Don't you want to know what that means?"

"Knowing Josiah, those chips are trackers or filled with viruses that will bring down every computer in the community and alert the peacekeepers."

Kolbe asked calmly, "Why would he have chips like that?"

"It's Josiah, why would he not?" Carolyn said, her voice pleading.

"I have to know," Kolbe said.

The two stared at each other for a long time.

"Tell her," Carolyn said, practically stomping her foot. "Tell her that he lies, that they're probably tracked and filled with viruses."

"I will," he said, quickly tucking the frames back under his T-shirt and subtly holding them with his left hand.

"Josiah, I swear, if you hurt anyone else I love," she mumbled under her breath as Kolbe pulled my arm to come with him.

Behind us, the screen door slammed shut.

"She's really mad," I said.

"I don't blame her. Grandfather was awful, particularly to her," he said.

I was silent. Mr. Northup's son married a slave. The thought of it must have disgusted him. No, Carolyn was worse than a slave. She was like me, altered and born from a machine. We were barely human. Slaves of the past were unaltered, born of their mothers. They were full persons, only considered less. We actually *were* less. Or at least I was.

"He was always kind to me," I said, again defending Mr. Northup. It wasn't his fault his son had married a gestate.

"I'm glad," Kolbe said. "But he's done a lot of damage in this family." His grip tightened around the frames he held under his shirt. "Seems like he still is."

"You don't know that."

Kolbe sighed and said, "I'm pretty sure. Why else would he have mysterious microchips hidden in frames?"

"Didn't your mom just say the same thing and you disagreed with her?"

"I didn't disagree that they were likely dangerous. She's probably right about that. But I still want to know what's on them."

We walked in silence, listening to the distant sound of dogs barking and children playing.

Tentatively, I said, "May I ask you something?"

"Sure," Kolbe said, his left arm still holding the side of his shirt. His right hand swung freely.

"Why did you tell Dr. Maggie and her husband that my name was Zelie?"

"That's your name," he answered.

"Gestates don't have names," I said.

His body stiffened and his right arm didn't move as freely.

"I mean that's not the name you use for me," I added quickly. I hadn't meant to upset him.

"It's the name you told Talia."

"But you don't use it. You call me the name your grandfather calls me."

His neck flushed red.

"What is it?" I asked.

"Azalea Rose fits you better," he answered without looking at me.

"Then why not tell the others that's my name?"

He wiggled the fingers on his right hand. It was a subtle movement most wouldn't have noticed, but I did. I was trained to notice.

"I guess I didn't want to share that with other people."

Kolbe stepped hurriedly onto the porch and knocked. I wanted to ask him what he meant by not wanting to share that with other people, but there was no time. He opened the door and entered. Ms. Vivian was moving toward the door. She smiled when she saw him. He was used to letting himself in, that was clear. I stepped in behind him and closed the door.

"This is a nice surprise," Ms. Vivian said with a broad smile, her white teeth creating a stark contrast against her dark skin.

Kolbe said, "We have something to show you."

At the tone of his voice, her smile faded. "What is it?"

"We'll show you in your bedroom," he said, lightly tapping the hard frames under his shirt.

Her expression became one of tired concern. "Lock the door behind you."

Kolbe turned and locked the door. Then he followed Ms. Vivian into the same room that contained the safe room I'd hidden in. They quickly closed the drapes, which I noticed were thicker than those in Kolbe's house.

She sat in a rocking chair similar to the ones at Kolbe's. She held out her right palm. He handed her the framed photographs.

"Nice pictures," she said.

"The frames are even nicer," Kolbe said, reaching his hand and sliding open the tiny compartment.

She studied the contents without removing the chip. "These frames came from Josiah's house?"

Kolbe nodded and opened the other frame in the same way.

"Do you know what they contain?" she asked, looking at each of us in turn.

I shook my head. "During the night when he was sickest, he wanted the pictures. I put them on Kolbe's desk. He would look at them and say 'They're the truth,' over and over again."

She handed the frame back to Kolbe and then stood. "If they're the truth, we'd better figure out what the truth is."

"Mom said to remind you that Grandfather has many secrets," Kolbe said. "That these likely have trackers or viruses or bombs that are going to explode as soon as you touch them."

"Paranoid people often have a reason," Ms. Vivian said, reprimanding his sarcastic tone. "Your mom knows your grandfather far better than you do. You should respect her concern."

She opened her closet doors and slid the clothes to one side, this time toward the safe room that hid me a few days before. On the other end of the closet, she opened another door to another room. This one contained several screens and computers. The air in this room was chilly. The space contained her air-cooling system. On the screens were images of the woods and two of the streets bordering the settlement.

"You aren't concerned about what Kolbe's mom said?" I asked.

"Oh, I'm definitely concerned," she said, turning on a screen that was archaic. "Which is why I'm using a computer that's not connected to the network."

She sat down in a sturdy wooden chair. I was sure Kolbe had made it for her. She opened a drawer and used a tool that looked like tweezers to remove the tiny microchip from the frame containing the picture of Mr. Northup and his young son and wife.

Ms. Vivian delicately placed the microchip into a larger rectangle and connected it to the computer.

She clicked around on the screen until it became filled with column after column of numbers and letters. Often the sequence of numbers and letters repeated itself within the same column. Sometimes there were multiple blanks across some of the rows. Ms. Vivian scrolled to the side; it went on for several screens. At the very end, two columns appeared unchanging from entry to entry. She scrolled down page after page. The two columns were different from one another—they contained a different sequence of letters and numbers, but they were each the same all the way through the database. Those two columns were the same the whole way down. None of the others were.

"There must be millions of entries here," she said as she continued to scroll.

"What does it mean?" Kolbe said.

When she leaned away from the computer, he stepped back slightly. The cool air rushed through the open door behind us.

She tapped her right index finger against her puckered lips and let out a long exhale. "It means your grandfather was definitely not in the training department."

Thirty-Two

"These are genetic codes … a list of alterations," Ms. Vivian said.

I felt my stomach tighten at the thought of alterations, of the world I came from that told me who I really was. The world that told me I was nothing and deserved nothing.

She scrolled to the left, where there was a column of numbers only. "This first column must be the serial numbers of gestates," she said. "Each of the other columns must be a record of the specific alteration they received."

"It can't be a list of gestates," I said, staring at the screen.

"It has to be. These last two"—she scrolled quickly to the far right of the spreadsheet—"are identical. That only happens with the alterations given to gestates, never with borns. Even immunity to illnesses must be altered based on a person's existing genetics."

"I didn't think gestates had that many alterations," Kolbe said.

He was right. We were given only two, the two that made us who we were.

"I didn't think so either," Ms. Vivian said, her voice sounding confused.

"What's on the other chip?" Kolbe asked.

Ms. Vivian saved the data to her computer and then removed the chip holder from the computer. She placed that chip into a tiny plastic container she pulled from the drawer of her desk. Kolbe opened the other frame and Ms. Vivian removed the chip. A minute later we were looking at more numbers and letters, but this time one column was all numbers and the other was all letters, or more specifically, names.

I gripped the chair Ms. Vivian sat in, my hands holding it so tightly my skin turned white.

"That makes no sense," Kolbe said. "Do the numbers match up with the serial numbers on the last database?"

Ms. Vivian nodded. "I memorized the first one. Those two, at least, are the same."

"So, that other file can't be a list of alterations for gestates," Kolbe said. "These are the names of borns."

They were of course the names of borns. What else could they be—gestates didn't have names and vintage borns weren't altered.

Ms. Vivian was still, her eyes staring at the screen.

"I don't understand," she said. Touching the screen, she caused the spreadsheet with the list of names to shrink to the side and the other spreadsheet to open.

"Why would there be two columns with the exact same genetic code for everyone? Even to be immune to viruses, there must be some difference somewhere among the population." She scrolled down the list while keeping those two columns on the screen.

They never changed.

Kolbe said, "There must be some other alterations you aren't aware of."

Ms. Vivian sat taller. "It's possible. I've been out of that world for a while. We monitor things from here, but maybe we missed something. Though …." She moved back to the start of the list, the part that listed everyone's serial number. In the next column were numbers only.

"These are dates of birth," she said, scrolling. "They go back to when I was young, long before Robert and I came here. I should've at least known about the major alterations, especially ones significant enough to give to every born."

She stared at the screen. "I wonder," she said, scrolling over to the two far-right columns, which were identical. She copied the first row of both columns so that she had one cell of each column, then she shrunk the spreadsheets. A moment later another database opened, one with genetic markers on the left and explanations on the right, along with multiple possible variants beneath it. For instance, under hair color, there were thirty-two variants. It was odd, how every born of every generation looked almost exactly the same as every other member of their generation, when there were so many options.

She scrolled to the bottom of the sheet, where there were two genetic codes with no variants. Next to the first one it read:

"Decreased empathy / increased apathy"; next to the second, "Increased need for guidance / decreased ability to think independently."

I turned away as my eyes began to sting at the descriptions—these were my alterations.

"Those are the same," Kolbe said in a hushed whisper.

I turned back and stared at the screen. He was right. The sequence of numbers and letters that Ms. Vivian had copied from the other spreadsheet, the one listing born alterations, were the same as those listed on the spreadsheet in front of us.

"That makes no sense," Kolbe said. "We saw the names attached. Gestates aren't given names."

"Tell me again what Josiah said," Ms. Vivian said, still focused on the screen.

"He said 'It's the truth' and he kept repeating 'The pictures are the truth,' " I answered, my throat so dry my words came out as a whisper.

"I have to ask him," Ms. Vivian said, her voice frantic as she clicked through databases until the screen was black and she was pulling the microchip from her computer. She put it beside the other one in the plastic container and urged us out of the narrow hidden room.

Behind us, she closed and locked the door to the secret room, practically running from the bedroom and out of the house. Kolbe, with his long legs, was able to keep pace with her without running; I had to jog every few steps to keep up.

"What do you think it means?" Kolbe asked.

"Shhh," she said, glancing around, "don't talk outside."

I didn't know what he'd said that he shouldn't have said. She was on edge in a way I hadn't felt since I'd been here. I realized now it was a feeling I felt often in my prior life, but not here … not until now.

Kolbe appeared startled; he wasn't used to any of this.

"We need to speak to Josiah," Ms. Vivian said in a hurried hush. "And pray he's aware enough to answer us, and pray even harder that I'm wrong."

"Wrong about what?" I asked.

"That everything I thought I understood—that we all understood—was a lie," Ms. Vivian said as we ran up the steps of Kolbe's house.

Thirty-Three

"Hi, Aunt Viv!" Talia exclaimed as we burst through the door of the family's house.

"Hi, sweetie," Ms. Vivian responded, not stopping as she went directly to Kolbe's personal room.

"Viv?" Carolyn said as we entered the room.

Each of us started coughing and gagging at the smell of toxins hitting our systems.

"Do you know what he has?" Ms. Vivian asked, ignoring the smell of toxic death to go near her best friend. "It can't be what I think it is, but if it is … all of it's a lie," she whispered.

Carolyn's eyes grew wide. "Kolbe, shut the window. Talia, go outside, please. The smell is too much for you to be in here."

"If it's too much for me, it's too much for you," Talia said.

Her mom placed a hand on her arm. "Go outside. Make sure no one listens."

"Why would anyone listen?" Talia said. "And how could they if the window's closed?"

Carolyn lowered her voice. "Whatever your grandfather had … we have to be careful. I'll tell you what I can, later. For now, please go inconspicuously guard the house. Pick some flowers or pet the neighbor's cat."

Talia hesitated for a moment. "Don't leave the window closed too long," she said before leaving the room.

Carolyn nodded to Kolbe, who quickly closed the window. In the distance, the screen door slammed.

"What was on the microchip?" Carolyn asked.

"There were two chips and two databases," Ms. Vivian said. "We need him to tell us what they mean, because if it's what I think it is, the world just turned upside down."

Carolyn's eyes matched the concern in her friend's expression.

"Josiah, wake up," Carolyn said, rubbing a damp rag across his face and arms.

His eyes fluttered open, startled and scared.

"Azalea Rose, go to him," Kolbe said.

"I'm here, sir," I said, kneeling beside Mr. Northup. "We're in your family's house, remember?"

The look of terror subsided and he gave a nod.

"How are you feeling, sir?" I asked. He looked even worse than when I last saw him.

He croaked, "Tired."

Ms. Vivian moved directly above me. "Josiah, we found the databases."

His eyes went to her. A look of confusion, followed by fear, washed over his face.

Carolyn came closer so he could see her. "It's okay, Josiah. She's been a sister to me since I came here. She helped me raise the kids after … when they only had me."

He wasn't focused on her; he was focused on me.

"She hid us that first night we arrived, do you remember?" I said, taking his frail, icy hand in mine.

"Do you trust her?" he asked, searching my eyes.

I squeezed his hand, hoping I could warm it and thus warm him. "Kolbe trusts her and I trust Kolbe," I said, realizing that was the truth. I trusted Kolbe more than I'd ever trusted anyone else, including Mr. Northup. With Mr. Northup, I'd always felt there was something hidden, something he wasn't telling me. Perhaps this was it—his life of secrets before he reached the age of uselessness.

Ms. Vivian spoke again, her voice hurried. "I compared the codes to the list of genetic alterations used by the gestation firms. The codes on the database didn't make sense."

Mr. Northup shifted his eyes to her, but didn't speak.

She continued. "The last two codes on the database of born alterations aren't alterations that are ever given to borns. That's what the database is, right? A list of alterations for the borns, with the second database matching up the names of the borns to the alteration list."

"That's what it is," he said, his voice uneven, his breath ragged.

Ms. Vivian paced anxiously, rubbing her hands together as she sped from one side of the room to the other.

Carolyn said, "What do you mean, the alterations listed aren't ones given to borns? Borns receive any alterations they want." She was watching her friend's frantic pacing.

"There are two they don't want. Two nobody wants," Ms. Vivian said, her voice full of meaning.

Carolyn silently stared at her friend.

Kolbe remained still, the muscles of his biceps pushing tight against his T-shirt. He said, "The last two alterations listed on the database were for alterations that only gestates receive … or were ever supposed to receive."

Carolyn tilted her head, and her eyebrows pulled together as she spoke to her son. "The ones that supposedly make gestates less than a person?"

Kolbe nodded slightly.

"Gestates don't receive any alterations," Mr. Northup said, his voice garbled.

I stared at him. "That's impossible, sir. It's the alterations we receive, along with being gestated by a machine, that makes us less than human—that make us what we are."

"And what are you?" he asked me.

I swallowed hard. "A human, but not a person. A human worthy only of servitude."

"Do you believe that?" he asked.

"I-I used to," I said.

A faint smile crossed his lips. "I thought my daughter-in-law would fix you," he said with a laugh that came out as a ragged cough. "The gestates aren't altered in the ways you were told, the borns are."

"What!" Carolyn demanded, her voice beginning as a gasp and ending as a shriek.

"I shouldn't have kept that from you, from all of you … it was a mistake," he said meekly.

"You knew I was unaltered and still you fought so hard against Joshua and me?" she asked, her brows pulled low in anger.

Kolbe's body jerked straight, his eyes wide, staring at his mother, but he remained silent. He was the only one here who didn't know what his mother had once been. That she had once been a servant, gestated by a machine.

Mr. Northup said, "I thought I was right. … I was wrong."

Carolyn crossed her arms and said, "Did Amelia's death finally teach you that?"

"Joshua, Amelia, Azalea Rose … they all taught me," he said, looking at his hand in mine.

"Me?" I asked.

"You were a beautiful little girl," he said, his voice full of emotion. "We didn't treat you that way," he said to Carolyn. "I would've, but Amelia protected you. She raised you as her own, despite my commands. And of course, you didn't wear one of those bands, not in my house, so she could do as she pleased. And she did," he said with a kind smile at the memory of his wife.

"She fought against me. She protected you. But no one was there for my Azalea Rose," he said, shifting his attention to me. "You were a slave, nothing more. It wasn't the life you should've lived. Alone, uncared for."

"You were there," I said.

"And I did nothing," he replied.

"Other than steal the databases," Ms. Vivian said, still pacing.

Mr. Northup offered a ragged chuckle. "I did do that. On my last day, before I entered the stage of uselessness. I expected them to come after me because I stole the files, but they never did. Instead, they started dissolving me … not because I stole the files, but because I was no longer of any use to them. Ironic that they thought I was so useless, yet I held the key to bringing down the world." A chuckle caught in his throat, turning into a cough.

"Bring down the world?" I asked, my body beginning to tremble.

"Imagine if they knew … if they all knew," Mr. Northup explained, his voice tired.

Ms. Vivian stopped pacing and began rubbing her hands together in frantic worry. "Why? Why were those alterations given to borns and not gestates?"

Mr. Northup inhaled a ragged breath, and then said, "It was fifty years ago. The robot alterations, as we called them, had been discovered. The government was pushing heavily for the use of slave labor ... for gestates. Those pushing wanted them to be given those alterations to make them easy to control." Mr. Northup paused to catch his breath. "My team pointed out the foolishness of that. Altering embryos often results in their death. Back then we lost one out of four, on a good day. It didn't matter that we had hundreds of millions frozen decades before, it was a waste—I hate waste. I made the recommendation that we make the parents pay for that waste, not the government."

I shivered at the touch of his hand in mine. I knew nothing of who this man I had risked my life for ... left Hastings for ... truly was.

"*You* told them to give the borns those alterations?" I said, my voice uneven.

"The gestation firms were losing too many gestate embryos. I pointed out it wasn't worth the loss for two unnecessary alterations."

"Unnecessary?" Ms. Vivian asked, her dark brown eyes focused on him.

"Genetic alterations were never needed to control slaves before. Why start now? The parents who wanted their offspring altered were already demanding alterations. The risk of death to those embryos already existed and that loss was

315

taken into account in the fees charged to those selecting the alterations. It was with the borns we could create any alteration they wanted … or we wanted. We already had the sequences. Why not use them?"

"It was that easy for you?" Kolbe said with disgust.

"Yes," Mr. Northup said, his voice hard. "Control was needed to avoid the chaos. We needed some who could rule … more who would follow. The gestation machines had been heavily invested in, but people wanted their children born of a woman, not gestated by a machine. What was to be done with those machines? We couldn't waste them. We needed more physical laborers, labor that no one wanted to do and so the gestates were created."

I winced at his callous tone. I wanted to pull my hand away, but I didn't.

"Why have gestates? Why not use the borns as slaves?" Ms. Vivian asked, her voice curious.

"We didn't want an entire country of slaves," he said.

Kolbe scoffed and said, "Not an entire country of slaves, but a country of half slaves and half robots."

"It's easy for you to judge. You didn't exist before the Age of Systematic Reason. None of you did. We removed all the evils the world had. The crime, the pollution, the hunger, the total lack of fairness, it all went away." Mr. Northup's voice was unsteady.

"How is removing the humanity from someone ever going to make the world better?" Kolbe asked. "Or enslaving an entire group of people. When has that ever made things better?"

"It often has," Mr. Northup said, "for those not enslaved."

My body jerked. It was an involuntary movement, an automatic response to the darkness coming from the frail man. "You cannot enslave someone else without enslaving yourself," I said, my voice low as I stared at Mr. Northup's bone-thin hand in mine. "You said it yourself … so much has been lost."

He squeezed my hand. "Yes," he whispered, his voice breaking. "Things have been lost."

No one spoke for several moments, until finally, Mr. Northup said, "We had to have order, and to have order we had to get rid of differences, and so we did. Those in politics mandated laws requiring all born children to be altered in such a way that no one had any advantage over anyone else. Such advantages were considered unfair, and they were … for some to be born with brilliant minds and others to be born unable to tie their shoes. There's no fairness in that, so we made things fair."

Carolyn said, "Life isn't fair, and those who tell you it is are lying. That's what Amelia always told me."

Mr. Northup grimaced in what was supposed to be a smile. "Yes, she told that to anyone who would listen. It was a dangerous belief, but she didn't care. I've never met anyone as stubborn as her," he said with a longing. "Most didn't agree with her. Most believed we could create fairness if we created sameness. Perhaps we were wrong, but we were doing what we thought was best."

Kolbe said, "You thought it best to take away caring, to take away free will … to take away *humanity* from an entire group of people and then lie to them about it?"

I didn't face him, but I was sure if I did, I would see his jaw clenched in outrage.

"We had to maintain control. We couldn't do that if they were not compliant."

"And attachment?" Kolbe said, not needing to say more.

"Love makes you go to extraordinary lengths … we didn't want that … it would create chaos and discordance," he said.

"You're holding the hand of a girl who was a slave, a girl you clearly love, while trying to justify creating slaves and not allowing others to love," Kolbe said, his voice hard.

Mr. Northup appeared noticeably weaker, his face even paler. "We did what we thought was best," he said.

Kolbe groaned in disgust as he stomped out of the room. The screen door slammed behind him.

Mr. Northup turned his head to face the window. Rays of sun were streaking in. He looked as if he would cry if he had the strength.

"What about the vintage borns?" I said softly. "They weren't altered or beaten … would they not create chaos?"

He exhaled loudly and turned his head painfully to face me. "We never forced anyone to be altered. They chose that. We welcomed the birth of vintage borns, and specifically created alterations that would not be passed down to offspring. But we knew the unaltered gestates would be needed to care for the infants. That task could not be left to the borns."

"Your system is working flawlessly, so why steal the database?" Carolyn asked, her tone steady. Her heart wasn't broken by learning the truth of who Mr. Northup was; she'd always known.

He replied, "They killed Joshua and they made Azalea Rose a slave."

I watched the faint pumping of blood in the hand I held. The hand was so frail it appeared dead, except for the subtle pulse I saw between the thumb and fingers.

I lifted my gaze. He was watching me, waiting for a reaction. His expression appeared hopeful, as if he expected me to be grateful he cared enough about me to steal the database as an act of revenge for the life *he* forced on me.

I gently released his hand. I did not want my anger to flow into him. I stood, beginning to leave the room.

"Azalea Rose?" he said, his voice strained.

I stopped and folded my arms tight against my chest. I tried to keep my words from shaking, tried to keep the tears from forming—tried and failed. "*They* didn't make me a slave, *you* made me a slave."

Thirty-Four

The evening air was clean and fresh. The scent of honeysuckle came and went on the faint breeze. I hadn't gone out the front door as Kolbe had; instead, I went out the back. I headed to the path of live oaks which had existed for hundreds of years and would exist for hundreds more if they were allowed to.

My mind was swimming with uncertainty. Everything I thought I knew—truths that were indisputable, no matter how much I wished they weren't—had been proved lies. But I didn't feel any great relief. Only more confusion. I was still gestated by a machine. That part had not been a lie, but did that matter? Did that make me less than a person? Now that I knew it was the borns, not the gestates, who were altered in those awful ways, did I believe they were less of a person?

The first morning in this community, Ms. Vivian told me I had always been a person. Now Mr. Northup seemed to be saying the same thing, and not just because they believed me to be, but because I was. What did that mean for Salt and her parents? Were they now human robots?

"Where are you going?" Kolbe asked, his feet beating against the soft ground.

I admired the low sun casting a pink hue throughout the sky while waiting for him to catch up.

"I'm not sure," I answered, wanting to add that I wasn't sure of anything, but instead I remained still.

A hawk had landed nearby, its talons clutching a lizard. It adjusted its sharp claws against the wiggling reptile. A moment later the bird took flight with the lizard securely grasped.

"How did you know where I was?" I asked, beginning to move again along the path created by the giant oaks.

"I was out front when I heard the back door close. After Aunt Viv left, I realized it was you who had gone out the kitchen door. I wanted to make sure you were okay."

"It's unsettling how much you and your family keep track of me. No one has ever done that before. I mean the AIs monitored my location, but that was only to make sure I didn't run. Were you trying to make sure I didn't run?" I asked, suddenly wondering if that was the reason he cared so much.

Kolbe laughed. "No, I wasn't afraid of you absconding into the night."

"Then what is it?" I asked.

All around us, birds swooped into the tall grass, feasting on insects.

"You were basically just told your entire life was a lie. I thought that might be a lot to deal with and that you might like to talk about it," he said.

"You learned the truth about your mom too," I said, glancing at him from the side as I continued to follow the live oaks.

"I always knew the truth about my mom."

I looked at him in surprise.

"Not that she was a gestate, but that she was my mom who loved me and was unafraid to speak her mind. If someone had told me she was altered not to love or think for herself, I would've known it was a lie. She's completely unaltered."

"It makes sense now," I said, feeling my heart aching again for Hastings. "Why his parents never cared about him. I always thought it was because he looked funny to them, or didn't behave the way he should. But they didn't care about his sister either. I thought there was something wrong with me. That I was too stupid to understand things, and all along it was them. They couldn't think for themselves. They couldn't return their son's love."

"You're talking about the family unit you served?"

I nodded. "Hastings always wanted to play, to be hugged, to be loved, but he never was. Not by anyone other than me."

"At least he had you," Kolbe said, trying to sound encouraging though he sounded hurt.

As the sky turned from pink to purple, I felt a storm rise in me. "I wasn't enough! I was broken, I *am* broken. He deserved more. Much more! He deserved to run and play, to be put to bed at night by his parents, not a stupid screen telling him a bedtime story. That isn't fair to him, to any of them!"

"Do all borns and vintage borns get bedtime stories?"

"The young ones do because clearly their born parents are unable to care enough about them to do it themselves!"

"The young ones," Kolbe repeated to himself, his voice sounding relieved.

I huffed; his lack of outrage was only making me more angry.

"Life isn't fair," Kolbe said, his voice no longer a whisper. "No matter how much Grandfather tried to pretend it was."

"He made it less fair. Do you think he understands that?"

In front of us a cardinal disappeared into the tall grass. "I'm not sure. I think he at least realizes things aren't the way he'd hoped."

"So why didn't he change it?"

"How would he have done that?" Kolbe asked.

"Told the truth, shared the database with others, exposed the lies."

"Let me show you something," he said, quickening his pace a little so that he led the way through the tall grass. Very soon we were at the end of the live oak trail. At our feet was concrete, mixed with stone and bricks.

"This is the ruins of the first house on this property," Kolbe said as the sight in front of me became clearer. All around us were the remains of walls no higher than our knees.

I went forward, stepping onto broken stones and bricks.

"What happened to it?" I asked.

"It was built by slaves a very long time ago. About a hundred and fifty years ago, anything made by slaves was outlawed. So it was blown up. For a long time, it was left like that. Knee-high walls surrounded by mounds of rubble. At some point in the last hundred years or so, people from my community started collecting the debris, using it to help build the community. The fireplace in my house is made from some of the bricks."

"That's good, to use it," I said, trying to understand the point of his story.

"Do you know what happened less than a hundred years after it was blown up?"

I shook my head.

"The first gestate was created. Of course, that man was not considered a slave. He was considered a successful science experiment. Over time, more and more gestates were created and they were made into slaves. The world went from outlawing anything made from forced labor to creating an entirely new group to enslave."

The evening air settled around us as the glow of the sun faded. The sound of history crunched beneath my feet—a history some were determined to forget and, so, repeat.

"Is it inevitable? People doing what they can to dominate others," I said, feeling the rough mortar as I reached my hand to touch the outlines of the house.

"I don't think so. I think the mistake is not learning from the past, or pretending past mistakes don't exist. When that happens, we repeat them over and over again, in new and even more disturbing ways."

The birds were gone. Now bats swooped overhead in the gray sky.

"I've always thought bats were like gestates," I said. "And borns were like birds."

"That's an odd comparison."

"No, it's a perfect comparison. Bats live in the shadows, working in jagged, uneven lines, but they're the ones who keep the world running. Birds are out in the open, making a big show of things with their bright feathers and attention-getting songs. They do some helpful stuff, but not as much as bats. Bats never stop to show off their voice or their drab bodies, they just get the job done."

"I don't think that's what birds are doing," Kolbe said with a faint smile.

"After having spent my life around borns, trust me, that's what they're doing," I said.

"It's getting dark. We should go back," he said, his hands in his pockets.

I didn't move. "I'm not sure how to talk to him. He did this to me … to Hastings"—my voice cracked—"to everyone."

"He forgot the past, they all did. He loves you. He didn't understand what he was doing."

"But he did it anyway," I said.

Kolbe nodded. "Yes, and that can never be forgotten. But it can be forgiven."

"There has probably never been a bigger lie in the history of humanity, and it came from him," I said with a choked voice.

"There have been bigger lies," he said in a sorrowful voice, "but that doesn't matter, not right now."

"We have to fix it," I said, scared by the meaning of my words.

He shook his head. "You've done enough," he said. His blue eyes refused to leave mine, as if he was willing me to accept his words and would not look away until I did.

In the distance, we heard footsteps running toward us, and Talia screaming our names … still his eyes did not leave mine.

Thirty-Five

Everyone in the community was following us as Kolbe and the three other men carried the box—the coffin, as they called it—that held Mr. Northup. My legs felt heavy, but that didn't keep me from walking directly behind the box. I didn't want to be away from him, even though he was dead and even though I'd been angry at him before he died. I'd asked Kolbe if I could be one of those carrying the coffin, but he thought it best if I didn't. I was glad of that, now that my legs felt heavy and my steps unsteady.

The coffin was simple: a rectangular box made of pine. On the top was a carving done by Kolbe. There were two pieces of wood, one longer and one shorter. The shorter piece was laid horizontally over the longer piece; both pieces were carved with roses. The roses made me smile in spite of my tears; how Mr. Northup had loved his roses. The roses that he named me for, whose scent even now filled my senses, though I was sure there were no roses near us. But still, I smelled their perfume and every time I did, peace washed over me. I could not explain it, but I was grateful for this peace. It was in those moments, when my steps felt lighter, that I believed everything would be okay. In every other moment I felt so lost it was difficult to think.

The Meadow of the Remembered, as Kolbe had called it, was on a low hill. There were no actual hills in this part of the country. This meadow, surrounded on two sides by a slow, winding stream, was the closest thing to a hill they had. At its base, near the stream, cypress trees flourished, their knotted knees preventing the stream from encroaching. In front of us was a path of bright green moss lined with wispy ferns. Here, before the hill, we were covered by the cypress canopy. The air coming off the stream felt cool. The scent of roses remained. We climbed six steps made of stone cut into the side of the land. Just as there were no hills, there was no stone in this part of the land. These stone steps must have come from the ruins of the old house.

We were far from the houses, in an area of the community I'd not seen before. Yet on the hill in this remote part of the community, the lawn was perfectly maintained. The grass was short, not covering my feet. In the distance there was a fresh mound of black dirt. At the sight of it, my heart felt tight, but I remained near the coffin, near Mr. Northup.

Beside me, Carolyn held Talia. She hadn't stopped crying since the three of us arrived at their home the day before. We were there in time for his last breath … I held his hand as he stopped existing. Yet I still felt him, as if he was walking beside me. That was impossible, but it felt so real that several times I turned, expecting him to be there, easily keeping pace with the rest of us, no longer held back by a body saturated with poison. He wasn't there; it must've been some part of my mind that didn't want him to be gone. Still, it felt so real.

Music began playing when we stepped into the meadow. It startled me. I'd never known that music could be created by humans. The music that the Parker-James family unit listened to was created by computers. The sound was so different that it was difficult to compare it to what they had listened to. This seemed alive, like it lived and breathed, lifting me with it as it wound toward the sky. Around me, voices began to sing. Sorrow. Their voices evoked sorrow in me, and yet it was as if the voices refused to give in, as if they were fighting against the sorrow. It seemed there was hope, not in a general sense but in a specific one; like there was hope for Mr. Northup, as if they believed he wasn't dead. Did they feel his presence as well? Perhaps they were as delusional as I was.

Kolbe and the others set the coffin near the hole. Without thinking, my knees bent, bringing me to the damp earth. I knelt beside the coffin, my hands upon it. The music continued to surround me while the men placed straps through the handles of the pine box.

Talia leaned over onto the coffin, her mother's hand on her back. Talia's slender fingers traced the roses on the carving her brother had made.

The music wrapped around me.

Peace … again I felt peace.

Carolyn gently pulled Talia away from the coffin.

"We need to let him go, to allow him to rest," Carolyn said.

"I worry about his soul. I worry he won't be able to rest," Talia said as she used a cloth to wipe her dripping nose.

"That will be up to him, as it is up to each of us," Carolyn answered, rubbing her daughter's back.

"I hope he chooses well," Talia said, and sniffed.

Her mother leaned into her, their foreheads touching. "So do I, baby girl."

I didn't understand their conversation, but they'd had similar ones since he died. Conversations that made it seem as if Mr. Northup still existed, like all those who were dead existed. It was a strange belief; one I didn't have the energy to question or even think about.

Talia clung to her mother. Only my hand touched the coffin. I alone would not let him go. … With trembling fingers I lifted my hand from the wooden box.

The men who held the straps, including Kolbe, lifted the coffin and gently placed it into the hole in the ground. Each of the other men stepped back. One stopped to hug Kolbe, both of them crying as they released each other. I wanted to ask why this man, who didn't even know Mr. Northup, was crying, but I remained silent. That man stood to the side with the others. The rest of the community fanned out in front of us. Young and old were there, men and women. Perhaps there were some missing, but I didn't think so. So many had tears in their eyes, tears I realized that were partially for Mr. Northup, but more for Kolbe and his family. These were the ones they loved; these were the ones they were there to support.

Such things didn't happen where I was from. People there didn't care about one another. The truth of Mr. Northup's databases sank down upon my shoulders. The borns did not care because they were created not to, the gestates had been beaten into not caring, and the vintage borns had no one to show them how to care—at least not those in born families.

So much had been lost; Mr. Northup's words rang in my mind … so much had been lost.

Kolbe knelt beside me, staring at the pine box deep in the earth.

Each community member took turns dropping a wildflower into the hole. Each flower floated gracefully down, landing on top of the coffin with the rose-carved symbol. Soon it was covered with flowers so that only a glimpse or two of pine could be seen.

When all had passed and stood fanned out in front of us again, Carolyn said, in a strong clear voice, "Thank you for honoring us by honoring Josiah. Being with him as he passed from this life into the next was a gift that we're grateful for. A gift we didn't receive for my mother-in-law or my husband." She paused, steadying her voice. "Josiah was not always an easy man to love, but he was loved just the same. His wife never gave up on him. We learned in these last days that she was right, that he tried to undo some of the damage he did in this life. I hope that means he is with her now. I hope he chose as I'm sure she and Joshua did." She suddenly became too emotional to continue.

Kolbe sat straighter. "Thank you, friends, for the love you've always shown us … even when I wake up your children at three in the morning, bringing back a beautiful girl and my dying grandfather."

Suppressed laughter came from the crowd.

"I'm sure their arrival was concerning for some and scary for others, but you've welcomed them in each your own way, and we're grateful. Thank you for loving those we love, for being our friends."

Silence settled on the meadow.

Kolbe nodded to the men who'd helped him carry his grandfather. Each began to shovel dirt into the hole.

Slowly, respectfully, people began to step back. Many were going to other graves where the markers were weathered. Those with young children were the first to leave the meadow. Dr. Maggie and her family were among the first. Others began to trickle away, until only Ms. Vivian remained with us.

Time passed.

"I'll be at your house," she said quietly as she went toward a weathered marker. She placed her hand lovingly on it and then continued out of the meadow.

After a few more minutes Carolyn held out a hand for Talia. Talia, still crying, took her mother's hand. As Carolyn passed us, she placed a hand on Kolbe's shoulder. Silently, she and Talia left the meadow.

"It's hard to leave him here alone," I said, as the birds began to hop about in the distance.

"He's not here … not anymore," Kolbe said with a sigh.

After many more minutes, Kolbe brushed the dirt from his pants.

"Come on, Grandfather would want you to eat lunch," he said, offering me a hand.

I squinted at him. Yes, Mr. Northup would want me to eat. I accepted Kolbe's hand.

The sun was hot as we left the Meadow of the Remembered and made our way down the stone steps lined with vibrant ferns. The air under the cypress canopy was cool; the scent of roses was faint here, not like it had been in the meadow.

"This place is extraordinary," I said as we walked back, nearing the houses where families were gathering for their midday meal.

"It's different than where we come from," Kolbe acknowledged.

"It's the families," I said, understanding the truth I'd witnessed from my first day here.

Through an open window, I watched a father pick up his young son and carry him to the table, where the rest of the family was waiting with filled plates in front of them. The boy, who reminded me of Hastings when he was three or four, squealed in delight.

The comparison brought a twisting pain to my chest. Hastings had never experienced such a moment; his father had never carried him like that. The only time he'd ever squealed in delight was when I pushed him much faster than I should have in the stroller he'd almost outgrown.

"Yes," Kolbe said, breaking into my memories, "it's the families. They sacrifice for one another … they love one another."

I ran my right hand along my left arm. The arm was no longer covered in a long sleeve. The pale ring had darkened to match the rest of my tan skin.

"It's not their fault—the families where we come from," I said as the scent of roses returned. "The ability to care for one another was taken away from them."

"By my grandfather," Kolbe said with guilt.

"He wasn't alone," I said. "I wonder … if people knew what we know … would it change anything?"

"It might, but it might not. The vintage borns don't want things to change and the borns … if someone tells them everything's okay, they'll believe it. Grandfather made sure of that," Kolbe said.

"I doubt all vintage borns are happy with things as they are, and I bet some borns aren't as fully altered as others. The alterations don't always work, and of course all of the gestates would care," I said.

"Maybe," Kolbe said, clearly humoring me.

I inhaled deeply. The scent of roses was bringing me calmness, though my thoughts were anything but calm. "Do you smell that?" I asked.

"I smell lots of food cooking."

"No, I mean the roses. They're so strong."

He drew in a long breath and let it out. "I smell a faint scent of jasmine, but not roses. I don't think we have any roses here. They aren't the easiest thing to grow, despite how easy Grandfather made it appear."

I smelled the sweet scent, all the while seeing Hastings watching me, his freckled skin covered in a thin layer of sweat, a smoothie in his hands. "That's all I can smell. Like I'm surrounded by them."

"That must be from Grandfather," Kolbe said as we stopped at the edge of his porch. "People here talk about how, sometimes, when people die, they send a sign to those they love."

"A sign of what?" I asked, fighting the urge to run.

Though, I already knew what the roses meant. The roses mixed with the image of Hastings.

"I guess it depends," he said. "I think a lot of the time it means the person is okay, or maybe it's an indication of something they want the person on earth to do for them."

My throat was dry. I couldn't swallow. No sound would come. It didn't matter since my mind was not able to form words.

Beside us, the screen door opened and Talia burst out. Without warning, she wrapped her arms around me. "I miss him so much," she sobbed into my neck.

Kolbe ushered us into the house.

"Me too," I said, my throat so dry barely a whisper eked out.

"It isn't fair," Talia said. "So many people I love die too soon. I was so young when Dad died, and then we left, and then Grandmother died. And now Grandfather died so soon after we found him."

My face flushed hot. She was right; many of those she loved had died too soon.

"Come on, Talia," Carolyn said, prying her daughter off me. "Aunt Viv brought her turkey tetrazzini, not to mention all the food from the rest of the community. Let's eat something. It will help us feel better."

"But it isn't fair," Talia cried as her mother escorted her to the table.

"Life isn't fair, my darling," Carolyn said, lifting her daughter's hair away from her sweaty neck.

"It could at least be more fair," she complained.

Carolyn kissed the top of her daughter's head. "Imagine if you were back where we come from, where it's mandated that life be fair, at least to some."

The words sent a shiver through me.

"I don't want to think of that," Talia said sincerely.

"Nor do I," Carolyn said. "We've lost a lot, but even with our losses we have much more than most."

"Yes," Kolbe said, placing his hand on my back and guiding me to the table.

I stumbled forward. The scent of roses was stronger than the steaming food on the plate in front of me.

"Are you okay?" Carolyn asked, suddenly focused on me.

"Yes," I said, my eyes low.

She would be able to tell; she would know I was lying.

I sat at the expertly crafted wooden table, Carolyn and her family around me—a family I loved, a family I was now a part of.

So much … I would be giving up so much. I forced myself to take a bite of food. Swallowing was impossible without sipping some water. My throat was too dry. How could I leave this place? The roses, mixed with an image of Hastings, returned. … How could I stay?

Panic crashed upon me, pushing me down like the raging waves of a hurricane.

"Are you okay?" Kolbe asked, his voice concerned, his hand lightly touching my arm.

Everything … I would be giving up everything ….

"Yes," I lied.

End of Book One

Azalea Rose's story will continue in *unAltered*.

Also by Jacqueline Brown

The Light, Book One of The Light Series
Through the Ashes, Book Two of The Light Series
From the Shadows, Book Three of The Light Series
Into the Embers, Book Four of The Light Series
Out of the Darkness, Book Five of The Light Series
"Before the Silence," a Light Series Short Story
Awakening, Book One
Gifted, Book Two of the Awakening Series

If you enjoyed *Altered*, please consider leaving a review. You can learn more about the author at www.Jacqueline-Brown.com, where you can get your free e-copy of "Before the Silence" and join the mailing list.